BLUE MONDAY

BLUE MONDAY

Harper Barnes

The Patrice Press
St. Louis, Missouri

Cover: Art direction by John Cournoyer with photographic collaboration by Michael Eastman.

Library of Congress Cataloging-In-Publication Data

Barnes, Harper.   1937-
    Blue Monday / Harper Barnes.
      p.   cm.
    ISBN 0-935284-92-3 : $9.95
    1. Moten, Bennie, 1894-1935—Fiction.   I. Title.
    PS3552.A67386B5   1991
813'.54—dc20   91-30679
                                                    CIP

Published by
The Patrice Press
1701 S. Eighth Street / St. Louis MO 63104

Printed in the United States of America

For Roseann Weiss
In Memory of Milton Morris

I dreamed last night
I was standing at 18th and Vine,
I shook hands with Piney Brown
And I could hardly keep from crying.

Joe Turner, "Piney Brown Blues"

1

Plink

Plink

Plink

Plink

The tall man bent at the waist to pick up more gravel from the driveway of the small two-story frame house. He cupped it in the palm of his right hand. In the glow of the streetlight, you could see that the hand was long and thin and the fingers twisted a bit, like twigs, but they moved with a rubbery grace. He pivoted his thumb and index finger into his palm and, with their tips, plucked out a piece of gravel. He held it to his eye like a dart and aimed it at a second-story window.

Plink

Plink

Plinkplinkplinkplink.

The man waited, but there was no response.

He snorted and rotated slowly to face us. He stretched out his long arms so the overcoat thrown over his shoulders spread out like a cape. The overcoat was beige. So was the suit he wore over a maroon shirt open at the neck. So was his hat, high-peaked with a snap brim. So were his shoes. So was his skin.

He grinned. He was a little wacky from the whisky the three of us had been sipping, but still every move he made had an easy flow to it, Jesse Owens, Fred Astaire. The drink just made him looser in his grace. He swept around to face the house again and cupped his hands around his mouth.

"Libba. . . Libba Ann. . . Elizabeth Ann Monroe! You home, baby?"

The sound he made was technically a whisper, but it came from deep in his throat and was driven by his diaphragm so it carried in the still, cool air like the notes of a muted trombone.

The window slid up. A woman, irritation pushing the sleepy hoarseness from her voice, said: "Hey! Keep it down, you'll wake up momma. Now who the hell is it this time?" A pause. "Teddy? Oh, hey Teddy. Sweetheart, I just got in off the road. I'm tired."

"Princess, we need you. Yesterday was Blue Monday and the boys have been jamming since I can't remember when and we been through three piano players already. Pete's been playing off and on for seems like a week and he's starting to fade, too."

"What time is it?"

"I don't know, three, four in the morning. Now come on princess, we need you."

There was barely a hesitation.

"I'll be right down." She shut the window.

There was no moon that cloudy spring morning. Along about midnight, there had been a quick splurge of rain, soon over, soon soaked into the ground and concrete. It had been a very dry winter and spring, coming after a terribly dry year at the eastern end of what had come to be called the Dust Bowl. The shower, brief as it was, was a blessing after the Biblical winds that had swept in from the parched plains over the past few weeks and brought great brown clouds rolling across Kansas City like herds of ghostly buffalo.

The dust settled like a fungus on porches and car tops and wash hanging out to dry, and the wind forced it through cracks and under doors and into homes and offices so that it lay everywhere. Dishes were coated with it, eyeglasses grew dim, and dust rose from the streets in the wake of cars and trolleys like water spray after a rain. It made your eyes itch and your sinuses ache and the days dark and fearful. Finally, though, the winds had slowed and then came the spring shower and with it the hope that the twin locks of drought and winter were broken.

It was cold—barely above freezing—but it was a pleasure to stand outside, leaning against my four-year-old Ford coupe, shivering slightly, hands in pockets or under armpits except when busy with the pint of whisky we were passing around. There were three of us: Theodore (Teddy) Wellington, late 20s or early 30s, jazz drummer, man of grace; his nephew, Robert Creech, early 20s, high-school music teacher up far past his bedtime, alto saxophonist of some talent and more learning, and myself, Michael Holt, 23, newspaper reporter of six weeks standing, innocent as corn silk and heart-wrenchingly in love with almost everything I encountered in those days in my first real city, almost everything except the dust, but of course I was used to the dust.

I was from Kansas. Robert and I had gone to college together at the state university thirty-five miles west of Kansas City, and I had called him that day to give him the news on the front pages of the early editions of the two afternoon papers: the U.S. Supreme Court had halted the executions of two of the Scottsboro boys, convicted in Alabama four years earlier of raping a white woman. He was glad to hear from me and we agreed to get together after work. For me, that meant well past midnight.

Robert Creech and I had first met on a soon-defunct Negro rights committee and had become friends because of jazz. Our friendship had endured the discovery that both our families had come west from the same area in the Piedmont of North Carolina and that I, too, had ancestors named Creech.

Robert was about 5′ 8″, stocky, and colored a shade he called "beginner brown"—not black, but close to it. He wore glasses and cheap serge suits and plain-toed, practical black shoes that looked like mail order from Sears, Roebuck. He was a very quiet and very serious-appearing young man, except when he chuckled in his throat—"heh, heh, heh"—at something that amused him. He looked young and vulnerable, like the colored kid in glasses and knickers who had to carry his instrument case through the crowd of toughs on his way to his music lesson.

His mother in Memphis probably would have preferred a violin, but he ended up with an alto saxophone because that's all they had left in the grade-school bandroom. At least, that's what he told his mother. After he graduated from high school with all A's, his mother sent him to Kansas University because it was not too far away, had a U after it instead of an A & I, was in a state founded by abolitionists and had a reputation for treating white and Negro students equally. Robert and I met trying to make it live up to that reputation.

Undoubtedly, Mrs. Creech would have sent her son almost anywhere else—save Mississippi and Alabama—had she know that, four years later, he would end up in the same city with his high-brown uncle Teddy, who had shown Memphis the tail of his coat at a precocious age and run off with a medicine show. He had become a dancer and a drummer who, Robert told me, had sat in with Louis Armstrong and Earl Hines in Chicago one night when Zutty Singleton was sick. Around 1932, Teddy had joined a band that roamed the Southwest—Waco, Joplin, Salina, Tulsa. A year or so later the band folded for lack of work and Teddy ended up here. A man named Tom Pendergast had willed that the Depression pass over Kansas City, just as he had parted Prohibition to let his people through. There was plenty of work for a musician in Kansas City.

Teddy told me about himself in an affable, joking way, slapping his hands together, occasionally tapping me on the shoulder to make a point. He had a light, jazzy voice, and always seemed to be in motion, like a boxer staying loose before a fight.

I took a shot from the pint of whisky and passed it to Teddy. He took it with his right hand and his fingers seemed to wrap around the wide, flat bottle as if it were the handle of a baseball bat. I remembered something. I reached into the gutter with my right hand and picked up a small stone. I tried to pluck it from my palm with the tips of my right thumb and index finger, the way Teddy had done.

The fingers wouldn't reach, at least not both at the same time. I looked at Teddy's hand wrapped around the flat pint bottle. Not only did the fingers seem oddly bent, but there was a long cord of scar tissue ridged along the upper edge of his index finger and running onto the back of his hand.

One drink less and I probably would not have asked the question: "Teddy, what happened to your right hand?"

Robert made a reflexive "heh" sound in his throat, but there was no humor in it. Teddy craned his neck to look down at me. He stared, tight-lidded for a few seconds, and then slowly his eyes relaxed and his expression slid from anger to irritation to disappointed reproach.

"White people," he said. "If you think you know me well enough to ask a question like that, you are a fool." He smiled slightly. "Suffice it to say it happened in Chicago a long time ago and it hasn't hurt my fabled quicksilver drumming style a bit."

He reached up with his left hand and, like a double-jointed kid on a school playground, pulled back the index finger and thumb of his right hand to touch his forearm. "Bet you can't do that," he said.

The door to the narrow frame house swung open and, in a clatter of heels, down the front steps came Libba Monroe. She was wearing a dark blue scarf and a blue coat with the collar spread over the shoulders. As she approached, I could see that she was tiny—perhaps five feet tall, and slight. And beautiful. She had Swiss-chocolate skin, deep, dark oval eyes, a soft, slightly flattened nose and a smile so wide and toothy and glistening it hit like a first morning glimpse of the sea.

The smile froze when she saw me. "What's this?" she asked Teddy.

"This," said Teddy, almost formal, "is Michael Holt, who is a friend of my nephew Robert. I believe you have met Robert. And how was the Apple?"

She gave her head a slow shake and her shoulder-length black hair, thick and wavy, tossed at either side of the scarf tied at her throat.

"Things are sad back East, Teddy," she said. "It's like they took all the money out of Harlem and put a curse on the place. I'm glad to be home." She spoke with a touch of Dixie softness in her vowels, like Robert and Teddy, but her accent was essentially regionless and raceless, educated, slightly clipped in its consonants. It had none of the half-Southern, half-flatland rough-edged sardonic slur of most Negroes who had grown up in Kansas City—*Kans*sity—a slur born for the blues. Looking at her and listening to her, I could tell why Teddy called her Princess.

She smiled at me—not *the* smile, but a smile—and said she was pleased to meet me.

Robert climbed in the rumble seat. I drove and Libba sat between Teddy and me. She was wearing dark silk stockings and parrot-green shoes and she smelled of lilacs. The car was small, but so was she, and we barely touched. I drove west toward Paseo. I apologized the first time I brushed her leg in shifting gears, but she ignored both the touch and the apology.

"Who's in town?" she asked Teddy.

"Princess, let me tell you who's not in town. Lester Young is not in town. Bill Basie and Herschel and Lips and them, they're not in town because Bennie Moten's band is in Denver for a gig. Now Bennie Moten himself, he *is* in town."

"Why's that?"

"Bennie stayed behind to get his tonsils out. His throat's been hurting for a long time, and the boys were complaining on the road that he snored so much they couldn't sleep.

"A couple of other bands are on the road, but the Rockets are in town. Ben Webster. Baby Lovett. Julia Lee. Joe Turner and Pete Johnson, they're always in town. And I'm in town and you're in town, so let's jump!"

Teddy's long legs were angled up against the dashboard and he began slapping a steady, driving beat against his right thigh—*pop-pop-pop-pop*. Libba picked up the beat and began to hum—that's not the right word, think of the sound a bumblebee makes and give it the resonance of human bone. It was a fast tricky blues, one I'd never heard before and, I suspect, neither had she.

Our destination was less than ten minutes away, down the wide, oak-lined boulevard called the Paseo. At 18th Street we passed the Paseo Tavern, where I had met Robert and Teddy about an hour before. They had just come from a jam session at the Sunset Club, and that is where we were headed now, piano player in hand.

The Paseo Tavern was dark now except for the Budweiser clock in the window that read 4:15. Faint music trickled from someplace down 18th toward Vine—"sounds like somebody's still blowing at the Subway Club," said Teddy, stilling the beat of his hand for a moment to listen—but otherwise 18th had finally shut down for the morning.

But not 12th. We could see the lights and hear the music and shouting of 12th Street a couple of blocks before we got there and, at the intersection, it hit like an explosion. We turned right and for three short blocks—Vine, Highland, Woodland—12th Street was swarming with life, like a carnival midway on Saturday night.

Music blasted from half a dozen clubs or storefronts along the stretch of low brick and frame buildings and hundreds of people were on the sidewalks and in the street, drinking, eating, bouncing along, leaning in doorways of clubs to hear the music for free, shouting at each other—"Hey, baby, how you been?"—hugging each other and slapping flesh, dancing in the street. It was like the last few buoyant hours of Mardi Gras in a village that was deadly serious about Lent, or a roundup-time celebration in a wide-open frontier town, except this happened almost every night along 12th and 18th streets.

With his drumming right hand, Teddy switched from his thigh to the dashboard and drove harder into the beat. With his left he reached across Libba to flick little accents on the horn every time some heedless celebrant would wander in front of the car.

We drove slowly past Crown Drugs and the Boulevard Lounge and Jazzland, past James Barnes' Billiards and the Black and Orange Cafe and the Hollywood Theater, past Williams' Shoeshine Shop and Delia Gordon's Fish Market—catfish, ten cents a pound, thirty crawfish for $1—past Wesley Young's domino parlor and Ling Lee's restaurant and the Smokehouse, a couple of taxi stands, four or five liquor stores, three or four pawnshops and an ice cream parlor, and every place, open or not, was brightly lit.

Near the end of the three-block stretch, at Woodland, 12th Street was dominated by two facing signs. On the left, a theater-style marquee, black letters on a white background:

LONE STAR NIGHT CLUB
BIG FLOOR SHOW
Music by Lee Etta Smith and Her Aces

On the right, a red neon sign:

SUNSET CLUB

And beneath it, to the left of the doorway, a poster that must have been six feet high:

EAST SIDE MUSICIANS CLUB
prop. Piney Brown
SINGING NIGHTLY JOE TURNER
Pete Johnson
Tuesday night female impersonators Colored and White

We found a lucky parking spot in front of the open door of a pool hall on 12th just past Woodland. Teddy and I finished the pint of whisky. Teddy dropped the bottle in the gutter and the four of us worked our way through the crowd back toward the Sunset—Teddy and Libba in front, Robert and I just behind them.

At Woodland was a lunchwagon. A hand-lettered sign on the side read: "Ribs Crawdads Short Thighs Snouts All 10¢." Behind the lunchwagon was a little gray-skinned man, hunched over, his face partially hidden by a floppy cap too big for his head. Teddy reached out and tapped him lightly on the shoulder with an open palm. "How's it going, Seventeen?"

The old man looked up. He said, "Hey, skinbeater, hey there, Princess. I'm holding on, I'm holding on. Who you got with you?"

"Seventeen," said Teddy, "this is my nephew Robert and his friend, Michael. Keep 'em out of trouble, will you?"

"You got it, drummerman." He took a couple of steps toward us. The cap hid part of the right side of his face, but I could see that his right eyelid drooped and the eye behind it looked fishbowl dead. He was wearing the filthy old coat of a double-breasted suit over an undershirt.

Seventeen turned back the left lapel of the coat. In the felt backing was a row of straight pins. He took one out and pinned it to the lapel of my coat. He pinned another to Robert's.

"Now you young men is all taken care of. Ain't nobody going to mess with you while you wearing the badge of Seventeen."

Libba tugged at Teddy's sleeve. "Come on, baby, we're wasting time."

Teddy reached into his pocket and patted a coin into the little man's hand. "Thanks, Seventeen. Dig you later."

The Sunset was just past Woodland, between a small grocery store and a billiard parlor. As we were momentarily halted by the mob bunched in front of the club, I grabbed Teddy by the arm. I asked, "Seventeen?

What kind of name is that?''

Teddy spat the words over his shoulder. "Jailbird name."

He shook his head, and then turned toward me and said, "That's how many years he spent in Jeff City. For stealing a pint of whisky. From a white man's liquor store. He had a little folding knife in his pocket, so they called it armed robbery."

Teddy pushed ahead and we moved slowly through the mass of bodies to the entrance. Music was blasting out of a loudspeaker above the swinging doors. Teddy shoved the doors inward and we followed into a room filled with people and almost submerged in smoke. In here, the music was twice as loud as it had been outside. And the club was much larger than it appeared. The storefronts on either side of the Sunset were only about twenty feet deep, and beyond them the room opened like a fat T, so the back of the club was almost three times as wide as the front. To the left, before the room opened up, was the bar. Back past the bar, tucked into the far left corner, was a triangular raised bandstand, and small chairs and tables were scattered throughout the rest of the room.

The bandstand was small, but there must have been eight or ten musicians on it—drums, bass, guitar, three or four saxes, a trumpet, a violin. At the rear of the stage, visible dimly through the blue-lit smoke, was the piano player, a coal-black man with an unlit cigar sticking out of his mouth. He was pounding chords behind the trumpet player, who was making a series of high register runs, climbing, sliding back, climbing a little higher, long bursts of notes that swelled and ebbed above the very fast beat of the piano, the slapped upright bass and the thumb-chorded guitar.

There were perhaps 200 people crowded into the T-shaped room, mostly Negro, with small groups of whites seated at tables near the front, and three or four young white men standing at the edge of the bandstand, clapping to the beat and shouting encouragement to the musicians.

The later it got, Robert told me, the less attention people paid to Jim Crow laws and the unwritten rules of segregation that theoretically prevailed even at a very loose, Negro-run club like the Sunset. As Blue Monday jams wore on into the morning, he said, you could look around at the crowd and think you were in some imaginary city where there was no segregation. "But it's always there, waiting to bite you," Robert said, "as long as there's white people around."

As we worked our way into the room, Teddy flipped his head from side to side with the rhythm. There was no discernable melody. He yelled to Libba, "What the hell they playing?"

Libba listened. "Sounds like the chords to 'Vine Street Blues.' "

"Hell," said Teddy, "that's what they were playing when I left."

At one side of the bandstand was a big yellow-skinned man, well over 200 pounds, well over six feet tall, built like a Hollywood bed. He was wearing a shiny white shirt and a pair of high-riding iridescent green suit pants that draped over his shoes and were held from his chest by suspenders, like a pair of fishing waders. His wide moustache was squared off at either end and looked as if it had been painted on, like Groucho Marx's.

The big man waved in our direction and held his left hand, palm backwards, in front of the bandstand. The trumpet player concluded his run with a two-bar flourish and sank into the background to let the rhythm instruments rise.

The big man's voice exploded into the room:

Look a there who walked in my front door,
Look a there who walked in my front door,
Piano lady and the boss man of four/four.

There was microphone on a stand a few feet from him, but he didn't need it. His voice was powerful and resonant, almost nasal, but it had a hard, grinding edge to it, and it cut and skipped through the rhythm like a speedboat across a tidal rip.

Four in the morning, we all feelin' fine,
It's four in the morning, we all feelin' fine,
At 12th and Woodland, down the line from Vine.

He lowered his hand and took a step backward, and the trumpet player rose again like a released balloon. This time he was joined by the fiddle player. I'd never heard a violin played that way—the sound was somewhere between an alto saxophone and rubbed crystal. The bow came down hard every third or fourth note, splintering tiny strands of horsehair so that it hung in fronds from the front of the bow and waved as the fiddler played.

The trumpet would lay down four bars of a twelve-bar blues chorus and you could sense the words behind the notes—"Four in the morning, we all feeling fine"—the violin would throw it back at him, slightly changed—"It's four in the morning, and we're all feeling fine"—and then the two of them would finish the chorus together—"At 12th and Woodland, down the line from Vine." It went on and on like that, a taut and tricky duet, half dance, half duel.

Teddy and I and Robert squeezed against the rear wall only ten or twelve feet from the bandstand. We were drinking beer from big dime cans and I'd had the waiter add a fifteen-cent shot of whisky to mine. Libba was seated at a crowded table beside us, sipping ginger ale.

Robert grabbed my arm and gestured at a table a few feet from us, partly illuminated by an overhead spotlight that played on the front of the bandstand. Two men were seated at the table. One was light-skinned, lighter than Teddy, with high cheekbones like an Indian, and a thin, hawk-beak nose. He was wearing a black fedora with a long brim curved down in front.

The other man was bareheaded. His short, nappy hair looked as if it had been parted with a soldering iron. He was pudgy and brown-skinned, with a round face made even more moon-shaped by a slightly receding hairline. His high-lapeled tweed suitcoat was open but, although his forehead was pocked with sweat, the vest underneath was buttoned to the top.

Robert put his mouth near my ear. "That's Bennie Moten," he said, pointing at the pudgy man. "Best bandleader around."

Bennie Moten had a tall glass of dusty liquid in his right hand. It looked like a strong whisky and water. He took a long, grimacing pull from it. The other man was drinking something much darker—rum and Coke?

On the bandstand, after a dozen or more choruses, the trumpet and the violin sank back into the churning rhythmic underpinning and the piano player, chewing his stubby black cigar, began rising above it. He was using his powerful left hand like a claw to force percussion and a crude, repetitive melody out of the lower end of the keyboard. The bass player was crouching closer and closer to his instrument slapping it so hard the peg began to bounce along the wooden platform. The drummer was slamming away, his arms pinwheeling high above his head to pump the drumsticks down into the tom-tom. The big yellow man leaned close to the microphone and shouted, "Roll 'em Pete!"

And just like that the intensity and drive of the music rose even higher. The bass player and the drummer and the guitar man could do nothing but respond to it—the propulsion came from the piano player's left hand. The tempo was already fast and suddenly he was playing twice as many notes as before, eight to the bar, his left hand rocking on his wrist as he rolled his way up and down the keyboard, driving everyone before him. The big yellow man stood listening at the edge of the bandstand, his arms folded, wearing a wicked smile. His sleepy eyelids were half closed and his large, jowly head was making tiny, rapid movements back and forth to the boogie-woogie rhythm of the piano player.

The big man's eyes snapped open and his head stopped jiggling. A very young man—a boy, really, no more than fifteen or sixteen—was stepping on the bandstand next to the saxophone players, who were standing quietly, bouncing to the music, hands on their instruments, waiting their turn. The kid was carrying a cloth bag made of striped pillow ticking.

The big man reached out a hand to stop him. He tapped the piano player on the shoulder. The piano man turned for an instant, frowned when he saw the kid, shook his head quickly and forcefully, and returned to his instrument. The big man looked at the kid and shrugged, as if to say "What can I do?" The kid stood at the edge of the platform in the light. He was walnut brown, with a high forehead, close-cropped hair that fit like a skullcap, a wide mouth, a thin upper lip and a lower one that plumped out in a sensuous, almost feminine pout. His eyes were drowsy and a bit oriental in the way they drew back slightly at the corners.

Finally, he turned and walked into the darkness of the Sunset Club.

Robert laughed. "Did you see that kid? He's in one of my classes, when he comes. He carries a saxophone everywhere. His momma made the bag for it. Heh-heh—you got to dig him, he's not shy. I wouldn't have the balls to climb up on Big Joe Turner and Pete Johnson's bandstand."

Joe Turner stepped forward to the front of the bandstand and surveyed the room: Bennie Moten keeping time lightly with the heel of his right hand, Teddy's head popping back and forth like a jack-in-the-box yoked to a metronome, the young white men at the edge of the bandstand jiggling up and down, half the people standing now, hands clapping, fingers popping, feet slapping time, the whole room bouncing to the freight-train locomotion of Kansas City riding into dawn.

Big Joe rolled his head in a circle around his shoulders. Then he said into the microphone, "All right . . . all right . . . let's take it on out. Take it on out . . . take it on out—"

The beat never slackened. Pete Johnson came to the end of a chorus with a huge two-handed chord and the three saxophonists—two tenors and an alto—burst in to ride through to the end with a familiar riff. The blues that Big Joe Turner had launched right after we had walked in the door vanished into "Vine Street Blues," which had been there all the time, hiding in the chords.

It ended with a drum roll and a sky-piercing trumpet arpeggio. When the clapping and cheering and table-pounding and foot-stomping had died down, Joe Turner said, "Thank you folks, thank you, thank you. Now we're going to take five or maybe ten and when we come back we're going to have a new drummer and a new piano player. Thank you. . . thank you. . . ."

Libba rose from the table and walked toward the bandstand. She stopped for a moment at Bennie Moten's table, where a waiter was delivering fresh drinks. Libba spoke with the two men briefly, then stepped up to the piano, where she began fooling around on the keyboard. "Princess likes to warm her fingers up," said Teddy.

By then I was well into my third spiked beer. I didn't feel drunk—I felt very loose, almost boneless, and I was gripped by an exhilarating sense of focus, as if I and the objects of my consciousness— Bennie Moten, the kid with the cloth bag, Pete Johnson's left hand, the notes of a violin hanging crystalline in the blue-smoke air—were locked together and traveling at high speed through a dark tunnel called the Sunset Club.

I turned to Teddy. "Big Joe called you the boss man of four/four. What's that mean?"

Teddy smiled and clapped his hands together in front of him, cupped so that the expelled air made little firecracker sounds—"pop-pop-pop-pop."

He said, "That's the kind of question I dig. Now, I want you to listen careful to this, because I'm going to teach you something you didn't know."

Teddy began talking very intensely, his large hands gesturing at either side of his body, like a trainer working with a young fighter. He had to talk loudly to be heard above the noise of the bar, but as he went along his voice got even louder and more urgent.

"Now remember what that last drummer was doing? *Bam*bam-*bam*-bam. He's from New Orleans and that's a city boy's beat. One and three. *Bam*-bam-*bam*-bam." He flipped his right hand toward me to emphasize the strong first and third beats.

"To me," he said, "that's artificial. Drumming is like breathing, it's like the band's a body and you're the lungs, you're breathing for everybody else.

"Let me breathe in and out the way that man was playing. *Hunh*-hunh-*hunh*-hunh-*hunh*-hunh. That gasp, that strong intake, that's desperation, that's fear, man. *Hunh*-hunh. Something just scared the shit out of you—*hunh*! City music.

"Now the blues, the wonderful blues, man, the thing about the blues is that the beat doesn't always go in any one place all the time, it can bounce around, but one thing the blues likes to do, the blues those country

12

boys play down in Mississippi and Louisiana and Texas, is to slide toward the afterbeat. Bam-*bam*-bam-*bam*-bam-*bam*-bam-*bam*-bam-*bam*."

"Iambs," I shouted in drunken epiphany. "Those are iambs."

"Will you shut the hell up?" said Teddy.

I gulped down some more spiked beer.

"Now that afterbeat, bam-*bam*-bam-*bam*, you know what that is? Let me breathe it for you, in-out, hunh-*huhhh*-hunh-*huhh*. That sound, that heavy exhaling, you know what that is? That's a sigh, baby. Hunh-*hunh*. Got de blues so bad it hurt my tongue to talk. Sigh. That's a country sound, that's resignation.

"Now the blues do pop, but the blues don't swing, and neither does that city music, because it's all two-beat.

"The Blue Devils band, which is one of the best bands that ever was, they came out of Oklahoma and Texas, blues country. They were a backbeat band—bam-*bam*, bam-*bam*, and Bennie Moten's band was a city band, *bam*-bam, *bam*-bam. When Bennie heard those Blue Devils, he knew there was something there he wanted. So he started hiring those Devil musicians—Bill Basie and Jimmy Rushing and Big 'Un, that's Walter Page, and finally he got the crown jewel, Lester Young. And then what you had was the one-three jammed together with the two-four, bam-bam-bam-bam, *bam-bam-bam-bam*. What you had was rhythm. What you had was flow. What you had, my smart-ass ofay friend, was four/four, Kansas City style."

Teddy let his hands dangle at his sides, and flexed his fingers. He grinned. "Now I think I'm going to play me some drums.

He moved toward the bandstand. As he climbed behind the drum set, an expectant hush rippled through the room. It was broken by a shout from the far corner of the club:

"Don't get salty with me, you whore bitch!"

Heads turned. A tall, thick-necked white man in a big-shouldered, loud-checked suit stood against the back wall with his fist cocked. A waitress had her nose shoved up in his face, unflinching.

"Kiss my ass, you dope-pushing mother fucker," she shouted. "I seen you trying to unload those caps. That shit don't go in here."

Before the man could swing, two men grabbed him and pinned his arms from behind. He rolled his shoulders and threw one to the floor, then turned and began wrestling with the other man, forcing him to the back wall.

Somebody fell into me and I looked to the left and saw Big Joe Turner plowing his way through the crowd. When he reached the back wall, he grabbed the stocky man by the back of his shirt collar and jerked him away from the man he was wrestling. He lifted him a foot off the ground and slung him over his right shoulder like a sack of cotton.

The man's arms dangled lifelessly from the pull of the shirt on his armpits and he was limp, as if terrified to resist this sudden force. Joe Turner carried the man on his shoulder past the bandstand. The crowd parted before him. He reached the side wall to the left of the bandstand and opened a door I hadn't noticed before. The two figures were briefly outlined by a streetlight as Joe Turner used his arm and upper body to toss the man into Woodland Avenue. He shut the door and climbed back on the bandstand. It was over in less than a minute.

Unperturbed, Libba Monroe sat at the piano, sipping her soft drink with her left hand, winging little runs with her right. Teddy, using drumsticks, made chattering passes across his instruments—tom tom, snare, high-hat cymbal. He kicked the pedal on the small, battered bass drum a few times. Most of the musicians were back on the stand—only one saxophonist and the guitar player were missing. The crowd had thinned by about a third and Robert and I found a place to sit near the middle of the room. I finished my beer. I wasn't sure I wanted another. I was getting woozy. I sank back into the wooden chair.

Libba hit a deep bass chord. The other musicians and the crowd quieted. She nodded her head four times—one-two-three-four— Teddy picked up the beat on the cymbal, the upright bass walked in behind him, the horns came in with a riff, and they were off. At one point, I remember, Joe Turner sang again. Something about Froggy Bottom, where they sing the blues all night. And Libba took a long solo full of strange minor chords and oblique rhythms. It went on for an hour. It must have. I woke up with a startled jerk of my head. "What was that?" I asked Robert.

"That was them not playing anymore," he said.

I rubbed my eyes and looked at my wristwatch. It was a little after six. Teddy and Libba were coming back to the table.

"We better go," said Robert. "I got to be in my homeroom in about two hours."

Teddy wanted to stay. "I figure these boys are good for another couple of hours. I think Libba wants to go home. Princess can't spring back from these road trips anymore. We'll find another piano player, or just blow without one."

Outside, it was not yet fully light. The Lone Star across the street was closed, but there were still people on the sidewalk, most of them spilled out of the Sunset for a taste of morning air. We walked to the car, Libba and Robert and I, without speaking.

14

The lights were still on in the pool hall next to where we had parked. At a table near the front window, two men were shooting a game. One, clearly profiled as he stood chalking his cue, was the light-skinned man with the hawk nose from the front table at the Sunset. He put the chalk down to sip something from a coffee cup—whisky, I figured. He had taken off his black fedora and his hair swept back from his forehead in a thick, black pompadour. The other man had unbuttoned his vest and loosened his tie. As he leaned forward for a shot, his face showed clearly in the light from the green-shaded overhead fixture. It was Bennie Moten, the king of Kansas City jazz.

"Thought he was supposed to be in the hospital," said Libba as she climbed into my car. "Me too," said Robert, climbing in after her.

I dropped Robert off first. He talked with weary excitement of the cutting contest I had slept through. The two tenor men had gone head to head, each soloing for fifteen or twenty minutes, and then going back and forth at each other in tight twelve-bar choruses. It had been, Robert said, a classic Kansas City confrontation.

Libba was silent, but she seemed relaxed, and after Robert had gone she sank back into the seat and clasped her hands just below her knees, like a little girl. She had a soft, fulfilled smile on her lips and the earlier tension between us seemed almost gone.

"Teddy's right," she said. "The road really did get to me this time. Everybody back East is so poor and miserable and Harlem is turning into a slum. It used to be so nice, but nobody's got any jobs anymore, not even maids. And it seems like every time we tour back East, that Jim Crow trash gets worse. Washington, D. C.? Tell me about that place. It's like a Cracker city."

She shook her head. "The South, it's rough. Don't know where you can sleep, don't know where you can eat, and we're driving around all shoved together, six of us in one car and seven in another. Naturally, that's the one with little me in it."

She smiled for an instant, and turned her head to look at me. "It's nice to get home. At least in Kansas City I know the rules."

She turned to gaze again out of the windshield as we drove to her house. As she spoke, almost dreamily, her legs crossed in the black stockings, the hint of perfume still around her, her voice relaxed and became more Southern.

"Lots of time, here, I don't get home until nine or ten in the morning. Sometimes, after the band finishes its regular gig, I'll go home and take a nap for a couple of hours and come back down at three or four in the morning for more jamming.

"The best time is Monday, like yesterday. Blue Monday, they call it. Most bands have Monday night off, so they jam instead. The big floor shows take Monday off too, so the white tourists mostly stay away, and Jim Crow turns the East Side loose. You get mostly Negroes and hip white people in the audience, and if there's a white band in town, Benny Goodman, the Dorsey brothers, the white musicians show up to test themselves. The boys like that." She smiled again. "This girl likes it too," she said.

"The sessions will start early Monday morning, after the boys get off their Sunday night gigs. The clubs will serve breakfast and sometimes, like now, the boys'll keep blowing until Tuesday morning, with different musicians falling out for a few hours and then coming back again. I tell you Michael, this town is magic for a musician."

Her smile deepened. "Robert was right, those two sax men were really blowing up a storm, but it wasn't anything to what happened last winter up at the Cherry Blossom near 18th and Vine.

"The club had just opened. Bill Basie and some of them from Bennie Moten's band were working there in a small combo. Fletcher Henderson's band was in town. You heard of Fletcher Henderson?"

I nodded.

"Coleman Hawkins was Fletcher Henderson's head tenor man. Truthfully, Coleman Hawkins was America's head tenor man. He lives back East now, but he's originally from up the river in St. Joe, and he knows where the real saxophone players come from. He was anxious to test himself against the best.

"After his regular gig with Fletcher, Coleman fell into the Cherry Blossom. Within half an hour, the KC tenor men that weren't already there had arrived—Lester Young, Ben Webster, Herschel Evans, Dick Wilson.

"I was at home nodding, three or four in the morning, when Ben Webster came pecking at my screen. He said Hawkins had his shirt off and wouldn't quit blowing and they needed a piano player. I didn't hesitate.

"Sure enough, when we got there, there was Hawkins in his undershirt. He had run into something he hadn't counted on. Lester has a light style, but once he gets going, he can't be cut. Hawkins kept trying to blow something to beat Ben and Herschel and especially Lester, but he just couldn't do it. Fletcher's band was playing the next night in St. Louis, and Hawk knew he ought to be there, but he just couldn't leave until he blew something strong enough to beat those crazy KC tenor men. And he couldn't. He didn't give up until that afternoon and he had to get in his car and drive five or six hours straight through to St. Louis to make the job. The story is, he'd just bought a new Cadillac, and he burnt it out getting to St. Louis.''

It was a tale I was to hear several more times that spring in Kansas City. There were variations. The car had been an Oldsmobile, or a Packard, not a Cadillac. Buster Smith had been there/ had not been there. Herman Walder had been there/ had not been there. Big Joe Turner had been there, improvising words and music, and he was so strong he cut Hawkins too. Or perhaps not. It didn't really matter. It had happened little more than a year before, and yet it had already achieved the glow of legend, the truth beyond factuality. Coleman Hawkins, defeated in his undershirt, Lester Young still blowing strong, the death and display of Hector, the triumph of Achilles.

After letting Libba off, I drove back down Paseo and this time went left, west, on 12th Street. As I turned, I could hear faint music from behind me. In the mirror I saw that the sidewalk in front of the Sunset was empty.

A few blocks farther west on 12th, at Cherry, a man with a push broom was sweeping trash out the front door of the Reno Club, which featured colored acts for white audiences. The marquee read: "I'm a Nudist Direct from the Plantation Club in St. Louis.''

Just past Cherry, white Kansas City began, and 12th was its main artery. At Oak, construction crews were already pouring concrete foundations for the new city hall. Facing it on 12th was the just-completed Jackson County Courthouse, ordained by County Judge Harry Truman before he left for the U.S. Senate, blessed by Boss Tom Pendergast and built with Pendergast concrete. Within a few blocks of the courthouse were saloons that bragged "We Never Close,'' and any number of whorehouses that didn't either, although they were a little more circumspect about it.

At Main and at Walnut, in the middle of downtown, people were already going to work and the coffee shops and drugstores were crowded, open for breakfast. But 12th Street was a ghost of what it would be in a few hours, when the bars and restaurants started filling up again, and the horse parlors were open for bets on the early races at the Eastern tracks, when the hustlers and the gamblers and the whores and the pimps and the three-card monte men were positioned like mannequins in a department-store window to catch the eyes of the college boys and cattlemen and wheat farmers and conventioneers looking for a little action in this wide-open city they had heard so much about back home in Kansas or Nebraska or Colorado or Oklahoma.

For a couple of blocks, going up the hill west of Main, I got stuck behind a concrete mixer, gray and encrusted with droppings. Its huge caldron reared over my head, turning slowly, and I could hear the sound of wet concrete slopping around inside it, as if a huge obscene insect was digesting a meal.

The truck turned left at Wyandotte Street, just past the swanky Muehelbach Hotel, undoubtedly headed for the Municipal Auditorium being built a couple of blocks to the south with the help of a lot of money from FDR's New Deal. On the door of the truck cab was painted, in red, Ready-Mixed Concrete Co. Pendergast's, of course.

I was only a few blocks from "home," the old, once-elegant hotel with the tall iron pillars and the unsafe grillwork balconies out front, the lobby faded like tafetta left too long in the sun. That's where I had a room: three dollars a week, free parking in the rear, bath down the hall, no cooking, no guests, metal-frame bed painted brown, small maple chest with newspaper-lined drawers, writing table, closet, silver-painted radiator, bare overhead light, yellowing flowered wallpaper, a window to look out of, and a sink to piss in.

2

"Jesus Christ," said Patrick J. O'Malley. "You look terrible. Your eyes are bloodshot. You're sweating like a pig. You've got a piece of bloody toilet paper the size of a Kotex on your chin. Unless there's a hell of a wind blowing from the stockyard, I can smell your breath from here. Where'd you go last night? Out playing with the darkies again?"

O'Malley sat cocked back in his wooden swivel chair, his pole legs propped up on the vast oak desk that occupied about a fourth of the press room at police headquarters. It was the size of a snooker table and over the years had been so carved with calligraphy by the penknives of reporters and policemen that it resembled the Rosetta stone.

O'Malley peered at me over the top of the *Kansas City Star*. He was smoking a hand-rolled Bull Durham cigarette, and a little gold fleck of tobacco was stuck on his thin upper lip. His gray hat was shoved back so you could see the beginnings of his black, knotted hair and his china-white forehead sprinkled with freckles. O'Malley's eyes were coal black and he had a thin mouth, a sharp chin with a perpetual stubble and an Adam's apple that poked out of his throat like the elbow of a half-swallowed child.

I looked at my watch. A few minutes after 4 P.M. Not bad, considering I had slept until three. I was slightly late, but O'Malley was almost two hours early.

"What are you doing here?" I asked.

"I'm doing a follow-up on last week's slot machine raids," he said. "I wanted to catch the chief before he left for the day."

O'Malley was the police reporter for the *Kansas City Times*, the morning edition of the *Kansas City Star*. I worked for the third paper in town, the *Journal-Post*, an occasionally flashy afternoon tabloid that had about half the circulation and advertising of its jointly owned competitors. For

19

years, the *Journal-Post* had been tottering on the edge of the grave the Kansas City Star Co. was digging for it.

I had come to work for the *Journal-Post* in late February, after being turned down by the *Star* and *Times*. After a month in the glooms—writing obituaries—I had been transferred to a new vacancy on the night police beat. One thing about working for a dying newspaper—the turnover was rapid.

O'Malley slammed his palm down on the desk. The sound made my stomach flinch. I took a few steps and sank into an old green morris chair that, O'Malley once observed, had the grip of a whore's mouth.

"I tell you, Michael," he observed, "you always hear people talk about how awful a man looks with a hangover. In my experience, which is considerable, men usually look better and act with more grace and courage with hangovers. There is a glow about them, a heedless gait, and a wonderful, surrealistic, metaphor-seized way of talking.

"But you, my boy,"—he pointed at me with a long finger, tufted with hair between the first and second knuckle—"you look like shit." His tongue flicked out to lick the tobacco flake off his lip.

I closed my aching eyes and rubbed them and little lights bounced around in the dark like notes from Pete Johnson's piano.

"For God's sake," said O'Malley, "You're too young to feel that bad. Wait until you reach my advanced years."

O'Malley was right—his had been advanced years, at least the last ten or twelve, since he had scaled the wall of the seminary and wrapped himself in the arms, and legs, of Tom Pendergast's Kansas City.

"O'Malley," I said, "please shut up." I leaned over and was able to reach the coffee pot, sitting on the floor on an electric hot plate. I poured coffee into a dirty cup labeled Forum Cafeteria. It was my fourth cup of day. I found a Lucky in a crumpled pack in my jacket pocket. In those days I didn't smoke unless I was drinking or had a hangover, which meant I found myself smoking more and more.

"If you think it will help," said O'Malley, "I'll turn the radio down."

Until O'Malley mentioned it, I had forgotten the police radio, which meant I must be getting used to the place. The speaker hung on the wall, crackling with static and spurting information:

"Car 33, car 33, please respond to a burglar alarm at 932 Genessee. That's a hide warehouse. Braaacccckkkk."

After a while, O'Malley had said, you got so you could take a nap in the morris chair and snooze right through all the unproductive calls—shoplifting, tire strippers, non-fatal accidents, burglar alarms in the stockyards, dead people in the poor parts of town—only to snap awake the instant your subconscious was grabbed by a phrase that might mean a story—"presumed to be armed and dangerous," "possible homicide," "bank robbery in progress," "officer in need of assistance."

I finished my cup of coffee with a gulp and freed myself from the morris chair. O'Malley had gone back to reading his paper. I sat down at my end of the huge desk, my back to the door, and looked at what had been left for me by my colleague Nelson "Bulldog" Drummond, day police reporter for the *Journal-Post*.

There were three pages torn from the second edition of that afternoon's *Journal-Post*. Articles were circled with a blue wax marker. On two stories, Drummond had suggested how I spend part of my shift by underlining a word or two:

A stabbing, victim in *critical* condition at the General Hospital. No suspect as yet.

Unidentified male body pulled from the Missouri river.

And there were followups from both papers on the weekend raids on gambling joints. That was it. Drummond was supposed to leave a note with a lead or two on imminent arrests or warrants, or radio calls that had come in after his 2:30 final deadline. I had been dealt a very bad hand.

I tilted my head back and stretched my stiff neck over the top of the wooden chair, listening to my joints crack. By now, I figured, Drummond would be at least half drunk, sitting in some North End saloon frequented by cops, criminals, and combinations thereof, trying to coax a barmaid into bed by showing her the police thirty-eight he carried in a shoulder holster under his double-breasted pinstripe suit. If that didn't work, and O'Malley said it seldom did, he might try showing her his dick. That never worked, but it usually at least elicited some human response, some outside proof to Drummond of his own existence.

I needed help, fodder for the maw of a dying newspaper.

"O'Malley," I said, "what's going on?"

My first night on the police beat, less than two weeks before, O'Malley had determined that I had attended a non-Ivy-League college and thus could (A) comprehend the system he was about to explain to me and (B) probably be trusted not to use it to screw him. Then he laid out for me the rules of the press room.

"Your first responsibility, Michael, is to see that you do not get fired. Your second responsibility is to see that I do not get fired.

"The people we work for, and perhaps much of the public, influenced by novels and movies about the newspaper business, choose to believe we are competitors for something called 'scoops.' In truth, by the necessity of survival, we are partners.

"Let me offer an example. Suppose, around midnight, you are here and I am across the street in the Pleasant Dove having a beer and shuffling a few cards with the boys. A radio call comes in for cars to respond to a possible homicide at 5650 Ward Parkway, which even you are able to recognize immediately as the home of one Thomas J. Pendergast. Suppose a little later, just before my deadline for the final edition of the *Times*, I return to the press room and ask, 'What's going on?' Nothing, you mumble guiltily, your eye on what you believe is the main chance.

"Next morning, my paper will come out without a mention of the death of the most important man in Missouri. By then, of course, even those buffoons on the radio will have the story. And it will soon be all over the front page of the first edition of the afternoon *Star*. So there will be no glory in your also having it for your afternoon paper. But my not having it for my morning paper could be disastrous for me. If they didn't fire me, they would at the least set me to writing wedding announcements, and I don't even know how to spell *peau de soie*.

"So, my boy, no scoops. We share all information. That also eliminates a lot of redundant work. Makes it easier on both of us. We are a team. O'Malley and Holt. In fact"—he paused to raise a finger in revelation— "Pat and Mike."

I was soon to learn that the rules were a little more complex and devious than that, but still, my question "What's going on?" carried the expectation of an essentially truthful answer.

In response, O'Malley closed the paper and set it down.

"Everything's quiet, but don't worry, we'll come up with something. Knife victim's still alive, but he won't say who stuck him. No name on the floater yet. He'd been in for a few days. He must have come down on the spring tides from St. Joe. It doesn't look like a local job."

"Why not?"

O'Malley shrugged. "When the local boys drop them in the river, they don't come back up. Tom Pendergast lets them have the cement at cost. They use enough to sink an elephant."

"Very funny," I said.

"Who's laughing?" said O'Malley. "So anyway they took prints off the stiff a couple of hours ago and they're checking them out with the FBI. Ever see them take prints off a floater?"

I shook my head.

"You can't put too much pressure on the fingers because the meat is all soft and squishy. So you cut around the finger between the first and second knuckle and very carefully squeeze the skin loose. It will slide off like a rubber. Then you put the shells of skin over your fingers and press them into the ink pad.''

''Christ, O'Malley,'' I said.

''Don't be squeamish.''

On the desk, under the tearsheets left by Drummond, were copies of the final editions of the two afternoon papers. The first job of a reporter, I had been told repeatedly, was to read the newspapers from front to back. If you were going to be a reporter, you had to know what had already been reported.

I reached for the *Journal*. I usually read my own stories first, sometimes several times, partly looking for changes made by rewrite men or editors, but mainly just caressing them, enjoying the sensation that they were mine, like a baseball player hefting his testicles.

Only two of my stories had made the paper—a $35 holdup, no shots fired; a two-alarm fire, no injuries or deaths.

O'Malley tapped twice on the desk with his middle and index fingers.

''My boy, perhaps you should rest your eyes. They look like chicken embryos. I've read that thing from the weather report to the classified ads, and I can save you a lot of time.''

O'Malley stubbed out his cigarette and cleared his throat dramatically. O'Malley loved to read aloud. He was, he admitted, a frustrated actor. His ultimate fantasy was go to Dublin and audition for the Abbey Theatre. He read with a tenor lilt that was coated with irony—a Barry Fitzpatrick who was at least half wise to his own sentimentalities.

That hungover day, his game was welcome.

O'Malley snapped the paper flat on the desk and began with the front page.

''You don't care about the runaway steer or the attempt by the farmers of Kansas to nail down what's left of their topsoil. You certainly are not interested in how the silk-stocking editor of the *Kansas City Star* figures the GOP is going to beat Roosevelt in 1936.

''Otherwise, in the main news, Senator Truman is going ahead with his bill to create an additional federal judgeship for Kansas City, thus providing the Pendergast machine with another high-level patronage job.

''And here's the news on our latest kidnaping. Mary McElroy, the deplorable skinny daughter of our city manager, is making yet another hysterical plea to the governor to commute the death sentence of one Walter H. McGee, the man who kidnaped her and held her prisoner for so many excruciating days. O'Malley's law—kidnap a virgin, and you have made a friend for life.

23

"We also have a news flash on the celebrated crime that has made kidnapping so fashionable. Three years ago today, $50,000 in ransom was paid for the Lindbergh baby, who unfortunately by then was the late Lindbergh baby. And now Bruno Hauptmann, who started it all, is languishing in a New Jersey prison. I quote from the Associated Press: 'Rain drenches the earth, soft winds blow . . . One day follows another.' Oh, don't I just know it.

"Enough of that. Internationally, the Italians and Ethiopians are skirmishing again in East Africa." O'Malley looked up from the paper and winked at me. "No mention of essentially the same groups skirmishing in the North End of Kansas City."

"Well," he said, opening the paper, "how about a four-club golf set? $2.98 at Katz Drugs." He turned several more pages and I lit another Lucky, the last one in the pack. The first drag was full of sulfur from the match, and the second tasted worse.

"Attention please," said O'Malley, slipping into his imitation of the clipped radio-news voice of H. V. Kaltenborn. "The Nazi leader Rudolf Hess calls the rebuilding of the German Army, and I quote, 'one of the main pillars of the Nazi economic program because mustering the younger generation for army service creates jobs for the elders.' "

O'Malley nodded his head, as if struck by a new truth. "Why didn't Roosevelt think of that? Pay all those young men to lean on rifles instead of shovels."

"What else? Mother Mary Olive died. She was head of the Sisters of Charity in Leavenworth. A nun. I hope her death was painful.

"Oh, yes, I almost forgot. This should interest you. Obituary headlined 'Bennie Moten is Dead.' "

"Bullshit," I said.

"Not at all. 'Tonsil Operation Fatal to Negro Orchestra Leader.' "

"Jesus," I said. "I just saw the man this morning. What page is that on?" I reached for my copy of the *Star*.

"Ten. Near the bottom, just under Mother Mary Olive. 'Bennie Moten, 38 years old. . . .' "

"O'Malley, let me read it myself." I found the article. It was about four inches long, three inches longer than any obituary I'd ever seen for a Negro in a Kansas City daily. It read:

> Bennie Moten, 38 years old, 2125 Prospect Avenue, widely known
> Negro orchestra leader, died today at Wheatley-Provident Hospital
> of a heart attack during an operation for removal of his tonsils.
> Bennie Moten was born here, one of six living children of Mr. and
> Mrs. Ruben Moten. The father was for thirty-eight years a porter

with a wholesale liquor house here. Bennie started playing the piano
when he was 4 years old, and by the time he was graduated from
Attucks school and enrolled at Lincoln high school, he was profi-
cient at the keys.

He formed his first jazz orchestra in 1916 and found ready employment in dance halls on Vine and Eighteenth streets. Eventually, his
developed orchestras played at Electric and Fairyland parks, in
downtown hotel dining rooms and in most of the other dancing places
in Kansas City.

He began recording his 'hot' numbers for Victor phonograph and
traveled with his orchestra to many hotels and other dancing places
in the East. His 15-piece orchestra was to open an engagement in
Denver today and Moten hoped to join them several days after his
tonsillectomy. He composed several popular song hits.

At the bottom were listed surviving family members; wife, eight-year-
old daughter, brother, four sisters.

It was jarring, disorienting, as if something immovable in the periphery
of my vision had jumped into the air. The inexplicable sense of dread
that comes with a hangover rose in intensity. My forehead was suddenly chilly with sweat.

"O'Malley," I said, "this doesn't make any sense. I saw that man
at six or seven this morning shooting pool near 12th and Vine. Is there
a story in the *Journal-Post*?"

"Yep," said O'Malley. "Somewhere up front."

The *Journal-Post* obit was shorter, as stories tend to be in a tabloid,
but it was on page three, a position of startling prominence for the death
of a Negro. Usually, Negroes died unnoted by the daily papers.

Instead of attributing Moten's death to a heart attack, the *Journal-
Post* read:

> Moten suffered a sinking spell while on the operating table, which
> alarmed the surgeon in charge. A pulmotor was summoned from
> the general hospital and used for some time in a futile attempt to
> revive Moten.

"What's a pulmotor?" I asked O'Malley.

"It's a thing-a-ma-jig for pumping air into somebody's lungs."

"And where's this hospital, Wheatley-Provident?"

"Over east somewhere. It's a private colored hospital."

O'Malley got up and walked over to a large oil-cloth map hanging
from the far wall. He ran his thumb down the index.

"Let me see . . . here it is, 19th and Tracy."

"How far is that from Hospital Hill?"

Hospital Hill, in midtown a few blocks southeast of Union Station, was the location of the city's two "general hospitals"—No. 1 for white people, No. 2 for colored. The three daily papers referred to the white institution as "the general hospital." The colored one, when it was referred to at all, was "general hospital number two."

O'Malley stretched out a measuring tape that was riveted to the edge of the map. "It's a mile and a half, mile and three quarters. Five minutes at the most."

"Why didn't they use their own pulmotor?"

O'Malley shrugged. "Maybe they didn't have one." He did not seem terribly interested.

I wiped my damp forehead with the frayed cuff of my white shirt. "How could that man have gotten from the pool hall at 12th and Vine to the hospital and into an operating room and be put under the ether and have a heart attack or a sinking spell or whatever it was and die in time to make the afternoon papers?"

O'Malley shrugged again. "I don't know. I'll see if I can find out what time he died."

O'Malley picked up the handpiece of his phone and jiggled the cradle.

"Give me the coroner's office . . . Sweetheart, this is O'Malley of the *Times*. I hate to bother you with this, but have you got a time of death on that shine bandleader who kicked off this morning? Moten. No, not Morton, Moten, M-O-T-E-N. Okay, I'll hold on."

O'Malley began tapping his foot and singing softly, "I am a happy plowboy, I plow the fields all day, and da-da-da-da-da-da. . . ." He stopped. "Yeah. . . Yeah. Sure, sure. Thanks. I'll buy you a rose. I do? Well, let me know when I get to a dozen. Bye."

O'Malley hung up. "The lady says the official time of death was 10:30 this morning. Apparently, this man had a bad ticker and it just quit under the stress of the operation. They worked on him for ten or fifteen minutes with the pulmotor, but he was gone. Even if the dayside reporters didn't find out until noon, they had a couple of hours to check it out and phone in the story. Plenty of time for the final two editions."

I said, "He died at 10:30 this morning?"

I mulled that over. Four or five hours after I had seen him drinking and shooting pool, he was dead on an operating table. "O'Malley," I said, "aren't people supposed to be in the hospital the night before an operation?"

"White people are."

I stared past O'Malley at the dingy, off-yellow walls, at the two dust-encrusted windows reinforced with wire netting, at the red-and-blue Kansas City Southern Railroad calendar on the wall. The police radio sprinkled the air with up-to-the-minute reports on the imperfectability of man.

I dropped my cigarette in the tin spittoon next to the desk. It went out with a hiss in the brown gruel. Once, I had been told, there had been a brass spittoon in the press room, courtesy of the management of the *Kansas City Star*, but the cops had stolen it and Drummond had replaced it with this one, bought used from a barber shop for fifty cents. It was cleaned and half-filled with water early every morning by a janitor. Tobacco chewing was not as popular as it once had been, so people tossed matches and cigarette and cigar butts into the spittoon. On bad mornings, Drummond would sometimes throw up in it.

I stood up. "I think I'm going to make the rounds," I told O'Malley. He dismissed me with a flicker of his skinny fingers. His feet were back up on the desk and his hat was pulled over his eyes.

I left the press room and walked down a long, dingy corridor with offices on both sides. Black letters were stenciled on the wimpled translucent glass panels on the doors—Homicide, Detective Bureau, Bomb & Arson, Vice, Radio Dispatcher, Missing Persons. Most of the city's police officers were here on the second floor of Kansas City's seven-story, fifty-year-old city hall.

Light filtered dimly down from metal-shaded bulbs hanging from the fourteen-foot ceilings. Many offices were already closed and dark for the day, but at the detective bureau the lights were on and the door was open. Several plainclothesmen were typing up reports.

Just past the detective bureau, the corridor opened onto a balcony above a long, wide, oak-bannistered stairway that led to the first floor and the Fourth Street entrance to city hall. On the balcony at the head of the stairs was a small alcove that looked like a cashier's cage at a bank. Behind little square bars above a chest-high shelf, a police sergeant sat at a desk—the booking desk. There was a thick gray ledger on the shelf and a patrolman was standing outside the bars, writing in the ledger. Two old women, one in a black dress and shawl, the other bareheaded, stood silently nearby.

Arrests were logged in the book: name, address, race, offense, time of arrest and status of the offender—in jail, in the hospital, out on bond, released for lack of evidence, dead. The book was colloquially referred to as the police blotter.

I usually began my rounds with the police blotter and the desk sergeant, but that day I wanted a breath of fresh air. My mouth tasted bitter from tobacco and coffee and my stomach felt queasy. I started down the filthy, oiled-softwood stairway. The stairs trembled, and squeaked like baby mice. They had buckled slightly at the center over the years, and the bannisters leaned in on either side, so there was the sense that the stairway was a narrowing and perilous passage and that day I imagined that the whole edifice was ready to fold inward, bringing tons of stone blocks rumbling down, like a trick Egyptian tomb in a Boris Karloff movie.

I stepped outside onto Fourth Street. I'd left my jacket in the press room and there was an April chill, but it felt good against my sweaty skin. Fourth Street was busy, but not as busy as it would be in a few hours, when the produce trucks and wagons began arriving. The low brick buildings across Fourth Street from city hall housed a restaurant, a bar (the Pleasant Dove), the police garage, and five small grocery stores. A block to the east was the main city market, more or less where it had been since the city had been founded 100 years before on a mud-coated limestone ledge that jutted out of the Missouri River just below its confluence with the Kaw. Over the years, the commercial center of the city had moved eight or ten blocks to the south, but the North End reclaimed that distinction, briefly, for a few hours on either side of dawn.

The brick and cobblestone streets of the oldest parts of Kansas City, as in many settlements on rivers and on bays of the ocean, were canted at an angle to the rest of the city. The forty-odd square blocks of the North End followed the organic geometry of the city's first main street, the Missouri River, while the newer parts of the city had been laid out with compass and grid, and streets ran precisely north and south and east and west, regardless of the folding of the land and the coursing of the water.

Some years before, the city council had officially changed the name of the decaying old river enclave to the North Side, because "North End" had become irretrievably associated with gangsters and whores, drifters, grifters, gamblers, drunks, Negroes, Italians, and Eastern Europeans. All those elements were still there, along with cops, city officials, saloonkeepers, hundreds of fruit and vegetable peddlers and three save-a-soul missions. The city council's trick had not worked even in the realm of press-agentry—most people still called it the North End.

The North End and the nearby West Bottoms and stockyards, where the steel was forged and the cows were bought and sold for slaughter, were mostly in the first ward. Earlier in the century, the first had been Tom Pendergast's ward, and his older brother's before him. Now it was Tom Pendergast's city, and he let the Italian crime syndicate run the first ward and operate openly in the entire northern half of the city, as long as he got a piece of every bit of illegal action, from the plush casinos with the hostesses dressed only in cellophane aprons down to the sleaziest syphillis-ridden whorehouse and the poorest of nickel-ante crap game.

28

It was almost five o'clock. The day-shift police who had not already fled were leaving, and the evening men were arriving. Women with string bags and bad feet were moving slowly down Fourth Street from store to store, bruising the fruit and vegetables. A skeletal white-haired man in the remnants of an army uniform from the Great War was curled up asleep next to a lampost, as if it offered shelter.

A horn blared, and an old woman in a flowered dress tumbled back onto the sidewalk as a long black Buick rolled by, inches from the curb. The swarthy man at the wheel glared at her from beneath the wide, turned-up brim of his gray fedora as he passed, never slowing down. There were hundreds of men who looked and acted exactly like that in the North End, and by the spring of 1935 it was impossible to tell to what extent "Scarface" and "Little Caesar" had been based on them, and to what extent they were based on "Scarface" and "Little Caesar." One thing I knew: the ones I had met were far too stupid and unimaginative to come up with an act like that on their own.

When the Buick had skidded around the corner and out of sight on Main, a hunched-over man in a dirty white coat resumed scraping horse-turds off the street and dumping them into a garbage can he pulled behind him on wheels. Like the hoodlums, this man and several thousand others owed their employment to the Pendergast machine, which had been running its own thuggish New Deal for years, while much of the country was waiting in vain for the Republicans to let some money dribble down.

The chill was piercing my damp shirt, and the air had cleared my head somewhat. I turned to go back inside. I waved to the man in smoked glasses rattling coins in a tin cup beside the entrance to city hall. He waved back.

I made the rounds—booking desk, prisoner processing, radio dispatcher, a few other offices that were still open. It took me less than half an hour. O'Malley generally took a lot longer. He found gregarious delight in making the rounds—it was a major part of his social life. He loved flirting with the secretaries and trading jokes and lies with the cops. With several of them, he had little cutting contests going on to see who could display more vulgar callousness to human suffering. A couple of cops liked to goose people and O'Malley even put up with that and, when a chance arose, goosed them back. Somehow I couldn't conceive of Ernest Hemingway, who had been a *Kansas City Times* police reporter in this building fifteen or so years before, playing the game quite that way. On the other hand, city hall veterans said that Ernest Hemingway had been a lousy police reporter.

The door to the detective bureau, usually my last and longest stop, was closed and locked. I returned to the press room with leads for a couple of marginal stories and found two plainclothesman talking with O'Malley. The stocky one in the morris chair was in shirt sleeves and was wearing a shoulder holster nestled up into his armpit. It held a revolver with a barrel so long it poked him in the upper edge of his gut. He looked like Wallace Beery, only meaner.

The other man, older, skinnier, with pinched undertaker cheeks, had his double-breasted suit coat flapping open and was wearing a brown hat. He was sitting at the desk in my chair, in the middle of telling O'Malley a story.

"So," the older detective said, "Sweeney here calls this rookie patrolman over and says to him, 'This colored lady says her son is missing. Take her to the basement.'

"We follow to the head of the basement stairs. They go down there, and you can hear their footsteps down that long corridor to the police morgue. Then the footsteps stop, and it's quiet for a few seconds. The first scream is kind of low, like a moan, and then she really lights into it. Sweeney hits me with his elbow.

" 'Well, Kessler,' he says, 'I guess we got a positive ID on that dead nigger.' "

The three men laughed. Kessler looked expectantly at me. I smiled politely.

"I wish they were all that easy," said Sweeney, from the morris chair. He had a high, almost girlish voice, but he spoke with the hard assurance of a man who hadn't believed in anything since Tinkerbell.

"Got one in this morning. Going to be a lot harder to identify. I'd be willing to bet this one never even had a mother. He's forty, forty-five, who can tell how old spooks are? Throat cut like somebody opened it up just to see what was inside. Found him in an alley down around 18th and Olive. That's nigger dope-fiend territory. They get all full of hop or morphine and when they run out they get so desperate they'd suck the diarrhea out of a sick baby's ass to get the paregoric."

My stomach rolled at that image. Thanks very much, Sweeney, I thought.

Sweeney ran his sausage fingers through his light brown hair, which was combed straight back from his forehead. He took a handkerchief out of his pocket and carefully wiped his hand.

"Was this man a drug addict?" I asked.

"Don't think so," said Sweeney. "No marks on his arms or legs. Or on his neck, except of course for the probable cause of death." Sweeney snickered moistly through his nose. "Did you ever see them when they run out of veins and they shoot it in the side of the neck? Makes all this scar tissue. Looks like a goiter that dried up. I don't think he was taking the stuff. May have been selling it though. Dressed like a real sport. Hundred-dollar suit. Silk tie. Pearl cufflinks.''

"What's your next step?" I asked. O'Malley gave a quick chortle. Sweeney heaved himself up from the morris chair with his stubby, muscular arms.

"What's my next step?" he asked incredulously, his voice rising. "O'Malley, do they get these new kids right off the turnip truck?"

"Worse," said O'Malley. "College."

I was standing near the door. Sweeney came over to stand in front of me, hands on his hips. He was three or four inches shorter than me but he outweighed me by twenty or thirty pounds—some of it fat, more of it muscle.

"I'll make it real simple," said Sweeney. "What I got is a dead nigger, and somehow I don't think he was the president of Western University or some bigshot bandleader, so you and I both know it ain't going to make the papers. Found him in an alley in the colored Bowery. Had a pistol in his hip pocket—did I mention that? Hadn't been fired. Dressed like a big-time numbers man. This is what we call in the law-enforcement game a misdemeanor homicide. Unless some dinge walks in the door here and confesses and he's waving a straight razor with type A blood on it, we just classify this as the unsolved killing of John Doe, Negro male, forty to forty-five years old, no distinguishing features except for a hole in his throat big enough to stick your peter in and wiggle it around if you're so inclined. Unsolved. We'll stamp it ANK. Another Nigger Killing."

With a flourish, Sweeney jerked a black cigar out of his shirt pocket, bit the end off, spit the tip in the direction of the spittoon and struck a kitchen match on the desk. Lit, the cigar smelled like a septic tank, and my stomach rolled again. Sweeney stared at me.

"I tell you what, Holt. I'll show him to you. Come on, we'll view the remains. Every cub police reporter ought to visit the morgue. O'Malley, you want to come along?"

"No thanks, Sweeney," said O'Malley, faking a yawn. "I saw a stiff once. You showed it to me. Remember?"

Sweeney giggled. He tapped me on the shoulder. "You first, Alphonse."

It was a long walk down two flights of stairs. Sweeney, at my shoulder, gesturing in my face with his stinky cigar, chattered all the way about well-known corpses he had seen. There were five of them in one batch the day of the 1933 Massacre at Union Station, when Pretty Boy Floyd and a couple of buddies showed up with submachine guns to meet lawmen taking a prisoner to Leavenworth.

"Then," Sweeney said, "there was that election day last year when they brought in four dead citizens all shot up. Hey, they shouldn't have been handing out Reform Party leaflets." He giggled as we started down the narrow basement stairs.

The basement was even darker than the first floor, dark and damp. But, at the end of the long cement corridor, the police morgue was blazing with light. It was about twice the size of the press room. In the center, under the glare of an overhead light encased in a spherical metal cage, was a chipped, white porcelain-topped iron table, about six feet long. Underneath the table the floor sloped like a funnel to a center drain. Above the table, a long, jointed metal hose hung down like a broken arm.

In one wall were double doors that opened into the central courtyard of city hall, big enough to accept the rear of an ambulance, or a hearse. In the opposite wall were twelve large gray metal drawers, stacked three deep, four across. The room smelled of urine and feces, ammonia and formaldehyde, the stockyards and the chemistry lab.

Sweeney went to the wall of drawers and pulled on one, on the far right row, second from the bottom. It squeaked as it rolled slowly out. The head came into view first, face up. The man's kinky hair had been processed and greased to sweep back from his forehead in a pompadour but already the treatment was giving away to time and nature, and coils of hair stuck up in the air like busted springs. He had a large, curved nose, long, thin lips and high cheekbones. He appeared to be tall, although the lower half of his body was hidden by a dirty sheet. His skin was the bloodless gray of ancient bread mold, the gray, almost, of the drawer he was lying in. From where I stood I could see nothing wrong with the man except for the pallor.

"Come on up closer," said Sweeney. "Show you the wound."

I took a step forward, and then a second. I could see nothing, and then I could. His throat had not been slit. An almost circular hole had been cut in it, as if someone had wanted to ream out his Adam's apple. The hole was open like the gill of a beached fish and filagreed with red and white strings of tissue. Flaps of gray skin around the hole reached inward, as if they had been sucked in during a desperate attempt to breathe through this new mouth. The light shone pitilessly down into the hole, on the speckled blood and sputum and the tendrils of sliced muscle and ligament.

Dizziness came over me. I could somehow sense the blood descending from my head and, as if my body was perversely trying to maintain its hydrostatic balance, the fluids in my stomach began to rise. I clapped my hand over my mouth and tried to turn away from the open drawer but I was too late. A thin, yellow-brown stream of vomit shot from between my fingers, curled in the air like a lariat and splattered in a thin, curving line down the face of the dead man.

The rest of it ended up on the cement floor. After the first couple of waves, there was nothing left to come up, but the choking heaves continued for a minute or more. My throat tasted of bile and sulfur. Sweeney was giggling like an unhinged mockingbird. I pulled my handkerchief from my pants pocket with my left hand and wiped my face and my right hand.

Sweeney reached for the black hose, still giggling. He triggered the nozzle and washed the vomit on the floor toward the drain. He ran the water quickly over the toes of my black shoes. "You got a little on you there," he said gleefully.

Sweeney wiped his hands on a tgowel hanging on the handle of one of the drawers. He reached for the drawer with the corpse. "Seen enough?" he asked.

Almost involuntarily, like a man on the edge of a cliff drawn to jump, I looked again. The thin vomit was disappearing into the faded gray of the dead man's skin. I looked down at the face. It remains fixed in my memory: hawk-beak nose, lacquered hair, long, thin lips, high cheekbones.

Sweeney gave the drawer a shove and it rolled shut, but as the man's head, illuminated in the overhead light of the morgue, disappeared into the wall, it came to me that I had seen that face before. And recently. It was the face of the man I had seen that morning, the man in the black hat, shooting pool with Bennie Moten.

3

SATURDAY MORNING, APRIL 6

"Shvitz," she whispered.

"Swits?"

"Shvitz," she said. "Sweat. You certainly sweat a lot." She ran the back of her fingers down the damp Y of light brown hair on my chest.

"And shmutz." She reached up and rubbed my forehead. She examined her fingers and then turned them to me so I could see the black smudge.

"Shvitz and shmutz." She shook her head. "My mother warned me about goyim."

I turned to look at her there beside me, and the image is one I have with me still, more than seven years later, as I sit here alone with the events of that spring in Kansas City rolling through my mind like scenes from a magic lantern. She was naked, lying on her right side. She gazed softly at me with those large brown eyes that shone like sherry through fine glass.

Her dark brown hair, which held an undertone of red in the late morning sun that spilled through the window next to the bed, was cut almost as short as a man's and brushed back over the tops of her ears, and you could tell by the tautness beneath her soft, satiny skin that she had been a tomboy, but had grown beyond it. She had cheeks that grew pink without rouge, the apple-lipped smile of a child who had just cheated the tooth fairy, a sensuously arched nose, small but fully formed brown-nippled breasts that yielded a bit to gravity, a slightly curved tummy beneath a deep Italian Renaissance bellybutton, low, rounded peasant-girl hips and a dancer's taut calves. And that tiny raisin of a mole that grew on the inside of her upper thigh. At that moment, I was certain I was in love with her.

"Know something?" I said. "I thought for sure you'd find a boy

34

in New York.''

"There aren't any boys in New York," she said. "Just men." She grinned and stroked my cheek with the tips of her fingers, making me shiver.

"I'm kidding," she said, "Actually, they're make-believe men. All they care about is Wall Street. Half of them want to blow it up and the other half want to own it. I tend to side with the former group, but I get a little tired of talking about it. I get a little tired of talking, period.''

"I hadn't noticed," I said.

"Hah. *Touché.*" She leaned down and kissed me, her lips apart. Her breast touched my chest and when her nipple brushed mine another shiver went through my body. I rolled toward her, but she pushed me back. I was surprised at the strength in her small arm.

"Not so fast," she said. She kissed me lightly on the side of the neck and her breath stroked me like a feather. She moved to my chest and then went lower, her tongue between her lips, moistening my skin. She raised her head to look up and me and said, with a very serious look on her face, "Let's do this first.''

I had met Rachael Loeb the year before in Lawrence, at Kansas U, where she was taking a summer-school course in advanced French, commuting three days a week from Kansas City. She took three hours of A back to Barnard in the fall. Rachael was nineteen years old, very bright, very strong-willed, a political radical but not evangelical about it; one of her father's three daughters but, I gathered, the favorite. We had dated a few times that summer, but only in Lawrence because her father would have disapproved of her having a gentile for a beau, and her very Orthodox second-generation Ukrainian mother, she said, would have shrieked like all the Furies.

Our dates were in the afternoon—a student union tea dance, a matinee at the university theater, a near beer or two in town—friendly, tentative. We had once tried to play tennis, but she was so much better than I that it was no fun, at least not for me. We'd written a few times. We'd missed seeing each other at Christmas vacation—I was 150 miles away, with my parents in southern Kansas, writing letters to newspapers pleading for a job.

Now, she had taken the DC-2 back from New York because her father had had a heart attack and was in Menorah Hospital. Friday afternoon, she had called me at work. She said her father was fine and she would be free after the nine o'clock visiting hour. I took off work early, well before midnight, leaving my journalistic future in the hands of Patrick J. O'Malley, and she picked me up in front of city hall in a little green

Dodge coupe that her father had bought for his girls. We had a drink at the Muehlebach. The Coon-Saunders band was dispensing its usual schmaltz. Rachael insisted on staying through some fat tenor's syrupy version of "Yours is My Heart Alone," her parents' favorite song. They had a taste for schmaltz. Their favorite novel, Kathleen Norris' romantic opus *The Heart of Rachael*, had inspired the anglophillic spelling of their daughter's traditional Hebrew name.

She invited me to her house, the white-pillared colonial near-mansion her father had built five years ago just west of Ward Parkway. It was on a hill with a backyard tennis court that looked down on the clubhouse of the Mission Hills Country Club, to which he could never belong.

Rachael's sisters had driven in from Chicago and St. Louis two days before and had left Friday afternoon, and her mother insisted on spending the night at the hospital. No one was there but the maid, who had two rooms in the basement and secrets of her own. Rachael and I drank sweet wine in the living room and listened to her father's Caruso records on the Victrola until three or four in the morning. Then, at Rachael's instigation (as I recall), we ended up in her room in her grandmother's four-poster oak bed.

We made love for a long time, first frantically and then much more slowly, and fell asleep with our arms around each other. When we woke up around ten in the morning, we had our little conversation about shvitz and shmutz and then made love again.

Afterward, we lay on our backs looking dreamily upward at the flowered canopy that seemed to float above the bed.

"So," Rachael asked. "What did you do after you threw up on the corpse?"

Oh, Jesus, I thought. When did I tell her about that? Must have been late.

"Nothing, that night," I said. "The next day I went in early and talked to the police reporters on the day shift. I found out the big colored funeral homes pay people at the hospitals to let them know the moment some well-known Negro dies. They like the publicity. There was plenty of time for the obit to make the afternoon dailies. The editors thought Bennie Moten's death was big news, I guess because so many white people knew who he was."

Rachael nodded. "Even I have heard of Bennie Moten. His band once played at a party I went to, after a very rich kid's bar mitzvah."

I didn't say anything.

Seeing my blank look, Rachael said, "Oh, my goodness. It's like a coming-of-age party. *Pour les petits princes.* Go on with your story."

"Let's see. Bill McClellan from the *Star* talked to a deputy coroner who said Moten's heart had stopped on the operating table, and they couldn't revive him.

"Drummond from the *Journal-Post* got his story essentially from McClellan. He changed 'heart attack' to 'sinking spell' so his story would sound a little different. He picked up the extra detail about the pulmotor on a call to City Hospital. That's it.' "

"Was there an autopsy?" asked Rachael, rubbing her fingers lightly across my belly.

"Stop that," I said. "It tickles."

"It didn't tickle an hour ago," she said.

"Yeah, well," I said.

"Go ahead with your story," she said. "I'll be good."

"A couple of days later, I called the coroner's office and talked to a clerk. He said he had seen the coroner's report and it ruled natural causes. 'The man just had a bad heart,' the clerk said. 'And the operation was too much for him. Thirty-eight is pretty old for a tonsillectomy.' "

"Sounds reasonable to me," said Rachael.

"Yeah, but dammit . . . look. Two men are together until early in the morning, drinking. Twelve hours later, both of them are dead. With their throats cut."

Rachael said, "So the tonsillectomy was a, what would Dashiell Hammett call it, a 'cover job'? Did you spring that notion on the men down at the police station?"

"On Patrick O'Malley. I told him the man I saw in the morgue had been playing pool with Bennie Moten that morning."

"What did he say?"

"He said I was drunk that morning and was probably mistaken. Besides, he said, and I quote, 'All niggers look alike.' "

"Nice man, Patrick O'Malley," said Rachael. "My roommate from Boston says the Irish are either funny or dangerous."

I laughed. "O'Malley's very funny. I don't think he's dangerous, but he could be. And he's smart."

"He doesn't sound it," she said. "Somehow, I thought newspaper people would be a little more refined. Walter Lippmann, Dorothy Thompson."

"They're more like *The Front Page*, only not as witty," I said. "What are you doing?"

"Stroking your leg," said Rachel.

"Rachael," I said, "I'm not sure I can do this again." She smiled and proved me wrong.

A little before one, Rachael Loeb dropped me off at the Country Club Plaza. She had to go to Menorah Hospital. Later that afternoon, an aunt was taking her to Union Station. And I was going to Bennie Moten's funeral.

"See you at Easter," I said.

"See you at Passover, pumpkin." She blew me a kiss goodbye.

4

I took the Country Club trolley down to 18th Street, and the 18th-Street car east past the Paseo to Woodland. In my lap was the *Kansas City Call*, the Negro weekly that I had bought the day before when I saw the display headline:

Funeral For
Bennie Moten
Is Saturday

Musicians to Have Charge
Of Noted Bandleader's Rites

The story said an autopsy had been performed and Moten's death was ascribed to "coronary sclerosis, hardening of the main blood vessel." Yet another cause of death? The story also said Moten "was in the hospital to undergo an operation." Nothing about tonsils. Curious. Or was it? Maybe I was just being overly suspicious. I read through the rest of the long obituary as the trolley rocked along:

On tours east Bennie Moten's orchestra attracted large crowds in New York, Philadelphia, Baltimore, Chicago, Cleveland and other well-known amusement centers.

In Kansas City, he is considered the dean of orchestra leaders. Many musicians who are now playing in large and well-known eastern orchestras got their start with the Moten organization.

When the orchestra played in Cincinnati a few years ago, it was featured nightly over the National Broadcasting Company's network. He became popular with radio listeners instantly.

I glanced through the rest of the paper. Some of the news I had already read in the white papers, although not in such detail, and the *Kansas City Star* would not have headlined a report on the latest victim of heavyweight boxing contender Joe Louis with the words "White Boy Badly Battered." Other news I had missed: There had been fifteen lynchings in Southern states the previous year. All the victims were Negro men, accused of offenses ranging from rape to speaking disrespectfully to a white man.

On that early spring day, the clouds had moved in from the north and west and bunched in the sky over Kansas City, veiling the sun behind a thick, rolling, translucent curtain. As the afternoon wore on, the wind from the west, the dust wind, picked up momentum and whipped the clouds around like spooked sheep. This time, the wind brought with it the startling smell of moisture, the long-awaited promise of a heavy spring rain.

I could smell the rain in the air as I walked up the steep hill on Woodland to 19th Street. It was a little after 1:30, with the funeral scheduled for two, and already the mourners had overflowed the large church at the top of the hill and spilled onto the wide cement porch. Hundreds more were standing on the lawn and sidewalk and across Woodland on the playground of Crispus Attucks school.

Next to the church doorway, under a high pediment supported by white pillars, a brass choir was playing "Just a Closer Walk with Thee." Two black-suited deacons guarded the door. I used my press card to get past them and worked my way through the packed foyer and down an aisle to a wall on one of the long wings that opened out on either side of the main central building. The church, it occurred to me as I backed against the wall, was shaped rather like the Sunset Club.

Light filtered in through large stained glass windows behind the altar and at the end of either wing. Centennial M. E. was the silk-stocking church of Negro Kansas City, an institution of deeply polished woods, high chandeliers of crystal and gold and a pervading sense of bourgeois rectitude.

There were perhaps 1,000 people in the church. They sat in the plush-backed theater seats on the main floor and in wooden pews in the three-sided balcony, and stood against the walls and in the foyer. There were three or four generations seated or standing together, from little boys in short pants and bow ties and little girls with dark ribbons on their pigtails to men and women old enough to have lived in slavery.

In common was a formality of dress in basic colors—black suits, stiff white collars, voluminous dresses in black and Navy blue, pearls white against powdered necks. Many men were in formal band suits with epaulets on the jackets and single dark stripes down the pantlegs. There were several dozen white people, including at least one councilman and a couple of other politicians I recognized from city hall.

The black-robed choir sat in wooden pews that rose on either side of the altar, facing the congregation. In front of the altar, the silver-bound casket was raised on a mahogany stand and almost hidden behind banks and sprays of flowers. The humid air was thick with their scent and the perfume of the mourners.

At either end of the casket a man in a burgundy band uniform stood at attention, facing the congregation. The organ was playing and each note was prolonged with agonizing, unmelodic slowness.

Just after two, three saxophonists in burgundy uniforms played "The Old Rugged Cross." As they drew out the last notes, a strong, deep voice came from the rear of the church:

"I am the resurrection and the life. . . ."

A minister in black robes walked up the aisle, followed by a veiled and sobbing woman holding the hand of a little girl. The woman was on the arm of a man with the unmistakable unctuous air of a fancy mortician. They were followed by ten or twelve other family members, including a handsome walnut-skinned man who, despite his moustache, looked like a slightly younger, slightly thinner version of Bennie Moten. It was, I discovered later, Bennie Moten's nephew Bus, the man who was to take over the band.

The ceremony that followed surprised me at first. I suppose I had been expecting something like the legendary New Orleans jazz funerals, or at least the Pentecostal fervor I had heard from whitewashed country churches in North Carolina childhood summers, but this was more like a politely boring Methodist or even Episcopal service in Burlington or Greensboro, given to droning music and smothering metaphors. Three ministers spoke and, by the third, with the warmth and humidity and the perfume and the drone of voices and the plod of organ and choir, I grew drowsy. I tried to keep awake by surveying the crowd. I spotted Teddy Wellington and, tiny beside him, Libba Monroe, in seats a few pews behind the family. I was looking at Libba when I saw her smile with delight at something the preacher said:

"And now, we will hear from Mr. James Scott."

A little old man got up from a pew near the front. He walked with the support of a cane, and even so, he had difficulty making his way to the baby grand piano that sat above the rostrum between the choir pews.

He was short—not more than 5'3" or 5'4", with a plump body. He had a long face the color of cigarette tobacco, with thick straight shocks of graying hair above a high forehead.

Spreading the tails of his mourning coat, he lowered himself stiffly onto a high, round-topped piano stool. The man seemed to be in his sixties, and he spoke with a frail voice and the formal diction of a McGuffey's Reader. I recognized his name and vaguely associated it with an article I had read about the influence of Negro ragtime music on modern European composers.

"I am James Scott. The young persons among you may recognize me as the very old man who leads brass bands in Paseo Park in the summer. If you are somewhat older, you may recall me as the leader of an orchestra at the old Ebelon Theater on Vine Street, little more than a block from here." The little man smiled.

"I am led to understand the Ebelon building now houses an establishment called the Cherry Blossom, where musicians continue to play, including some associated with the late Mr. Moten. Some few of you may be old enough to remember when I appeared at such sinful places, playing on the piano a music called ragtime.

"In his youth, Mr. Moten too played ragtime. Indeed, he was briefly a student of mine, before his own restlessness took him beyond me, as jazz replaced ragtime as the profane music of the Negro people. Mr. Moten was one of those responsible for that change, and for many years I felt bitter about this."

The church had grown silent and even the nervous and bored coughing that almost inevitably punctuates a long funeral had ceased, as if everyone wanted to hear what the little man was saying in his dry, ancient voice.

"In recent years I have come to see that Mr. Moten had not deserted ragtime. I hear our old music in all of his compositions, in their daring rhythms and counterpoints. He had permitted ragtime to live, embodied in a new orchestral music that will be the basis for the concertos and symphonies and operas of our race, and even its sacred music, its oratorios.

"Sadly, Mr. Moten's music is now considered unfit for the house of God. Similarly, ragtime was long ago thought of as the music of the devil. But now that it is acceptable in polite parlors, I hope you will permit an old man the minor impudence of playing the music of his youth in honor of a man who himself once played ragtime."

He paused and took a long, slow breath. A child said "Mommy?" as if to begin a question, and was gently shushed.

"It is appropriate," James Scott continued, "perhaps even inevitable, that Mr. Moten was from Missouri, for Missouri was the birthplace of ragtime. I would like to play selections by three of Mr. Moten's fellow Missourians.

"The first, untitled, is by myself, James Scott of Neosho, Carthage, and Kansas City. It is newly written with Mr. Moten in mind. The second is by the late Scott Joplin, an adopted son of St. Louis and Sedalia. It is 'A Real Slow Drag,' the finale of Mr. Joplin's opera *Tremonisha*. The opera concerns the freeing of our race from ignorance and superstition. For reasons we can only guess at, it has never been performed in full.

"The third selection is by Blind Boone, the untrained Negro prodigy from the tiny town of Miami, Missouri. It is called 'Carrie's Gone to Kansas City.' "

The little man turned to the piano, slowly rubbing his fingers. He grimaced, as if they ached. His left leg curled up beneath him like a child's to hook beneath the piano stool. He spread his stubby fingers impossibly wide, like the ribs of a hawk's wings, and began to play his requiem for Bennie Moten.

It was like nothing I had heard before, at least nothing called ragtime, which to me meant tinny old player pianos pumped too fast, the pit music behind the Keystone Kops, "Ragtime Cowboy Joe." This music had implacable grace, little haste, notes rising and falling like wooden horses in unsymmetrical but precise progression; the last ride on the carousel. I looked across the church. Libba had her hands folded on top of the pew in front of her and her chin resting on them. She looked hypnotized, like a nocturnal animal bathed in sudden light.

The second piece, the one by Scott Joplin, was wistful, full of spaces, and it ended with the melancholy sound of a music box running down.

"Carrie's Gone to Kansas City" had a spare, ancient lilt to it, the lilt of the West, dust devils on the prairie, waterholes in the distance and the roll of wagon wheels. The Kansas City that Carrie was heading for was one that existed long before Bennie Moten and jazz, before ragtime had a name. It was the place where the West began.

As the final note decayed in the high reaches of Centennial M. E. Church, a woman began to sob. James Scott rose slowly and returned to his pew just behind the family. Shortly after that came the benediction, and the funeral was over.

After the casket had been carried out and the church had begun to empty, I walked to the altar. Among the flowers yet to be carried out was a large wreath in the plow-shape of a sixteenth note. There was a card attached. It read, "With deepest regrets, T. J. Pendergast and family."

A four-inch obit in the *Star* and now this, I thought. Bennie Moten must have been a man to reckon with.

The church was still more than half full. People were bunched at the entrance and on the single stairs leading down from the balcony. But the downstairs pews were empty—except for a young man, just a kid it appeared, sitting asleep at the end of a pew. A deacon walked over and lightly shook his shoulder. His jaw wobbled a bit but there was no other response. His eyelids stayed shut. The deacon shook again, harder, and finally the young man's eyes opened. They were large black circles. He blinked several times, shook himself, and then got to his feet quickly, with a little hop. He reached down to the seat and picked something up. It was a striped cloth bag. He put it under his arm and started to push his way through the crowded front door, and I remembered him. It was the young man who had been refused admission to Pete Johnson's bandstand, the saxophone player who was in one of Robert Creech's classes at Lincoln High School, Bennie Moten's alma mater.

Outside, under a sky of darkening clouds, a hearse and four long black limousines sat at the curb. Behind them, fifty or sixty musicians in the uniforms and formal suits of a dozen bands had formed in ranks of four stretching halfway down the hill to 18th Street. Cars were lining up behind the musicians.

As the cortege slowly pulled away from the church and turned right to head west on 19th, the huge band began marching and playing—sloppily at first, but quickly falling into step and key. It was the Chopin funeral march. I looked down 19th and as far as I could see the street was lined with mourners.

I saw Teddy and Libba standing nearby on the church lawn. Libba looked luminous beneath a flat black hat with a raised veil. She was wearing a thin black wool dress, black silk stockings and a single strand of small white pearls. Teddy, in his navy-blue band suit, had his arm around Libba's shoulder and he hugged her to him as the wind rose suddenly, bringing with it a damp chill. When he did that, I felt a quick stab of an emotion that was hard to define—sadness, regret, perhaps even jealousy. Perhaps it was just the spring wind, full of promise and a vague nostalgia. Something from a contemporary poet came into my mind, a line about April, "mixing memory and desire, breeding lilacs out of the dead land."

Teddy saw me. He took his hand from Libba's shoulder and, holding it palm down, made a slow sideways movement, as if slicing a few inches into the humid air. It was the most elegant, most blase wave I had ever seen.

44

I walked over and said hello. Teddy gave an almost imperceptible nod. Libba smiled, and I felt warmth rise to my face.

"Well, where's Robert?" I asked.

"Colored folks supposed to keep track of each other?" asked Teddy.

"Teddy, he's your nephew," said Libba. She looked up at me. "Robert's in the band. They didn't have any need for piano players."

Teddy squeezed her shoulder again. He said, "And I'm long past beating one of those damn bass drums."

"This is the biggest funeral I've ever seen," I said.

"I've only seen one bigger," said Teddy. "Last year, after they machine-gunned that big-time Italian gangster, Johnny Lazia. They say Pendergast had him killed because he was getting too much power, and then gave him the biggest funeral in the history of Kansas City."

We stood on the lawn and watched down 19th as the hearse and then the rest of the ungainly procession turned north onto Vine, two short blocks away. The wind from the west was picking up strength, carrying the sound of the funeral back to the church. The band ended the dirge and began playing "Nearer My God to Thee."

As the last of the marchers disappeared around the corner on Vine and the cars began making the turn, the sound of the band began to grow louder. The head of the procession must have turned off Vine onto 18th and be heading back this way. A few people began walking down the hill on Woodland toward 18th and then more got the idea, and began hurrying after them.

The long obituary in the *Call* had given me enough information to understand what was going on. The band was inscribing a mark on Kansas City, a mark that took in six blocks, touching the edifices of Benny Moten's life and music: his church, Centennial M. E.; his school, Crispus Attucks; the colored musicians union that he helped to found at 1823 Highland; the Cherry Blossom on Vine, where only last year his saxophone players—Ben Webster, Herschel Evans, Lester Young—had prevailed over the vaunted competitor from the East; the other dance halls and clubs around 18th and Vine where he had first gained recognition.

Teddy and Libba and I stayed at the top of the hill, looking down Woodland. Soon, three motorcycle policemen arrived at the intersection and blocked it. The hearse and the black limousines turned left, away from the church and toward the cemetery four miles away. The band stopped at the intersection, and stood in tribute, silent except for a muffled drum beat and the rumble like distant thunder of a solo bass horn, the ancient backbone of jazz.

The bass horn slowly mourned. It was a hymn, but unfamiliar. I turned to Libba. "What's he playing?" I whispered.

"Asleep in the Deep."

The horn player reached into what seemed to be the very bottom of his instrument and then, in a series of doomful steps, went even lower to find the notes a pole away from the trumpet ecstasy of high-C. It ended with a plunge to a note so low it was almost subsonic in the slowness of its reverberations, drawn out like the last surrendering rattle of death from the throat of a giant.

Then, the huge bass drums sounded twice, there was a matching roll from the smaller drums and a trumpet pierced the air. All the instruments came together in a fast riff and then quick-stepped up the hill, propelled by "Moten Swing."

When it was done, I turned again to Teddy and Libba and brought up the subject I had been waiting to talk about.

"You all remember the other night, when we saw Bennie Moten drinking with another man at the Sunset?'

"I do," said Teddy. "Do you?" He laughed.

"Through a glass darkly," I said. "And later, Libba, remember we were going to the car and you and I and Robert saw Moten shooting pool with the same man, a tall man with sort of a hooked nose wearing a black fedora."

"I remember," said Libba.

"Could that man have been a drug peddler?"

"Ha!" said Teddy. "He was indeed. A licensed drug peddler."

"Pendergast licenses drug peddlers?" I asked, quite prepared to believe it.

Teddy laughed again. Libba smiled and said, "Michael, that man's a doctor. Dr. Stone. He's supposed to be the best Negro doctor in town. He was Bennie Moten's doctor."

"They were also friends," said Teddy. "They catted around together."

"No kidding?" I said.

That put a halt to my train of thought. Or did it?

I said, "If Dr. Stone was a close friend of Bennie Moten's, he would have been at the funeral today. Was he?"

Teddy said, "I don't remember seeing him, but hell, there were hundreds of people here today. Libba, did you see him?"

She shook her head.

"OK," I said. "What if I told you that I saw that doctor last Tuesday afternoon dead in the morgue?"

Libba shook her head. "Nope," said Teddy. "Man that prominent, we would have heard about it. And they would have had two funerals here today."

I was thinking that over when Robert Creech walked up, unbuttoning the jacket to his blue and gold Lincoln High School band uniform. Teddy said, "Nephew, did you happen to see Dr. Stone at the funeral?"

"Stone?" said Robert. "He wasn't here. I heard he left town until it blows over."

"What blows over?" asked Libba.

"I talked to some of the boys in the funeral band and they say Dr. Stone messed up that operation. They say he cut the wrong thing and Bennie Moten bled to death on the operating table. They say that's why Dr. Stone left town."

Immediately, I thought of several more questions, questions that Teddy and Libba and Robert might be able to answer. But first, I decided, I wanted to talk to O'Malley.

5

The 18th-Street trolley swayed back and forth with a relaxing gait. I stretched my legs out on the three-passenger wooden bench that ran just behind the driver and gazed out the windows at the red-brick facades of 18th, more bourgeois than funky-butt 12th: colored dentists and lawyers and movie theaters and clothing stores and even a couple of Negro hotels and restaurants among the nightclubs that catered almost exclusively to whites. I tried to arrange my thoughts about the death of Bennie Moten in light of what I had learned in the police morgue and at the funeral. I was going to meet O'Malley later that day, and I wanted to lay it all out for him like a deal in showdown poker.

In those days I loved to ride the trolleys, which ran almost anywhere you wanted to go, and watch the city go by. The Kansas City streetcars had symbolized the big city to me for years, ever since I had come to town with my parents to the American Royal horse show and carnival, and had been kept excitedly awake half the night at the Muelbach Hotel by the streetcars squealing by.

When I got off at the Market Square turnaround across from city hall, I checked to make sure my car was still in the police parking lot. I usually left it there, except for those nights when, as O'Malley put it, I was too drunk to walk home.

Car thieves were so busy in Kansas City that insurance rates were about the highest in the country. I couldn't afford insurance, and I certainly couldn't afford to replace a stolen car on my salary of fifteen dollars a week. I figured it was safe in the lot, unless some policeman decided to steal it.

The car had been a windfall. It had been given to me at the end of my junior year by my father, who had received it as a legal retainer

48

from a Kansas bootlegger who got caught about once a month running liquor-store booze across the state line from Joplin. The 1931 Model A coupe was in good shape except for several gashes—bullet holes?—in the rumble seat. My father had given it to me the previous spring, when I graduated from college, and, despite his threats, had let me keep it when I quit law school after only one semester of being bored, at times literally to tears.

It was not quite four o'clock when I got upstairs to the press room, and Bulldog Drummond was still there, working his way through a flat bottle of amber liquid labeled ''Old Crony.''

''Not bad,'' said Drummond, after successfully suppressing his gag reflex, ''but it ain't worth ninety-eight cents a pint.''

Drummond wandered out with his bottle, on his way to Saturday night's indecent acts, and left me with a small pile of stories that looked as if he had chewed them out of the newspapers with his false teeth. I went through the pile and the rest of the tattered newspapers, called the fire alarm office, and went by the booking desk, the dispatcher, homicide, and the detective bureau. By 5:15 I was ready to phone in a half-dozen crime items, including another attempted kidnapping on the South Side (I got a good cop quote: ''The kid eluded his nappers by climbing to the top of an elm tree''), and a Sunday roundup on the Hurd killing.

A few days before, seventy-seven-year-old Mr. Hurd had shot and killed pretty young Mrs. Hurd. First, he had to escape from the ropes in which she had hogtied him so he would hold still while she burned his feet with his Zippo lighter. I had gotten a nice front-page piece in the Friday *Journal-Post*, with a half-page of pictures inside showing the Mexican rope thumbcuffs and other fiendish devices the late Mrs. Hurd allegedly had used while torturing the stingy old bastard, trying to ascertain where he had stashed his fortune.

O'Malley came striding in about 6:15 to take me to dinner. He often came down to the police station on Saturday, his day off, and came in early on working days. Although he could always cite a reason, I suspected the main one was that he was lonesome and the dirty old press room was one of his homes. His other home was with his mother, the Irish-immigrant widow of a Kansas City policeman, in a flat off Main that O'Malley called ''the sacred hearth of Jesus.'' It was, I gathered, a major Midwestern archive of gory religious artifacts. ''The woman's mission in life,'' O'Malley once said, not without love, ''is to have her knees bleed the length of Lourdes.''

That Saturday, O'Malley showed up in a thick black sweater with a high turtleneck that gaped at his turkey throat and a loud houndstooth jacket that was too narrow for his shoulders and too fully cut for his chest. On his head was a low-peaked, narrow-brimmed Kelly green hat with a yellow canary feather stuck in the band. He was swinging a shooting stick and whistling that trumpet flourish you hear at the racetrack. O'Malley had just come from Riverside Park, which was seven miles out of town at the end of the only four-lane cement-paved road in Platte County, Mo. People called it "Tom Pendergast's Road." Actually, Pendergast owned the racetrack, not the road. He had, however, sold the state the concrete to build it.

O'Malley was grinning as if he had hit the daily double. He opened the handles of his shooting stick and jammed the pointed end into the filthy softwood floor.

"You know, Michael," he said, easing his skinny buttocks onto the seat of the shooting stick, "Riverside Park is a marvelous institution. Where else in the country would a couple of thousand sportsmen come out on a chilly, overcast day like this one to watch horses run in a state where betting is illegal?"

"I thought you could bet at Riverside Park," I said.

"Oh, no, no, no, no. There is, of course, a window where you can invest in the improvement of the breed prior to each race. If it should happen that the particular animal for which your investment was earmarked improves to the extent that he wins the race, then you are per force entitled to a dividend. Today, thank the Lord, I invested wisely. Shall we go to dinner?"

He folded the shooting stick and threw it on the desk. "Better bring a wrap," he said, grabbing an old raincoat from the coat rack. "The *Times* predicted rain."

Unfortunately, the *Journal-Post* had forecast no precipitation, and my raincoat was in my room. I felt a sprinkle or two as we walked a few blocks through the North End, but I just turned the collar up on the coat to my Sunday suit.

There was no sign outside the restaurant, which was on the second floor of a two-story building, up a narrow flight of stairs. The door had a peephole in it. O'Malley gave the door two dramatic knocks and posed smiling as the peephole slid open. We heard the bolt being drawn. O'Malley winked at me and whispered, "The boys don't know Prohibition's over."

The heavy door swung open towards us. "Mr. O'Malley," said a man in a black tuxedo.

"Ciao," said O'Malley.

Inside was a long, narrow room with large wooden booths on either side of an aisleway. At the end of the aisle, spotlit from above, was a life-sized rough-stone statue of a child of six or eight, clearly male. His head was tilted back and water was spewing out of his mouth and falling over his body to gather in a cement scallop shell at his feet. As we were being led to a table past the crowded booths, O'Malley whispered to me, "Ask me later about the statue. Aren't the fucking guineas priceless?"

I hoped nobody had overheard him, since about the half the customers seemed to be speaking Italian.

We settled into a booth big enough for six. Almost immediately the waiter brought us large salads: lettuce with pitted black olives and little bits of salty ham. And he set before us a quart Coca-Cola syrup bottle filled with a red liquid. O'Malley poured us each a glass. He took an appreciative sip. I followed suit. It was a dry red wine.

I said, "I take it this place doesn't have a liquor license."

"I doubt if this place has an occupancy permit," replied O'Malley. He started in on his salad. "But really," he said, chewing, "I think a lot of this is just for show. Speakeasy swank."

The salad was very tasty, with lots of garlic in the olive oil and vinegar dressing. I took a few hefty bites, washed them down with wine, and said to O'Malley: "I went to Bennie Moten's funeral today. I found out some things you might find interesting."

"I doubt it," said O'Malley. "But go ahead and tell me. I shall eat."

"There must have been a thousand people there," I said. "Some white people, including councilman McKissick. A lot of flowers. And a huge wreath from Thomas J. Pendergast."

"How sweet," said O'Malley. "T. J.'s just another sentimental Irishman."

O'Malley gulped in a huge chunk of lettuce and I quit talking and hurried to catch up. We finished our salads in a dead heat. The waiter took the empty plates and replaced them with big platters of spaghetti covered with tomato sauce.

O'Malley twisted a gob of spaghetti on his fork and shoved it in his mouth, with loose ends sticking out. He looked like a Kansas mudcat trying swallow a ball of night crawlers.

I told O'Malley what I had found out at the funeral—that the man who had been drinking with Bennie Moten had been his doctor, and that the musicians had heard rumors that the doctor had botched the tonsillectomy and that Bennie Moten had bled to death on the operating table. "The doctor was not at the funeral," I said, "and I was told that he left town. But I think he's dead in the basement of the police station."

O'Malley swallowed and wiped red sauce off his lips with a white cloth napkin. "Eat your spaghetti," he said. I cut up and ate a few forkfuls, and took a long drink of wine.

"So," said O'Malley, "what your fervid little Saxon brain has come up with is that the doctor killed your musician, perhaps on purpose, and then somebody turned around and killed the doctor. Right?"

"Right," I said, taking another big bite of spaghetti.

"Why?"

"Something to do with drugs," I said, pouring myself another glass of wine from the Coke bottle. "I haven't got it all figured out, but Sweeney said the man in the alley might have been killed because of drugs, and you're always hearing about Negro musicians using drugs and you're always reading about doctors being arrested for selling drugs. Maybe Bennie Moten got in the middle of some narcotics transaction, and somebody wanted him out of the way. And maybe somebody also had proof the doctor was selling illegal drugs and blackmailed him to kill Moten. Then somebody killed the doctor to keep him quiet."

I expected O'Malley to laugh. Instead, for the first time, he seemed interested.

"That's ludicrously farfetched," he said. "But maybe it contains a germ of truth. The coppers have noticed a lot of heroin coming into town the last six months or so, and they aren't sure where it's coming from. New mugs in town, they figure. They've rousted a couple of street peddlers, fellows who are selling it by the bag, but apparently it is delivered in such a way that they cannot trace it back to its source. The street peddler gets a call in a phone booth, he's told to go to another phone booth by a certain route to see if he's followed. Leave the money here, pick up the dope there, that kind of thing."

"I don't know much about heroin," I said.

"Heroin," said O'Malley, sucking a tomato seed from between his front teeth. "Pain killer derived from morphine. Originally developed by the Germans as a morphine substitute, thought to be much less addictive. Turns out that heroin is five or ten times as addictive as morphine. It's been around for years, but it is just beginning to show up in large amounts for the dope-fiend trade. It's illegal now to make it in this country, and the new stuff comes from overseas, the Orient, maybe through Japan."

O'Malley took a long drink of wine.

"So what do I do now?" I asked.

"What you do now is be very careful," said O'Malley, licking his lips. "Big-time dope pushers murder people, even if they didn't murder Bennie Moten and the doctor, and I frankly doubt they did. That scheme is too jesuitical for dope pushers. But that does not mean they will not murder you, if they think you are poking into their business."

"So," he said, pouring more wine in my glass, "watch your step. But it might be worth trying to get a look at Bennie Moten's death certificate. Was it his heart, or was it his throat? A copy should be on file by now at vital statistics. You can't do anything about that until Monday. Then, you might go nose around that colored hospital. For now, eat."

I finished my spaghetti and pushed my plate away. Inadvertently, I belched.

"Sorry," I said. "Guess I'm full."

O'Malley smiled beneficently and cleaned the remainder of the sauce off his empty plate with a chunk of bread. As he popped that into his mouth, the waiter came over and took our plates.

"Fine meal," I said, stifling another belch.

The waiter slid two more plates in front of us—the fish course, O'Malley explained. The sole in white sauce was followed by the meat course—a thin piece of veal in butter and garlic. O'Malley kept eating and pouring wine from the Coke bottle. I ate as much as I could, and at the end I was stuffed and exhausted. I lit a Lucky, my first of the day, and offered one to O'Malley but he shook his head and rolled a Bull Durham. "Solidarity with the working class," he explained.

The Lucky and a small but potent cup of bitter coffee revived me enough to stand up and reach for my wallet.

"I had a good day at the track. Let me get the bill," said O'Malley, rising and beckoning for the waiter. He pulled a two-dollar bill and a one-dollar bill out of a money clip and dropped them on the waiter's tray. "Keep the change," he said. I never saw a check.

As we were leaving, we bumped into an odd group coming in. There was a tall, flush-faced white-haired man in a light gray flannel suit. He looked simultaneously distinguished and disreputable, like a congressman from the Deep South. With him were two swarthy men wearing gray hats with snapped-up brims, one folding up a damp umbrella, and a plump woman, feathered and beaded and peroxided, Tugboat Annie aspiring to Mae West. O'Malley seemed to know them all, particularly the white-haired man, but no introductions were offered.

Outside, the rain was not heavy but steady, and O'Malley held his raincoat high so we both could hunch under it as we walked back to the office. We had to pick our way through a tangle of horse-drawn wagons and small motor trucks bringing produce to the city market. The horses were skittish in the rain, their hooves slipping on the wet bricks, and once I was afraid a rearing horse was going to tumble on top of us, but he regained his footing.

The booking officer gave us a little salute as we passed his desk, going up the stairs. "The Crimson Kid just left, running," he told O'Malley.

"Good for him," said O'Malley. The Crimson Kid was a cub reporter for the *Star* who filled in at the police station on Saturday nights.

The press room was empty but the box was blaring: "Holdup in progress at the Pussycat Tavern at 2310 Troost. Officers in the vicinity please respond." I started to dash back out—I saw the chance the catch an arrest in action, maybe even a shootout—but O'Malley held my arm. "Take it easy. The Kid's ahead of you. By the time you get there, the robber will either be dead or gone. Give it fifteen or twenty minutes, make some calls and see what happened."

O'Malley hung his wet coat and hat on the rack and sat down at his end of the immense desk. I settled with a squirm into the morris chair.

"O'Malley," I said, "who was that tall, white-haired man in the restaurant?"

O'Malley was rolling a cigarette. "First," he said, "you're supposed to ask me about the spitting statue."

"OK," I said. "What about the spitting statue?"

O'Malley lit his cigarette and took a long drag. With smoke curling out of his mouth, he began speaking.

"As you are no doubt aware, J. C. Nichols, the South Side real estate tycoon, has brought many thousands of pounds of outdoor statuary to the Country Club district from Italy. The spitting statue you saw today was one of the first to arrive.

"It was in place for less than a month when some of the boys from the North End chanced to spot it on the way out to that golf club they frequent. One of them came back at night with a hammer and a tire tool and jimmied it loose. It ended up in his backyard, not far from here."

O'Malley took another drag off his cigarette and used his little finger to remove a tobacco flake from his lower lip. He was gazing above my head at nothing, his dark eyes taking on the dreamy look of a favorite persona—the Wise Old Raconteur. The words began rolling out like taffy.

"Several of the thief's neighbors wanted spitting statues of their own, and so he began taking orders. But, before he could fill the first one, word of the theft reached the ears of a man of great importance in the

North End, and indeed in the city as a whole.

"The thief was summoned and a few tiny but crucial bones were shattered. And the word got around quickly, so there are no more thefts of statues from Mr. Nichols' curving lanes, even though there now must be a couple of dozen of them scattered about."

Dramatically, O'Malley flipped his cigarette into the spittoon, where it went out with a quick sizzle.

"The man of importance decided, however, that it would be foolish to draw further attention by returning the statue, particularly since it made such a nice fountain. So he had it placed in his restaurant, both as a source of aesthetic pleasure, and as a reminder to patrons not to steal statues from Mr. Nichols."

"O'Malley," I said. "You mean J. C. Nichols called up somebody from the Black Hand to complain about a missing statue?"

"Oh, no, no, no," said O'Malley, holding up his hand. "Stop that. I suspect J. C. Nichols was not even aware that the statue was missing. He has many statues. The initiative came entirely from the other end. The point is for you to understand how Kansas City works, to understand what can be gotten away with, and what cannot. Rule number one: Don't steal from the rich Protestants in their part of town."

"OK," I said. "I get it. Now what about the white-haired man?"

O'Malley glanced to his left at the clock. "Make your phone call about the robbery."

I looked up the number of the tavern and called. A policeman answered. The thief had gotten thirty-four dollars from the register and was long gone when the police arrived. I wrote that down and turned back to O'Malley. He looked at me with a rather sad expression.

"The white-haired man is Dr. Foster. The syph doctor."

I must have looked puzzled.

"Syph," repeated O'Malley. "Syphilis. He treats the whores for syph and clap and keeps them from getting knocked up. He also treats some of the boys, the gun toters. They all get VD, since the only women who'll sleep with them are whores. They come in every few weeks for their silver nitrate or whatever."

O'Malley tilted his head back and scratched with the fingernails of both hands at the half-day's growth of black whiskers on his neck. He sighed.

"Dr. Foster was a friend of my old man's, back when Dr. Foster was legit and my old man had not been killed in that alley by a drunk nigger with a straight razor."

"I thought they never found out who killed your father," I said.

"Who else carries razors? Anyway, my old man walked a beat downtown along Grand, past the building where Dr. Foster had his office. They both loved the horses, and they got to be friends at the betting parlors around the corner on 12th."

O'Malley pulled his Bull Durham sack from his shirt pocket and stared at it for a moment. Then, he used his teeth to tighten the string loop at the top. He put it back in his pocket and licked his lips.

"I need another drink," he said, his eyes wandering back to the ceiling. "You know, Dr. Foster used to have a pretty ritzy clientele. You'd be surprised, this was before the silk-stocking doctors started moving out to the Country Club Plaza.

"One day, a woman came to him and asked for help. Respectable woman. Her thirteen-year-old daughter had been kidnapped and gang-raped by four or five hoodlums. The mother thought she had contracted syphilis.

"She was right. The girl was also pregnant. The mother probably knew that already. She begged Dr. Foster to get rid of the baby. He said he didn't believe in abortion, but the girl started crying and they both begged and finally he figured, what the hell, syphilis, rape, a child for a mother, what chance would the baby have anyway?

"So he did it. And the mother said she was eternally grateful and must have told everybody she knew about it because the Medical Society came by one day and told Dr. Foster he was no longer a member in good standing. They let him treat the whores and the hoodlums, but if he tried to practice with respectable people, he would probably find himself in jail."

"O'Malley," I said, "that's a damn shame."

"Yeah," said O'Malley. "On the other hand, he did murder that little baby."

I had no idea how to answer that, so I got up and made the rounds again. It took me half an hour. When I got back, O'Malley was still there. Somewhere, he had dug up a pint of whisky and he was glowing again.

"What's new, scoop?" he said, offering me a drink from the bottle. I declined and told him what was new.

"They finally got an ID on that fellow they fished out of the river last weekend," I said. "You know, with the soggy fingerprints. He was an American seaman. More precisely, a Japanese-American seaman. Born in San Francisco, twenty-six years old, lived with his mother who thought he was at sea and had no idea what he was doing in Kansas City. Do you think my city desk might want me to pursue it?"

"Pooh," said O'Malley. "Give them an item, and forget it. Who cares about some week-old Jap floater?"

O'Malley sat up in his chair and put the bottle on the desk in front of him. "Did you run into the Crimson Kid?" he asked. "Maybe jacking off in the men's room with *The New Republic*?"

The Crimson Kid had gone to Harvard, which was his first mistake as far as O'Malley was concerned. His second was that he was godawful eager, and his third was that he had left lying around some editorials he had written for his college paper. They called for peace and justice and a restructuring of the economic order, and they seemed pretty sensible to me, but O'Malley and Drummond and Sweeney and even McClellan rode the Kid about them every chance they got. He didn't seem to notice, which may have been his fourth mistake.

"I didn't see the Kid," I said. "I did see something surprising though. I saw the chief of police."

"Huh," said O'Malley, "that's news. Awful late for that bird to be in the office, and on a weekend. Was he alone?"

"No, he wasn't," I said. "He was with this guy I've seen around headquarters before, usually with the chief of detectives. He's a big man, swarthy. A long face that's getting moony. Probably in his thirties. Wearing a camel hair overcoat and one of those snap-brim hats, but this one looks like it cost fifty bucks."

"Charles Vincent Carollo," said O'Malley. I nodded, recognizing the name.

"Nickname: Charley the Wop," said O'Malley. "But don't call him that. Very important man. Let me think about this."

O'Malley tilted the pint to pour some whisky in his mouth and rolled it around like Listerine, diluting it with saliva. Finally, he swallowed. He put the bottle down, pulled out his top desk drawer and fumbled for something.

"This story is so recent, I haven't filed it yet." O'Malley kept massive story files in the cabinet to the left of his chair.

He held up a clipping. "From last Sunday's *Kansas City Star*. Let me read it to you."

"Jesus, O'Malley," I said, "can't I just read it myself?"

He frowned. "And I felt like declaiming. Have it your way." He slid the clipping across the desk and began whistling a familiar tune.

I remembered the article. It reported on gambling machine raids the previous weekend. The police had confiscated more than fifty of the machines, and the owners of the raided establishments were shouting foul.

One of their complaints was that many machines still operated in the downtown district. And these machines, they said, belonged to what they termed the "syndicate." Charles Carollo, a former business partner of the late John Lazia, was mentioned generally as head of the syndicate.

It is a recognized edict that none of the gambling devices may be displayed, connections or not, south of Thirty-first Street. The order went out some time ago and has been complied with swiftly.

Many marble games, in which balls roll into numbered holes, were still attracting Kansas City nickels last night in the downtown district. Most of them are known as "Rocket" games and pay off anywhere from ten cents to one dollar in nickels to the fortunate few who actually achieve the lucky combination. Recently, however, a new machine in which seven tiny aluminum horses, mechanically controlled, race under a glass cage, has gained a wide popularity.

Students of Junior College in the last week have provided an additional source of income for the machines, since one of the horse race games has been placed in a drugstore at Tenth and Locust streets, a block away. The students, between classes, crowd around this gambling game.

Another of the horse race games was found operating last night directly across the street from police headquarters, in the restaurant of the city market.

When I looked up from the article, O'Malley stopped whistling. "Well?" he asked.

"Well," I said, "I suppose, if I was the chief of police, and the *Kansas City Star* had implied those things about my department, I might do something to prove I wasn't the lackey of the syndicate."

"And how would you do that?"

"I guess I would confiscate a few syndicate machines. But I would want to explain things to Charley Carollo first. And then I would do it on a Saturday afternoon or evening so I could get it in the big fat Sunday *Star*.

"Uh huh. And which syndicate machines would you confiscate? Or borrow for a few days?"

"I guess I would pick the ones mentioned in the story."

"I certainly would think so," said O'Malley, with a gay grin. He picked up the phone. "Give me the Detective Bureau. Hello, is Detective Sweeney there? . . . *We're off to Dublin in the green* . . . Hello, Sweeney? O' Malley here. Listen, what time are the race machine raids? Oh, I just thought there might be some . . . yeah . . . Can't locate the Crimson Kid, huh?"

O'Malley winked at me.

"Yeah, Sweeney, that's too bad," he continued. "Well I'll be a monkey's uncle. A raid, right under our noses. . . Naw, I don't know where the kid is, probably checking in with his commissar. But Holt's here. . . right, if you can't get the Sunday *Star*, the *Journal-Post* is better than nothing. . . Fine, I'll pass it on."

O'Malley put the receiver down and spread his arms wide, as if he had just prepared me the most marvelous feast of bread and fish.

"They were just going to call," he said. "They've been trying to locate the Crimson Kid but he's lost somewhere. They had to go ahead and hit Tenth and Locust because the proprietor wanted them to get it over with, so he could lock up and go home to bed. But the city market restaurant is open all night. They would like to go ahead and make the raid now, if that's convenient with you."

The raid went like a cotillion. Detective Sweeney chatted with the midget behind the cash register while four burly uniformed cops carried the machine carefully out the door, which was held open by the fry cook. "Mind you don't slip on them wet bricks," warned Sweeney. He gave me some nice quotes: "Let this be a lesson to the criminal element in our community. We will enforce the law with an even and just hand. We will play no favorites. No one is immune from the law."

When I got back to the office, O'Malley was gone. I gave the story to the city desk in time for the final edition and was about ready to leave when the Crimson Kid came in. He looked bedraggled and distraught, and his long straight hair was wet and curling at the edges. He started to tell me a sad tale about someone breaking into his car while he was in the tavern and not only taking his spare tire but using his jack to steal one of the wheels right off his car. Well, he went back into the tavern but. . . .

I took pity on a fellow cub reporter and interrupted him to tell him about the raid. It was already well past his midnight deadline for the final, but he might be able to get a few quick paragraphs in for the 1:30 replate, thus partly saving his ass without significantly diminishing my accomplishment.

At the front entrance to the station, a newsboy was already selling early copies of the *Star*. "Hot off the presses," he said. It would be at least another half-hour before the tired old *Journal Post* was on the streets.

I bought a Sunday *Star*, made a mental note to put the nickel on my expense account, pulled out the society section to cover my head from the rain and ran the half block to the Pleasant Dove with the rest of the paper under my suit coat. Inside, I ordered a double shot of whisky and spread the paper out on the table in front of me. I leaned close to read in the tavern's dim light.

First, I checked sports. Paul Dean and the World Champion St. Louis Cardinals had beaten the St. Louis Browns in the first game of their annual exhibition series. Good news. Like almost everybody else who lived west of the Mississippi, I was a Cardinal fan.

I went back to the front page.

A woman had been treated at the general hospital after shooting herself in both thumbs "toying with a revolver." The Crimson Kid had neglected to tell me about that one.

A prolonged fight was expected in Congress over the New Deal bill to establish "social security."

But the main story concerned the weather. "Break in the Drought" read the subhead, and the top headline was positively exultant:

It Rains At Last!

6

The clerk at the bureau of vital statistics was asleep. Her thin arms were on her desk and her head was on her arms, her wispy light brown hair trailing over them. It was a little after two o'clock. I coughed a couple of times and got no response. There was a bell on the counter and I popped it with my fingers. She woke with a start and looked up at me. She was about thirty years old, thin, pretty in a weary way. She stood up and brushed her hair back from her face with a hand.

"What do you want?" she said, rubbing her eyes.

"I want a death certificate," I said. "On a man who died six days ago."

She pulled a comb and mirror out of a black patent leather purse and began working on her hair, combing it back to trail down her neck.

"You a relative of the deceased?" she asked, glancing at me over the hand mirror.

"No."

"Then you can't see the death certificate," she said, poking her comb back in the purse and pulling out a lipstick.

"The hell I can't," I said. "I'm a reporter. Holt of the *Journal-Post*."

"Holt of the *Journal-Post*," she said, in a mincing voice. "La-de-da."

She stopped spreading the deep red lipstick, which was turning her thin mouth into a Cupid's bow, and looked at me more closely. "No, you ain't. I never seen you before." She went back to greasing her lips. I took a deep breath and let it out slowly before I spoke again.

"I'm sorry. I'm new. Here's my press card."

I pulled out my wallet and dropped the card on the counter. She finished making her mouth into a bow, the lipstick arching well above the line of her thin upper lip, and patted it lightly with a Kleenex. She inspected herself in the hand mirror. Her tongue went up and scrubbed

61

the lipstick off her front teeth. She walked slowly over to the counter and looked down at the picture on my press card. With three fingers of her right hand, she flicked back the brim of my hat. She looked at my face.

"You ought to grow a moustache," she said. "Make you look older." She leered at me with coquettish contempt. "But maybe you can't grow no moustache." She turned and walked back to her desk. She pulled a stick of Juicy Fruit out of her purse, unwrapped it and shoved it in her mouth. When she began to chew the gum, I could smell it all the way across the room. "What's the name of the deceased?" she asked.

"Moten. M-O-T-E-N. Bennie. He died last Tuesday."

She turned and walked toward one of the scarred wooden file cabinets that lined the walls. Her skinny hips swayed beneath a long black skirt that was shiny at the seat. I could see her brassiere strap beneath her filmy white blouse. She was not wearing a slip.

She flicked through files for a minute or two. Finally, she turned back to me. "Nobody by that name. Sure he died in Kansas City, EM OH, not Kansas City, KAY AY ESS? She gave me a smart-aleck little smile.

"Yes, I'm sure," I said. "He died at 10:30 A.M. April 2 at Wheatley-Provident Hospital."

She raised her eyebrows. "Shit," she said, between her teeth. I flinched. It was not a word I was used to hearing from women. "Wheatley-Provident. A nigger. Why didn't you say so in the first place? Brother, you are new."

She snapped her gum. I'd always wished I could do that. She went to a corner of the room where two ancient file cabinets leaned together like a couple of drunks. She fought open a stuck drawer and rifled through files.

"Nope," she said. "He ain't here neither." She had one of those western Kansas whines that sounds like a sandstorm scouring an old tin silo. "You sure you got the name right? I got some Mortons in here. No Bennie, though."

"No, ma'm," I said. "Maybe it's not here yet."

"You say he died six days ago. We got everybody, Negro and white, from July 1, 1886, until the day before yesterday. Maybe Mr. Moten ain't really dead." She gave me a big fat smile. In doing so, I was glad to see, she smeared lipstick on her teeth again.

"Dammit," I said, "this is supposed to be an office of public records. And this is important. Let me speak to your boss."

She snickered. "Important, huh? Well, my boss has gone for the day. You want to complain, you could see the city manager, if he's not home protecting his daughter from those cute hillbilly kidnappers. Building next door, three flights up.'' She stood staring, hand on hip, chewing her gum, until I turned and left.

I went next door to the old red-turreted city hall, but I only went one flight up, to the police press room. My colleague Bulldog Drummond was there with a couple of uniformed cops and Bill McClellan of the *Kansas City Star*. O'Malley was not due for a few hours.

The foursome was playing pitch on the big desk. As usual, Drummond had already started drinking and his eyes were watery beneath a ludicrously large black hat that looked as if it had been designed for Tom Mix.

''Hey, kid,'' he said gruffly as I came in. ''Take off your hat and stay awhile. Watch this.'' He pulled a card from his hand and snapped it down on the desk. ''High,'' he announced, laying down the ace of hearts. ''Low,'' he said, dropping the deuce of hearts on top of the ace. ''Jick.'' Jack of diamonds. ''Jack.'' Jack of hearts. ''Joker. . . and game.'' He threw the last card down so hard it skidded off the desk.

''You cheating scumbag,'' said one of the cops as Drummond raked in four nickels. The policeman got up and wandered out.

The pot had been lying on top of the latest edition of that day's *Journal-Post*. A banner headline announced that the Senate had just passed Roosevelt's $4.8 billion work-relief appropriation. I turned the paper around so I could read the story.

''Know what T. J. Pendergast said about that relief bill?'' Drummond asked, scratching at the day's growth of beard he was somehow able to maintain at all times. ''He said you could buy a lot of votes for five billion dollars.'' He yawned. ''Almost three o'clock,'' he said. It was 2:35. ''Time to get out of here. Where you been today, kid?''

''Vital statistics,'' I said, hanging my brown hat on the rack. ''Looking for a death certificate they said they didn't have.''

Bill McClellan said, ''Mike, are you still worried about that colored bandleader?'' McClellan was a gruff but essentially sweet-tempered man who had been in the press room so long and was so respected that a rookie patrolman met him at the front door every morning and parked his car in a reserved space next to the chief's.

''Yeah,'' I answered. ''I think he was murdered, but I'm having a hell of a time getting anybody else interested. The floozy at vital statistics said they don't even have a death certificate on him.''

''She did, huh?'' said McClellan. ''You make a pass at her?''

''Hell, no,'' I said.

''Well, that's your problem right there. Didn't O'Malley teach you anything?'' He picked up his phone and tapped the cradle. ''Give me vitals, please,'' he said. He put the phone back in the cradle. ''Line's busy,'' he said. ''I'll call later.''

Bulldog Drummond pushed himself up from the desk. He pulled a piece of *Journal-Post* copy paper out of a pile of clippings. It had some notes and numbers on it.

''Come here, kid,'' he said. I walked over to the desk. He tapped his index finger on the notes and breathed whisky in my face.

''A tip came in from Hanrahan in the Independence Bureau. This seventy-one-year-old lady, she's on relief, spends her days roaming around the alleys picking up pieces of tinfoil, selling it to junk dealers.''

Drummond was seized by a cough. He beat it back with a long pull off the pint he pulled out of his drawer.

''So,'' he said, swallowing and wiping his mouth with his sleeve, ''Sunday night, two mugs break into the old lady's place while she's out roaming the alleys. They lady goes to the cops and reports that they got $300, and she's scared they're going to come back for the other $400 she's got stashed away.''

''Sounds like a rat police item to me,'' I said.

''Listen, kid, I'm not talking about the burglary, I'm talking about this old broad being on relief when she's got all that money stashed around the house. The county relief administrator has been out all day, but I got his home phone number and his wife says he'll be home at six. You call and ask him what he intends to do about this blatant swindle of public funds.''

He dropped the pint bottle in his jacket pocket and reached over and patted me on the arm.

''That old broad will be off the rolls slicker than snot, and we'll have us a nice offbeat crime story. Make sure you give me credit. Okay, kid?''

Drummond snorted, leaned forward past me and spit a projectile of mucus into the spittoon. ''Got to be going, kid,'' he said, lurching for the door. ''You make that call now.'' I looked over at Bill McClellan, who was hanging up the phone again. ''Still busy,'' he said. ''A wonderful human being, Mr. Drummond. Just leave him a note that you couldn't reach the guy.''

I went through the papers and left to make my early rounds. I spent half an hour listening to a cop expound on the evils of the ''send me a dime and in four weeks you'll get back a thousand dollars'' chain letters that were the national fad that spring, briefly replacing dance marathons, and it was almost 5:30 by the time I got back to the press room. McClellan had left, but O'Malley was there in his usual pose,

Ichabod Crane legs and size 12A shoes propped up on the desk, reading his paper.

"Ah, young Michael," said O'Malley. "I have a message for you from McClellan. That girl at vital statistics checked again and they really don't have a death certificate on a Bennie Moten or anything close to that. She also said you were a drip."

"So what do I do now?"

"Stop being such a drip," said O'Malley. He winked.

"Seriously," he said, "You could try to get the coroner's office to let you see the original, but they will probably just give you a runaround about going through channels and send you back to vital statistics. The coroner's a Jackson County office, and they got damned independent and rule-conscious under Judge Truman."

O'Malley pulled up his right pantleg and scratched under his right sock. He gave a sigh of tiny pleasure.

"But the death certificate is also a state record, and the coroner has to send a copy to Jeff City. You could call them. I'll find the number."

The records clerk at the state office building in Jefferson City said I could have a copy of any death certificate for a quarter, and it would take a couple of weeks for them to mail it to me. No, it would not help for me to drive down, since the problem was their shorthandedness, not the U.S. mails. I was not sure I would learn all that much from a death certificate anyway, but I mailed them a quarter.

I also mailed a penny postcard to Rachael. The note read "WRITE!! Love, Michael." It was all I could think of that didn't sound sappy. When I got back from the corner mailbox, O'Malley said, "You got anything to work on?"

"Yeah," I said, "Drummond wants me to get some old lady kicked off relief."

"I'd wait until just before Christmas on that," said O'Malley. "What else?"

I told O'Malley what little I had found making my rounds, and he left on his. I unloaded a couple of 12th Street tourist holdups and the arrest of an apparently very stupid prostitute for soliciting a banker in broad daylight on the Country Club Plaza, and then, with some time to kill, I decided to follow a piece of advice O'Malley had given me the night before.

I reached the administrator of Provident-Wheatley Hospital just as he was ready to leave for the day. His name was E. Willard Johnson, and he had a very prissy, round-toned way of talking. I said I was trying to get in touch with a Dr. Stone.

"Dr. W. E. Stone," he said. "Dr. Stone is not here. Dr. Stone is on vacation."

"Oh," I said. "When did he leave?"

"Last week. Rather suddenly. He was exhausted by an emotionally draining operation and asked to leave two weeks early on his vacation. We shuffled schedules and managed. We always seem to manage."

"Where did Dr. Stone go?" I asked, interrupting a long sigh.

"Mexico," said Johnson. "A remote gulf resort in the Yucatan. He cannot be reached."

That's convenient, I thought. Particularly if he was dead. "Why do you wish to converse with Dr. Stone?" asked Johnson.

"To ask him about one of his former patients, the late Bennie Moten."

"Oh," said the administrator. there was a long silence. "Well, in that case, I'm afraid we have nothing more to talk about. The relationship between a doctor and his patient. . ."

"Dead patient," I said.

". . .and his former patient is sacrosanct. I expect Dr. Stone to return sometime the first week in May. He may be a few days late, since the train service in Mexico is notoriously slow and uncertain."

"Not to mention the banditos," I said.

"Precisely," said Johnson. "But I certainly shall leave him a message that you called. Holt, was it, of the *Kansas City Star*?"

"Michael Holt, *Journal-Post*," I said. I thanked him and hung up. Incommunicado in the Yucatan. Sounded like a rumba.

I sat there with my thoughts, listening to the spittoon congeal. I did not seem to be getting anywhere with this double murder that nobody else believed happened. I was ready to slip across the street for a quick drink when O'Malley saved me the walk. He came strolling in, followed by Detective Sweeney. They were laughing and passing a bottle.

O'Malley did a slow, tipsy lope over to his chair and sat down, elevating his feet onto the desk. Sweeney tumbled into the morris chair like a tree frog succumbing to a pitcher plant. He had a stupid, half-dazed grin on his face and I figured he might be stuck in there for the night. He looked as friendly as I had ever seen him, and I decided this was my chance.

"Detective Sweeney?"

He turned his grin in my direction.

I said, "How do you go about exhuming a body?"

O'Malley drawled, "Well, Andy, first you gits a shovel and goes out to de seminary."

"Hush, O'Malley," I said. "What about it, Sweeney? How do you go about legally getting a body dug up?"

Sweeney's mouth hung open as he pondered the question. Then grinned again. "So that's your deal, is it kid? Personally, I like 'em to wiggle a little bit when I jam my roscoe in. How dead you want this broad to be? I could probably find you something down in the basement. That too fresh for you?"

He chortled, and the sound was like a plumber's helper working on a stuck drain.

"I'm afraid he's serious," said O'Malley.

Sweeney's face grew solemn, and when he spoke it was as if a Victrola was playing. "A writ of habeas corpus is required, signed by a duly appointed or elected member of the circuit court in the district in which the corpse resides. Or resided. Or is buried." He looked puzzled. "Anyway, you need a habeas corpus writ."

O'Malley said, "How about an all-purpose writ?"

"Shit," said Sweeney, "could I use an all-purpose writ. Like a license to steal."

"You already have one of those, Sweeney," said O'Malley. "You're a member of the Kansas City police department.

Sweeney made that sludgy laughing sound again. When he had finished, he said, "Who do you want dug up, kid? There's a couple of judges around here'll sign anything as long as there's something in it for them. You might have to give them sloppy seconds."

"I want you to dig up Bennie Moten, to see how he died," I said.

"Who's Bennie Moten?" asked Sweeney. O'Malley just shook his head.

I explained the whole thing to Sweeney. As I spoke, Sweeney scratched the side of his neck with his thick fingers, leaving red marks that were slow to whiten. He wiped his forehead with a handkerchief he somehow extracted from his hip pocket. He seemed to be sobering up.

When I was finished, he said, "Now wait a minute, kid. Big funeral and all that. Police escort, councilman in attendance, wreath from T. J. Pendergast himself. I don't care if he was a jig, we'd have to get approval of the family on this one. That might be a little rough. Sounds like there might be some other angles here, too. I think we better let that bandleader lay."

"OK," I said. I'd figured that would be his answer. "Then what about digging up John Doe, Negro male? You don't have to ask any family for permission on him, right? Dig him up, because I think he is the doctor who operated on and killed Bennie Moten."

"Kid," said Sweeney, "why don't you leave this thing alone?

Somebody must have wanted that man to be dead real bad to cut his throat open like that, and they probably don't want you tripping around trying to find out whodunit. Besides, kid, it's another dead nigger."

"Two dead Negroes," I said.

"If they're connected," said Sweeney. He wiped his brow again. "If they're connected, and if one of them was a killing at all. Kid, I'd just forget about all of this. I tell you one thing, no judge in Kansas City is going to let you dig up anybody on the basis of that blue-sky tale you just told me."

Slowly Sweeney rose from the morris chair, like a cork coming out of a bottle. He had to push with his arms and his face grew pink with the effort. Finally, after catching his breath he said, "Anyway, Holt, if we dug that man up and showed him to you, you'd just puke on him again."

He laughed. "I tell you what. I can't show you John Doe, but I can show you his personal effects. Maybe you can find some clues." Sweeney winked at O'Malley. "I got to warn you, we'll be down there right next to that nasty room where they keep the dead people."

"Let's go," I said.

"Fine," said Sweeney. "See you later, O'Malley."

I followed Sweeney down the squeaking stairs and into the basement. We stopped in the narrow, damp corridor before we got to the entrance to the morgue, at a room-sized cage with a combination lock on the door. Inside were metal shelves with wire baskets on them, like the ones you get at the YMCA to put your street clothes in. At the back of the cage a chest-high metal counter ran across two rows of what looked like large safety deposit boxes.

Sweeney turned the combination dial to the right and the door clicked open. He ushered me into the cage.

"What was the date on that again?" he asked.

"April 2, last Tuesday," I said.

"Hokey-dokey, let me see here." Sweeney ran his fingers along the shelf and then pulled down one of the wire baskets. It was about half-full of clothes. He led me back to the counter at the rear and set the basket down.

"Go ahead," he said. "Maybe you can find yourself a nice pair of shorts." He took a ring of small keys off a spike at the rear of the counter and bent over to peer at the locked boxes.

I started going through the basket. Unfortunately, I could not remember what the doctor was wearing that night. Except for the fedora, and there was no hat in the basket.

The shoes were on top of the pile. They were expensive-looking brown patent leather slippers, and stuffed in one was pair of knee-length dark brown silk stockings. Next was the underwear, shorts and a singlet, both cotton. The white dress shirt was silk, though, with a high collar and French cuffs.

Sweeney straightened up and tossed a set of pearl cufflinks and a gold stickpin on the counter.

I pulled the suitcoat out of the basket. It was green sharkskin and the label was ripped half loose, as if someone was interrupted trying to tear it out. It gave the name of a men's store in San Francisco. I held the coat up so Sweeney could see the label.

He nodded. "Yeah, we saw that. We called San Francisco, but they wasn't missing any niggers."

I went through the pockets of the coat and the pants, but I found nothing. I was folding the coat when I felt a tiny stab in my thumb. I looked down and saw a small drop of blood. I sucked it off my thumb and then picked up the coat to see what had pricked me.

I found it right away. In the left lapel was a straight pin, stuck through a pinch of cloth as if by a tailor. I stared at the pin for a moment and then tapped it with a finger, as if to make sure it was there. Then I put the coat and the rest of the clothes back in the wire cage.

"Congratulations," Sweeney said. "You handled yourself like a real pro when you saw that blood on your thumb. Shall we go, Alphonse?"

7

I overslept, hung over from a long debate at the Pleasant Dove over what O'Malley kept calling "your quote murders unquote." As I was hurrying across downtown to work, not watching where I was going, I stepped off a curb and my right heel flattened a horse turd. I slid to the pavement and my foot ended up about six inches from the wheel of a passing Ready-Mixed concrete truck. I jerked my leg back just in time to avoid a flying glob of gray Pendergast goo, sat on the curb and watched five more concrete trucks lumber by on Main, probably headed for the vast and eternal creek-paving project just south of the Plaza.

When I got to my desk at 3:12 that afternoon, I was not surprised to see that Drummond had already gone, and that he had been busy that morning:

> Widow on Relief,
> Exposed as Hoarder,
> Stricken from Rolls

The article from the early edition of the *Journal-Post* was the only clipping (or rather ripping) that he had left me. And I did not come up with much else on what turned out to be an extremely slow night, even for a Tuesday.

When O'Malley came in about 5:30, he and I went across the street for the first of several beer breaks. By 10:30, I had called in a couple of rat items and taken off, trusting O'Malley to pass along any subsequent criminal activity to my paper's late rewrite man, an old police-beat buddy. I grabbed another quick beer for the road at the Dove and I was mellow as Jello at a few minutes past eleven, when I pulled up to the curb at the bus stop in front of Lincoln High.

Several hundred people were gathered on the broad front lawn of the old red-brick school that had produced half the great musicians in Kansas City. Robert Creech waved from the edge of the crowd and came over and got in the passenger side, carrying his saxophone case.

I said, "We didn't get crowds like that for band concerts in Pittsburg, Kansas."

Robert leaned forward to wriggle out of his band jacket. "Pete Johnson and Ben Webster and Bennie Moten weren't alums of your high school," he said. "And maybe you all had some other kinds of heroes to look up to." Robert rolled the blue-and-gold jacket lengthwise and tucked it into the case, over and around the saxophone. Carefully, he shut the case and held it in his lap. The case was made of grained black leather, worn at the corners but expensive looking. A small pewter plaque held his initials: RCC, Robert Carver Creech. The case had been, I knew, a high-school graduation gift from his mother, who was graciously signifying that she had finally given up trying to make him a scientist or a doctor. By then, it was probably clear that his temperament would lead him toward teaching music rather than his uncle Teddy's jazz-band wanderings.

"You think we can find Seventeen?" I asked.

"I talked to Teddy after you called last night," said Robert, "and he tells me Seventeen can be scarce this early in the week. But we'll try. You really think you can learn anything from an old half-blind ex-convict?"

"Maybe," I said. "The dead man in the morgue had a pin in his lapel. Maybe Seventeen remembers giving a pin to the man who was with Bennie Moten. That would almost prove I was right about the doctor being murdered. And maybe Seventeen saw where they went after they left the pool hall, or saw someone pick them up. Seventeen could tell us a lot of things."

"That sounds pretty fanciful," said Robert. "But I still hear rumors about that tonsil operation, and that doctor sure did disappear right afterward. If Bennie Moten was murdered, and if it had to do with drugs, I'd like to do something about it."

Robert sighed and lightly slapped his sax case with his right hand. "I am sorry to say that there are kids in my high school, boys sixteen, seventeen years old, who are starting to use dope. Not just smoking tea—real narcotics."

I looked out on the lawn of the high school, where boys in suits and ties or sweaters and neatly pressed pants chatted with girls in their Sunday dresses. I said, truthfully, that I found it hard to believe. Robert shook his head and yawned. He took off his round horn-rimmed glasses so he could rub his eyes.

"Long day," he said, wiping his lenses with the front of his white shirt. "Drive on down Paseo to 12th, we'll check around the Sunset first."

I made a U-turn and headed west for Paseo. "Hey, listen, Michael," Robert said, eagerness in his voice. "I talked to a couple of the fellows in Lawrence today. I think they're finally getting some action."

I glanced over at Robert and I could see in the dim light that he was smiling. He turned the smile toward me, but shyly, and I sensed his eyes pulling away. No matter how close we got, there was always a touch of something guarded in his manner.

"I bet they're falling all over each other giving us credit," I said.

"I guess we're unsung heroes," said Robert. "I don't mind. Do you?" He looked over at me.

I turned north onto Paseo, heading downhill along the divided boulevard through a slash of parkland. It was supposed to rain again that night, and mist was making halos around the street lights Pendergast had installed in Negro neighborhoods shortly before the last election. "I guess I don't mind not getting credit," I said, doubtfully, backing off the foot throttle and letting the engine slow us as we started down a steep, curving hill. The engine snarled and rattled and backfired twice.

"Still looking to be the next John Brown?" said Robert. "Heh, heh, heh."

"I suppose," I said. "Would that make you John Brown's buddy?"

"Heh, heh," said Robert. "You're the buddy, buddy. You got into it because of me. Besides, I ain't molding in no grave. Not even for equality."

In the fall of 1933, I had followed the directions on a hand-printed leaflet to an anti-discrimination meeting, where I had met Robert and learned that Kansas was not as much of a Free State as its history might suggest. We also got to talking about jazz and I was fascinated to meet a Negro who knew, and even sometimes played, the music I was coming to love.

As a boy in North Carolina before we moved to Kansas, I had had several Negro friends. Although deep inside we must have known that we would be separated at the first tickle of manhood, that seems an eternity away when you are seven or eight, squirming your naked toes together in creek-bank mud, waiting for a bream to bite in the middle of a long Southern summer.

Robert Creech, I discovered, had had similar doomed friendships in Memphis—Mississippi River fishing chums he hadn't seen since puberty.

In Kansas there was no legal segregation, as there had been in North

Carolina and Tennessee. But Negroes were not treated as equals, not even at the state university, where they couldn't eat with the white students in the cafeteria or swim in the pool or play on most of the college athletic teams. Even when they were sick, they were hidden behind beaverboard in a back corner of the university hospital.

After the equal-rights meeting, Robert invited me to come listen to his records. He had a hand-cranked portable phonograph in his room, on the second floor of a big old ramshackle boarding house in the colored section just north of the river. The west wind sizzled through cracks in the walls and moaned around rotting cornices. There was one indoor toilet that was always stopped up and two outhouses in the backyard, where chickens and sunflowers ran wild. It was a funky hovel, but it reminded me of my favorite uncle's Tobacco Road farmhouse in North Carolina, and I loved being there. Robert and I spent hour after hour sprawled out on his bed, looking out the window past a huge sycamore at the Kaw rolling by, sipping Cokes from thick ice-cold bottles, listening to Louis Armstrong and Duke Ellington and Bessie Smith and talking of a better world.

"Watch it!" said Robert, raising his knees and grabbing for the saxophone case on his lap. I hit the brakes as a man came out of the mist on Paseo just above 18th Street. The car swerved briefly on the damp pavement and the man skipped by me and onto the raised median as I straightened it out and slid to a stop at the red light. More people strolled across Paseo, and through the closed window of the car I could hear music coming from both directions along 18th.

"What's going on in Lawrence?" I asked.

As the light changed and I continued down Paseo, Robert filled me in on what had happened since early March, when the Kansas legislature had told the university to quit its Jim Crow practices.

"The chancellor screamed, just like he did when we were there," said Robert. "He said parents wouldn't send their kids to KU from Missouri and Oklahoma anymore, bullshit like that. But some students and professors and three or four ministers and a few people from Lawrence met at the Unitarian church and they formed a council on race relations. They're going to make sure the university does what the legislature told them to do."

It had been a year and a half since Robert and a dozen other Negro students had tried to get a council like that going, with little success other than bringing in a few white students, myself included. Robert had even brought Roy Wilkins, the editor of the *Kansas City Call*, down to Lawrence to speak, and only seventeen people had shown up.

"I guess we planted the seeds," Robert said. "And maybe they took notice of our little agit prop. Heh, heh, heh."

Robert was referring to the minor brawl that had resulted when he and I decided to eat lunch together at a table in the student union cafeteria. Negro students were expected to eat in a separate section, an unwritten custom that was enforced by a gang of Greeks who had lost their frat house to a bank foreclosure, and who hung out in the union, drinking coffee, playing pitch and cribbage, whistling at co-eds and harassing Negroes and foreign students. We were getting the shit kicked out of us by four or five of them until a large Negro cook ran out of the kitchen waving a cleaver, and our attackers dispersed. The student paper put the story on the front page, and both of us had given depositions to a legislative investigation that we figured would never come to anything.

"Just up ahead," said Robert. "Go right."

I backed off the accelerator to slow down for 12th Street, and the car backfired. A man on the sidewalk instinctively ducked and swiveled his head cautiously in my direction. I fiddled with the choke to thin out the mixture. In response, the car backfired again. This time, the man just laughed. I put the choke back where it had been.

Robert grinned. "You know, too bad you were the only one had to go in for stitches. I hate missing the chance to integrate a Jim Crow hospital."

"Maybe you'll get another shot at it," I said, turning right and driving slowly along 12th Street. It was even more brightly lit than on Monday, since nightclubs that catered to whites were open, but there were far fewer people on the sidewalk. Almost all of them were white. We did not spot Seventeen near the Sunset or the Lone Star, or anywhere along the four or five blocks of nightclubs.

"It's early and Tuesday's the slowest night of the week," said Robert as I pulled over just short of Brooklyn Avenue, beyond the noise and glare. "Sometimes Seventeen's over at the Reno Club, but I checked the *Call* and they got no show tonight. Head on up to 18th."

I turned right on Brooklyn and drove up a dark street of small houses and flats toward the lights of 18th and, like a castle on a hill, the girders and fences of Muehlebach Field. It was the home of the triple-A Kansas City Blues and the Negro Kansas City Monarchs, with their foxy pitcher Satchel Paige, who Robert said was better than Dizzy Dean. (I assumed that was racial chauvinism, since nobody was better than Dizzy Dean.)

We didn't see Seventeen or his lunch cart as we drove down 18th, nor when we slowed at Vine to look up the hill toward the Night Hawk.

"Let's drop by the Subway," said Robert, gesturing toward a parking place just ahead on 18th. "Maybe Teddy and Libba have seen him. You said you wanted to talk to Teddy anyway, about that fellow in the morgue."

The sidewalks along 18th around Paseo and Vine were populated but not crowded this early in the week. Again, most of the people were white, except for a small group of young Negroes lounging outside the shoeshine parlor of the Street Hotel a half-block west of where we were parked, and a well-dressed crowd coming out of the last show at a colored movie theater up Vine.

I turned off the ignition. "You going to play that thing tonight?" I asked, curling my keys in my palm and tapping Robert's horn case with my index finger.

"Let's lock it in the rumble seat, all right?" said Robert.

"Chicken," I said, reaching for the door. "Wait a minute," Robert said, grabbing my arm. "I got something to tell you. You might be a little cooler around Teddy, try not to ask him so many personal questions."

"Why?" I asked.

"Teddy doesn't much like white people. If the usual reasons don't seem to be valid, he'll find new ones."

"Yeah?" I said.

"Yes," said Robert. "In your case, Teddy's decided you're a nigger lover."

I coughed. I could feel my face getting warm. "Well, Robert," I said, swallowing, "is that necessarily a bad thing?"

Robert nodded his head slowly. "Yes, it is." He turned the door handle. "Let's lock this horn up and go hear some music," he said, pushing open the door and letting in a blast of blues from the loudspeaker above the shoeshine stand.

To get to the Subway Club, we went through a swinging door at the back of a chop suey restaurant on 18th. The club must have been a speakeasy in the 1920s, or at least the entrance was designed to give the flavor of one. A narrow stairway had been gouged out of the limestone that lay under much of Kansas City, and at the bottom we turned right at a rough stone wall and walked through an arch, to find ourselves at one end of a limestone tube, ten or twelve feet high, twenty or so feet wide and forty or fifty feet long. A head-high wooden partition ran along the stone wall to the left, with the bar set against it and, farther along, a raised wooden bandstand.

It was a few minutes after twelve, and the band was warming up for the midnight show. The place was about half full. Twelve or fifteen white men and a few white couples were seated at the tables near the bandstand. Negroes were seated at four of the six tables in the back that were clearly demarcated by a three-foot aisle. Robert and I took an open table next to the arched entrance and ordered beer from the waitress.

Libba Monroe sat at an upright piano on the corner of the bandstand nearest to us, facing the far wall. Her black hair spilled over her neck and glistened in the overhead stage lighting. She was pulling poignant minor chords out of the keyboard while the white trumpet man exercised his lip with random runs, shrieks, and growls. The other horn men, an alto and a tenor, stood quietly. There was also a bass player, a tall, thin, ginger-skinned man who had to lean down to finger his instrument, and Teddy Wellington at the drums.

Libba, Robert told me, had another three weeks off until her band opened a month's stay at Fairyland amusement park. Teddy was again between bands, which suited his temperament as long as there was freelance work around.

Piney Brown had hired the two of them and the bass player for a couple of weeks to be the rhythm section at Subway, which was famous for its wide-open jam sessions. "I think that trumpet player's from the Dorsey band," said Robert. "They played St. Joe over the weekend. He must have driven down to steal ideas."

The yellow-skinned waitress brought us two bottles of Country Club beer and I threw a quarter and a nickel on her tray. She gave a little half-curtsy at the dime tip, and as her short black skirt flounced up, it appeared that she was wearing nothing beneath it but a tiny red G-string. That was tame compared to the Chesterfield gambling club, where they wore cellophane aprons with nothing underneath but their pubic hair, shaved into the outline of one of the suits in a deck of cards. The white girls wore diamonds and hearts, the colored girls clubs and spades.

The trumpet player quit his runs and stood, licking his lips, as Teddy laid down an almost sleepy four/four on the high-hat cymbal with his brushes. Libba hit a chord and then another, the bass player came in with a strong plucked note on the second and fourth beats and the tenor man stepped to the front of the bandstand, which looked big enough to hold twice as many musicians. As he started in, breathy and languorous, the chatter of the crowd died down. I thought I recognized the tune and looked over at Robert.

" 'Memories of You,' " he said, just loud enough for me to hear. "Sax man is Ben Webster, used to be with Bennie Moten too. Ben

Webster." He laughed. "They call him Frog."

Ben Webster was a handsome brown-skinned man with a rogue's wide moustache, shaved to devilish points. He was dressed to kill in a red-checked yellow vest over a pin-collared pink shirt and a red tie with small yellow polka dots. When he turned so the stage lights shone on his popped-out eyes, you could see why they called him Frog, although Frog Prince might have been more appropriate. On this slow, nostalgic tune, his tone was creamy and sensual. Every note came out in a cushion of breath, and when he swept into the upper register, he sounded as passionate and sexy as Johnny Hodges, Duke Ellington's alto man.

Slowly, as his solo wound its way through an almost pornographically languid series of twists and thrusts, he turned his slim body so he was facing Libba, as if he was playing just for her, and then he launched a long, upwardly sliding note that ended in what sounded like a love-startled gasp. It hung in the air for two beats and then Libba lightly mocked it with a similar but dissonant chord.

Teddy gave the bass drum two quick, angry kicks.

Webster grinned around his mouthpiece and began blowing again, dropping back down into the middle range, as if accepting the rejection with good humor.

"Did you see that?" I asked with delight.

"What?" asked Robert, his face serious as usual, and it occured to me that my imagination might have created the little playlet. Or maybe Robert was so intent on the music he missed the romance. Libba took a long, lyrical solo, precise and formal yet infused with passion, Chopin with the blues. Then, startlingly, she took off on a tangent, throwing in a quotation from "Fascinating Rhythm," and ending her solo with eight bars of boogie-woogie. The alto man and the nervous white trumpet player took their turns, and then the three horns came together to ride the tune to the end.

Robert got to his feet, yawning. "It's almost one, I got to be in school tomorrow. Here, finish my beer."

I did, in one long gulp. Outside, it was still misty but there was no rain. Robert said he was chilly in his shirt sleeves. When I handed him his saxophone case from the rumble seat, he took out his band jacket and put it on. Robert's rooming house was five blocks away, chosen because it was halfway between 18th and Vine and Lincoln High, and he said he wanted to walk.

"Besides," he said, "you'll lose your parking place." The crowd in the streets had increased and cars were cruising along 18th, looking for a space. I crossed 18th with him and watched as he walked up Vine past the glare of Lucille's and the Cherry Blossom and the Night Hawk into the glowing mist, the handle of his saxophone case tightly gripped in his right hand, the long shawl collar of his band jacket turned up so it rose behind his head like a cowl. I tried to spot Seventeen around the clubs, but Robert was the only Negro on Vine street, except for the uniformed doorman at the Night Hawk.

As I walked down 18th, I thought of the hurtful phrase Robert said Teddy had used to describe me. I had heard it plenty of times from white people, sometimes directed at me and clearly intended as an insult, but I was having trouble figuring out its thrust coming from a Negro.

I had been a small boy in North Carolina when I first heard someone called a "nigger lover." The speaker was a truculent street-corner lint-head who hung out in front of the shadier of the town's two drugstores, and the insult was directed at my father, who took hold of my hand and walked silently by. Dad, a Midwesterner who had met my mother at Chapel Hill and stayed on in her home state, was one of the few lawyers in Alamance county who would defend a Negro against a capital charge. One day, when I was ten, he came home at noon and sat at the kitchen table, drinking bootleg corn whisky out of a quart Mason jar until it was empty, tears spilling from his eyes.

A Negro client had just been declared guilty of the murder of a white man, a cotton-mill foreman who had been blown up during strike. The Negro was a janitor, almost retarded, and it was very doubtful that he could have planted the bomb, but the mill owner also held a partial deed to the county prosecutor, and the janitor was the only suspect the police could catch. My father had been hired for the defense by the National Textile Workers Union, which also sent in two lawyers from New York. It soon became clear they only needed my father because he was a member of the North Carolina bar. It also became obvious, as they goaded judge and jury with speeches insulting the South and proclaiming man's inherent right to revolt against oppressors, that they were not interested in pleas and stratagems to save the man's life, and certainly not the outright ass- and Confederate-flag kissing my father was capable of as a last resort.

"They wanted a martyr to the Marxist cause," my father said, perhaps overstating their intention in his anger and grief. "And so they turned him from a poor, ignorant swamp Negro into the Red Menace."

On the day the man was executed, my father decided to bow to the pleas of his family and come to southeastern Kansas to take over his ailing great-uncle's law practice.

Back down in the Subway, the tables were filling up. I stood just inside the arched entrance and listened as the band punched into "After You've Gone." Ben Webster put on a muscular, hard-charging exhibition of Kansas City jump, as unlike the breathy kiss of his previous solo as a prize fight is unlike the act of love. Webster had just finished his solo to cheers and clapping, and the trumpet player was making skittering, preliminary jabs above Libba's lithe chords when someone brushed by me on the left and I heard a crash. Four men in a flying wedge were coming through the arched entrance, knocking people and tables out of the way as they stormed down the center aisle of the club. A waitress tripped trying to get out of their way and a tray full of drinks smashed on the floor.

Behind the wedge came a fifth man, pearl gray hat pulled over his eyes, collar of his long gray overcoat covering his neck, following his advance guard right up to the stage. "What the hell is going on?" shouted the white trumpet player, snatching his instrument from his lips, and I could see his spit flying through a spotlight. Libba and the tall bass man stopped playing, but Teddy kept his cymbals sizzling and kicked a series of defiant explosions out of the bass drum. A light shone down on him from the top of the partition just behind the bandstand, and his back-lit face was like a fierce mask, his eye sockets dark holes, his thin lips tight with anger. He kicked the bass drum again, even louder than before, and then there was another explosion that was literally deafening as it echoed inside the cement and limestone cavern. The light above Teddy shattered with a brilliant flash, and I was momentarily blinded with the image etched in my eyes of Teddy ducking into his drum set as glass showered down on the stage.

I closed my eyes and squeezed them shut for several seconds and when darkness had begun to close in on the sunburst at the center of my vision, I opened them slowly. It was another five or ten seconds before I could see or hear much of anything through my battered eyes and ears. I swallowed and blinked a few times and then watched as Teddy pushed himself up from his scattered drums. Libba was still seated at the piano, glaring at the man in the gray fedora who stood in front of the bandstand, his right hand raised to shoulder level and wrapped around a piece of shiny black metal. Now, the only sound was a low, confused murmur of voices and then there was a high-pitched scream and a man shouting, "Shut up, Martha, that man has a gun."

Without turning his head, the man in the pearl gray hat said, "She knows that, buddy." He did not seem to raise his voice, but I could hear him clearly, even with my ears still ringing from his gunshot. He waved his pistol at the musician nearest him, the trumpet player, and said:

"You get on down from that stage. Nobody's going to hurt you, just get on down. And the rest of you. Off the stage. You too lady. Frank, you and Charlie get that piano down to the floor."

The trumpet player and the alto man hurried off the stage and into the crowd that had backed away from the bandstand. I looked for Ben Webster, but I couldn't see him anywhere.

Teddy picked up his snare drum and cymbal from the bandstand floor and lugged them toward the back wall.

"You, too, lady," said the gunman. "Get off that piano bench."

Libba did not budge. I could see the right side of her face, perspiration glistening off the dark skin of her high sculpted cheek, and she had a look that I had seen a few weeks before, on the face of a striking steel worker blocking the way of a mounted policeman in the West Bottoms. *I shall not be moved* was what the look said.

"Listen, black bitch," said the gunman, "you get the fuck down. We got to move that piano."

Teddy carefully set the cymbal and drum down near the back wall and turned toward the gunman, who was about fifteen feet away. Teddy didn't say anything, but he took a step toward the gunman, and then another, and Libba did not move. The gunman turned his head toward Teddy, the gun still held high and pointed at the ceiling.

A man dragging a woman by the hand slipped past me and through the arch, and I heard them run up the stairs.

Two of the hoods had jumped up on the bandstand and were standing on either side of the upright piano. The other two hoods flanked the gunman. One of them shoved back the brim of his hat and reached inside his coat. The crowd pressed back from the bandstand, and a man's Okie voice said, "Aw, shit. Ma'am, why 'on't you just do what that feller tells you?"

"I think it's the principle of the thing, Kyle," said a woman.

The profile of Libba's face was outlined as clearly by the remaining stage lights as if it had been cut by a silhouette artist. I could see a smile begin to take over her lips. She slowly shook her head, as if to shake away the smile, but she rose from the piano bench. She stood erect, her face expressionless, her neck high and straight like Nefertiti, and swept off the bandstand with her hand holding the folds of her long black skirt. When she had stepped down from the bandstand, she turned to Teddy and said, "Come on baby, let's go home."

Behind me, I heard the clatter of heavy footsteps coming down the stairs.

Teddy had not budged, and he was not smiling. He was looking straight at the gunman, whose face was in the long shadow cast by the brim of his gray hat. Teddy was sliding his hands together in front of him and I sensed that his long dancer's legs were tensed, as if he was ready to leap.

"Listen, white man," Teddy said, drawling out the words, but with bands of tension beneath them, "Don't you go calling a black woman out of her name."

"Nigger, who do you think. . . ." The gunman did not finish his sentence as a shout came from my left.

"Who you calling nigger, you Dago motherfucker?"

I turned and saw, standing in the crude stone arch, a stocky dark-brown man in his shirt-sleeves with his vest unbuttoned and his tie hanging loose. The gangster turned. "Who the fuck . . . ." The sentence died like a lost erection. "Piney Brown," murmured a man to my right, and then I recognized the club owner from Blue Monday at the Sunset. The gangster finally spoke. "Mr. Brown. Sorry. The, uh, ATF. We got to, ah, get those boxes out of here."

"Well, you do that, Morelli," said Piney Brown, advancing down the aisle toward the bandstand. "But first . . . you been calling this lady names?"

"Yeah, well, I'm sorry about that, I got a little hot under the collar."

"Did you apologize?" asked Piney Brown, now standing a step or two from the gunman. "Sheeeeit," said a man near me.

The gunman sighed and put his gun away. He nodded to Libba and touched the long brim of his hat. "I apologize," he said.

Teddy cleared his throat. "You apologize what?"

"I apologize, Ma'am," the gunman said. Piney Brown stepped onto the bandstand and announced that the show was over for the evening. "I'm sorry, folks," he said, "but a small emergency has arisen. I'm going to have to ask you to leave right away. The waitresses will clear the tables."

The people seemed happy to get out as quickly as they could, and it only took about two minutes to empty the club. I stayed where I was, standing in the shadows just inside the stone arch entrance, and nobody bothered me or the three Negro men in suits who had stayed at a table on the other side of the arch, near the bar. The bartender stayed too, and only then did I notice he was holding something under a towel on top of the wooden bar. Teddy got the rest of his drums off the bandstand and two of the hoods rolled the upright piano to the edge. With Piney Brown watching, the other two hoods helped them lower the piano to the cement floor. Wheels squeaking, it was rolled back against the wood partition.

Then the four men lifted up the three risers that made up the bandstand and carried them out of the way, uncovering six long wooden boxes sitting on the concrete floor. With a man on each end of a box, it took three trips to carry them through the arch and up the stairs. The boxes were unfinished pine, about five feet long, and stamped on the side with "U.S. Army."

Without speaking, Teddy and Libba sat at a front-row table and watched until all the boxes had been removed, the bandstand reassembled, and the piano replaced. Piney Brown walked over to the bar and poured himself a shot of whisky. He tossed it down and then took two full shot glasses over to the table, putting one in front of Libba and one in front of Teddy. It took Teddy about thirty seconds to drink both of them.

When the bandstand was back as it had been, the gunman apologized again to Piney Brown.

"Tell your boss this was a bad idea," the club owner said in reply. "Tell him we ain't going to do this again."

"You tell him yourself," muttered the gunman, not very loudly, as he turned and left, followed by his companions. Piney Brown helped Teddy replace his drums on the bandstand and then the club owner walked over to the end of the bar, reached behind it and poured himself a couple of shots of whisky in a thick-bottomed old-fashioned glass. He took the drink to the table with the three men in suits.

Teddy and Libba got up to leave. As they walked in my direction, I heard Libba's creamy laugh. "Yeah," she said, "you're right, baby. Soon as that gun went off, Frog was out of there like Jack the Bear. We may never see Ben Webster again."

I stepped into the light. "Teddy," I said.

Teddy kept his eyes straight ahead and took Libba's arm with his right hand. "What the hell you want, pink boy?" he said, continuing past me toward the stairs.

Libba stopped and looked back, forcing Teddy to halt also if he wanted to keep holding on to her arm. She squinted in the dim light and then smiled. It was still not quite *that* smile, but it sent ripples through me.

"Hey, Teddy," she said, "it's okay. It's that friend of your nephew, the one who likes to nap while I'm playing."

"So what?" said Teddy.

"I need to talk to you," I said. "About Bennie Moten."

Teddy looked back at me over his shoulder. "Even if you find something out, the white law's not going to do anything about the murder of a black man. This ain't no detective story. Let's go, Princess."

"Don't bother the artists," said Piney Brown, rising from his chair. "Friend, you don't sound like you're a cop waiting for a bribe after all, so get on out of here."

I followed Teddy and Libba up the stairs and cut ahead of them in the restaurant to hold the front door. Libba snatched her arm away from Teddy and went through ahead of him, nodding to me as she passed, and I caught a brief whiff of a smoky perfume and heard silk rubbing against silk. Teddy followed, brushing by me. Outside, it had turned chillier, and the mist had cleared. Teddy turned up the collar of his suit-coat and walked down the street toward Vine, his left arm touching Libba's shoulder. She took the dark blue scarf from around her neck and put it over her head, tying it at the throat.

I came up behind Teddy on his right. "I've got a car," I said. "I'll give you all a ride."

"We'll get a cab," said Teddy, taking Libba's arm again as they paused at the intersection of Vine. "Damn," said Teddy. "They're not supposed to do that." He was looking catty-cornered across the intersection at the Negro taxi stand near the side door of the Street Hotel. There was a black-and-maroon Monarch cab at it, but a group of white people was getting in it, and there were no other Negro cabs in sight.

Up Vine to our left, two yellow-painted cabs were idling in front of the Night Hawk. Another yellow cab came toward us on 18th and Teddy gestured at it, almost as if by reflex. His open hand turned into a fist as it cruised by without slowing down. "Fuck you," he muttered. His voice got louder. "Did you see that? There was a spade driving that cab. Thanks, Brother."

"Teddy, don't be so contrary," said Libba, again pulling her arm loose from his hand. "I'll take a ride from Michael, if you won't. I'm getting cold."

Teddy snapped his head around and glared at me. "All right," he said. "White people took my cab, and I can't get one of theirs. I guess you owe me a ride. Take us both to Libba's house. You got anything to drink in that rattletrap?"

8

I turned around in the alley next to the Street Hotel, briefly scattering a crap game, and headed east on 18th. I had to cut into the other lane to go around a Buick sedan with white government plates that had just double parked in front of the Subway. "You're not going to find nothing!" shouted Teddy from the rumble seat as men in trench coats began spilling out of the sedan. Teddy knocked on the window between us. As soon as I had rolled it down, he began issuing commands as if my little Model A were his Dusenberg Phaeton.

"Up ahead," he shouted. "See it?" I nodded.

"Get a quart," said Teddy.

"Maybe he'll buy you a chauffeur's cap," murmured Libba, who was sitting next to me in the dark, smelling like lilacs and smouldering pine needles. I pulled to the curb in front of the Black and Orange cut-rate liquor store, adjusted the hand throttle to keep the car idling and ran inside. I came back with a quart of rye for $1.87, hoping Three Fathers was a cut above Old Crony. Teddy immediately twisted off the cap and took an exploratory sip. After a grimacing swallow and a scornful grunt, he took a longer drink. I got back in the driver's seat and, as I pulled away, he offered the bottle through the window to Libba. Libba said she would pass, thanks just the same.

I turned right and started up a steep hill. In Kansas City, as in virtually all river cities, uptown is uphill. We were rising from the old river valley, going south toward the newer, and nicer, sections of town for whites and Negroes both. But first we passed through two blocks of mostly abandoned brick and frame buildings that squatted around an overpass of the southbound railroad tracks: warehouses, a low wooden water tower, a vacant bar and lunchroom, an old feed store with the words PURINA HORSE CHOW on the side in flaking white letters. I heard the sound of breaking glass.

"Pull over," said Teddy, his vocal cords hoarse from the whisky. He coughed and swallowed. "Pull over right here."

I eased to the curb. About twenty feet in front of us were three boys aged ten or twelve. They turned to face into the headlights, standing their ground, seeming more curious than frightened.

Teddy handed me the bottle and stood up in the rumble seat. I took a swallow and grimaced. It tasted just like Old Crony, harsh and corrosive, with the rotten organic aftertaste of unaged distilled corn.

"Where you boys from?" Teddy shouted.

The one in the middle, the largest, let a large stone fall from his right hand, and I heard it smack the pavement. "I asked where you from!" repeated Teddy.

The largest boy mumbled a familiar-sounding name, but for an instant I thought I had heard it wrong.

"*Palestine?*" shouted Teddy. "They throw rocks at windows down there?"

The boys did not respond. They continued to stare into the headlights, as if waiting to learn the reason for this inexplicable interruption by a Negro in a rumble seat.

"You boys go on home," shouted Teddy. "You're in Kansas City now. You don't want to be acting like Southern white trash."

The largest boy stared at Teddy for a few seconds, looking baffled, then turned and began walking—as slowly and deliberately as a boy of that age could walk—up the street away from us. The others followed him. They angled across the the sidewalk and then, as if they could hold back no longer, they broke into a run and disappeared between two dark buildings.

"Palestine, Texas," said Teddy, reaching through the rear window for the whisky bottle. "Little boll weevils come up on the Katy from de land o cotton. Those boll weevils are going to get in your hair someday, white man." He tapped a loud military drum roll on the roof of the car with his fingers. "Country niggers can do more damage to a city than dynamite," he said.

"Teddy, it's not their fault," said Libba. "Turn left on the second street, Michael."

"I'm not talking about fault, Princess," said Teddy, his fingers still for an instant. "Everybody knows whose fault it is. That's the blues."

He slapped the roof. "But listen, baby, the blues is prologue. I'm a jazz man myself. Straight-ahead four/four, like those riots last month in Harlem." Teddy laughed deep in his throat and starting tapping a steady jazz beat. "One, Two, Three, Four, Rev-o-lu-tion . . . you hear what I'm saying?" He cackled above the beat.

"Two men were killed in that riot," said Libba. "Both Negroes."

"We'll see what happens next time," said Teddy, ending his roof-tapping with a fusillade. "Garveyites want to go back to Africa, leave these American cities to the white man. I say take these cities away from the white man. It's his turn to live in Shitheel, Alabama, and pick cotton and sing dem blues. You want another drink?"

Libba did not say anything, and then I realized Teddy was poking the bottle through the window toward me. "Thanks. In a second," I said, needing both hands to make the turn onto the well-kept residential street where Libba lived.

"Sixth house on the right," she said. "Turn in the driveway." I nodded and grabbed the bottle with my right hand long enough to take a quick drink before I slowed down for Libba's house.

"Myself," said Teddy, taking the bottle back and rubbing his palm over the top, "I always wipe my bottle after another man's had a drink out of it. Don't white folks do that?"

I turned right just past a street light, and the front wheels crunched onto the gravel driveway. As I pulled on the brake, I looked back at Teddy and he had the bottle to his lips again, but he was smiling around it, and his eyes flashed as he looked in my direction. He took another drink and rolled the whisky around in his mouth and swallowed.

"You trying to get inoculated with some of my spit?" Teddy asked. "Trying to pick up a nice, non-lethal dose of Negritude?" Teddy winked, and I realized he reminded me of someone else, but I wasn't sure who.

"Teddy, come on inside," said Libba. "And stop being so rude. Michael, you got to forgive Teddy, he probably hasn't been to sleep for a couple of days."

"I haven't been to sleep for a couple of years," said Teddy, opening the door for Libba.

Libba smiled and touched my forearm with her left hand. "Why don't you come on in too? That way, you can have a drink of your whisky and we can talk about Bennie Moten. Teddy, hide that bottle."

The house was not locked. Libba went in first, and then held the door for Teddy and me. There was a long, narrow hall that went into a kitchen past a stairway on the left. To the right, through an archway, was a small living room. The doorway was half blocked by a baby grand piano. As Libba closed the door and turned the night latch, I heard the floor creak above us, and then a woman came down the stairs. She was wearing a white nightcap over gray-white hair, cut short like bird feathers, and a dressing gown covered with tiny pink flowers.

She was as short as Libba, and had the same high cheekbones, but she was very slight of build and had a thin face. Her skin was the color of powdered cocoa.

She stopped at the bottom step and said a frozen-faced hello to Teddy, who by now smelled like a leaky whisky barrel. I got a suspicious look until Libba introduced me as a college friend of Teddy's nephew— "You remember, Momma, the music teacher?"—and then she smiled and extended her hand and said she was pleased to make my acquaintance. The slimness and delicacy of her frail hand, the politeness of her greeting and the Southernness of her voice stirred a nostalgic image in my mind of my North Carolina grandmother. I had adored her, and she had died when I was seven.

"Elizabeth," her mother said, "you send your friend home soon and come to bed. You been staying up 'til dawn way too much." She said good evening and turned and went back up the stairs, her right hand plucking a couple of cotton balls of out of a pocket of her dressing gown. As she disappeared past the top of the stairs, I saw her tuck one into her right ear.

Libba smiled and shook her head. "Mama's been saying that since I was sixteen and fell in love with a piano player in a jazz band," she said softly. "You all go on in the living room." She went to the kitchen. After a glance at me, Teddy reached into the front of his high-waisted pants and, shivering wickedly and wiggling his hips, pulled out the quart of whisky. He followed Libba into the kitchen.

I stepped past the piano into the living room. It looked like home. In the middle of the room, a nappy dark-green couch and a matching well-stuffed easy chair faced each other across a worn oriental rug. Beyond them, a small black stove sat on a black metal hearth, with an exhaust duct leading through a metal circle in the wall. A full bucket of coal sat next to the stove.

In the far right corner was a straight-backed wooden chair with a flowered wool sampler covering the seat. In the left corner, beyond the sofa, was a Victrola in a chest-high, dark mahogany cabinet. The lid was opened, and the thick, goose-necked metal playing arm was raised so the steel needle was pointing upward.

Teddy came out with a tall iced-tea glass two-thirds full of whisky and water, and Libba followed with a tray holding two more glasses and a pitcher of water. She set it on a small, high table next to the easy chair. "No ice," she said. "The iceman comes tomorrow."

Teddy set the bottle on the tray and eased familiarly into the chair.

The fire made it warm and cozy in the living room, so Teddy and I took off our jackets and Libba hung them in the hall closet under the stairs. Teddy kept his hat on, shoved back a couple of inches on his high beige forehead.

"I'll take one drink," said Libba, sitting at the end of the couch away from the stove. "Make it very light. What about Bennie Moten?"

That was the first time I realized that Libba spoke in the same economical, angular, provocative way she played the piano, changing directions abruptly without transition or explanation. It invited directness in reply.

"I think Bennie Moten was murdered," I said. "And then the doctor who cut his throat was killed, too. I'm sure I saw the doctor's body, in the morgue at the police station."

"Dr. Stone?" said Libba. "I still haven't heard anything about him being dead."

Teddy poured a shot of whisky in the bottom of a glass and added about six ounces of water. "He's sure as hell not in town," he said, leaning forward to hand the drink to Libba. "And, if he is alive, he's wise to lay low for a while. The boys say he was too drunk to hold the knife steady. They say Bennie died with his mouth full of blood."

Teddy sat back down in the easy chair and poured down about a fourth of his drink. He smacked his lips. "This shit's starting to taste better," he said. He looked up at me.

"Robert tells me you're looking for Seventeen," Teddy said. He seemed to have mellowed a bit from his earlier jitters and anger. On the other hand, he had not offered me a drink.

"That's right," I said, taking a step away from the stove, which was overheating my back. "The dead man in the morgue had one of those Seventeen pins in his lapel. His body was found the day Bennie Moten died. I figured maybe Seventeen could tell me if he gave a pin to Dr. Stone, or to anyone who was with Bennie Moten, and if he saw anything else that night that might mean something."

"Yeah?" said Teddy. "Seventeen may not tell you much. He hasn't been very trusting of white folks since he got railroaded for shoplifting from that kike's liquor store."

"Teddy, don't you say that word," said Libba. He nodded without looking at her.

"Yeah, okay, Princess," he said. "White man's liquor store." Teddy yawned, but I couldn't tell if it was because weariness was descending or to release tension left over from confronting the hoodlum. Perhaps both.

He said, "Seventeen probably doesn't remember who he gives those pins to." With the fingertips of his left hand, Teddy rubbed the ridge of scar tissue on his right hand as if he were half-consciously stroking a cat.

"Or maybe it was just a regular old pin," said Libba. "Maybe he had been wearing a boutonniere, or been to the tailor. Michael, are you going to sit down?" She patted the middle of the couch with her left hand.

I nodded, and walked over to the table next to Teddy and poured myself a stiff drink, half whisky, half water. I sat down at the other end of the couch from Libba. I could smell her perfume again, sweet and smoky. Her dark blue satin dress was belted at the waist and cut deep in front like a choir robe, with wide, flat lapels that crossed her full breasts and slid apart when she moved to reveal the cleft where they began.

She saw me looking at her and for an instant our eyes met. Embarrassed, I turned to Teddy. "Did Bennie Moten have anything to do with dope peddlers?" I asked.

"Hell, he kept the dope peddlers away," said Teddy. He pushed his hat back further on his forehead. "Listen, man, he kept all that shit away so you didn't have to have any truck with those people, cats pushing dope, gangsters, strong arms. When I worked for him, I once saw him pull one of those little .22 pistols out from under his vest and chase this white dope pusher out of the dressing room at the Pla-Mor ballroom."

Teddy put his glass to his lips and swirled whisky around in his mouth before he swallowed. An undertone of red was rising into his tan cheeks and forehead, and his right knee was beginning to bounce. He seemed to shift moods as fast as Libba moved from idea to idea. Maybe, I thought, that's why they make beautiful music together, and I felt another inexplicable stab of jealousy.

"Michael," said Libba, glancing from Teddy to me, "you know the way Piney Brown ordered that hood around in the Subway? I've only seen one other Negro act that way and get away with it in this city, and that was Bennie Moten. It was known that he was Pendergast's man, and those wise guys didn't mess with him. Right, Teddy?"

Teddy nodded, rubbing his temple with his left hand while he swirled the drink in his right. "I'd say Bennie had considerable power, particularly for a colored man. I always heard, and I made sure to conduct my ass as if it were a fact, that you better not get on the wrong side of Bennie Moten. I know that was true if you wanted to work in Kansas City as a musician. If you were from out of town, Bennie got a cut of the take. He was in control."

I took a long drink and decided I wanted a cigarette. "Do you mind if I smoke?" I asked, perfunctorily.

"Mama does," said Libba, closing the subject. "Bennie Moten ran things, but he ran them clean."

"There was a wreath from Pendergast at the funeral," I said. "Does Pendergast come to the clubs? Did Bennie Moten know him?"

"Hell, no," said Teddy. "The way I hear it, Pendergast is in bed before we begin the first set. But Bennie knew somebody who knew somebody who knew Pendergast, I'll tell you that. Just like Piney Brown. One reason Piney Brown's got so much power is he runs all the policy on the East Side, and Pendergast ends up with a cut. You got to figure some of the money Bennie took in ended up in Pendergast's pocket, too. Pendergast runs things here, all the things, and that's not such a bad deal."

Teddy set his drink down on the small table and rose to his feet, stretching his lanky arms. He had removed his celluloid collar and opened the top of his old-fashioned dress shirt, and his red silk foulard hung around his neck like an Oriental scarf. Teddy's irises were a deep, dark brown, and even the whites of his eyes were shadowed with beige. As he stared down at me, I could see they were bloodshot as well.

"Kansas City is a lot better than Chicago," he said. "This town is run by a machine, but out here the politicians control the gangsters and not the other way around. They're some mean motherfuckers in Chicago, you do something they don't like and they'll cut your throat in a minute, like they did to that singer Joe E. Lewis. All he wanted to do was go to work for another cat in another mob and they cut his throat from ear to Adam's apple and left his tongue hanging by a thread."

Teddy shoved his hands in his pants pockets and walked slowly to the hallway, his eyes downward. He turned on his heel, smartly like a drum major and came back, apparently lost in thought.

"Maybe the local gangsters aren't as benevolent as you think they are," said Libba. "They sure as hell don't mind killing each other, or killing innocent people during an election."

Teddy stopped in front of Libba and began flexing his right hand as if he was squeezing a ball. "I don't know," he said. "You always hear about the Chicago Outfit trying to muscle in down here. Maybe they're trying to push dope down here. I'm sure as hell seeing a lot more of it around lately, not just morphine but that fucking heroin. Maybe Bennie got in the middle of some deal those Chicago boys were trying to pull off and they had his throat cut."

"Is that what they did to your hand?" I asked. "Cut it?"

Teddy looked at me. He squeezed his right hand so tightly his knuckles paled, but the scarred index and middle fingers poked up from the fist like sticks out of a bird's nest.

Libba said, softly, "Tell him what happened, Teddy."

"I'll punch him in the teeth, that's what I'll do," said Teddy, looking me in the eye, but with more weariness than anger in his voice.

"You said you'd tell me about it sometime," I said. Teddy shook his head and sighed. "Yeah, I guess I did."

He let his hand relax at his side. I couldn't avoid looking at the scar. It looked like something that had wriggled under his skin.

"I tell you this," he said. "If these boys are from Chicago, you better think twice before you go poking into their business."

Teddy looked into my eyes. "Did you know they killed a nosy reporter back there in Chicago, shot him down in the middle of Clark Street? You start snooping around, they'll get you too."

"Teddy," said Libba. "Tell him what happened to you."

Teddy's eyes flicked over to Libba and they stared at each other for a moment. Then Teddy picked up his drink, added another splash of rye, sat down in the easy chair, cupped his right knee with his scarred hand and told me what had happened.

"This Irish weasel, O'Bannon, worked for Al Capone," he said, his eyes shifting between me and Libba. "Used to hang out in the Deuces, where I played. He owned half the place, and he had eyes for my girlfriend, Terry. She was very young and very sweet."

"St. Teresa," said Libba.

Teddy gave her a twisted smile and continued. "She was our singer," he said. "He'd tip her a ten or a twenty to sing a song for him. He liked several little ditties, but his favorite was 'Melancholy Baby.' He wasn't trying to be funny. O'Bannon was not a funny man.

"One night he was drunker than usual and he and his three buddies stayed until four in the morning, an hour after closing time. He wanted to have a private concert and he was throwing twenty-dollar bills around like confetti, so Terry and I and the piano player and the bartender stayed on to entertain them."

Teddy took a sip of whisky and set the glass on the table. He was looking over our heads now, gazing across the room. "She sang 'Annie Laurie' for him and he took out a fifty and folded it in the middle and set it upright on the corner of the table. It was one of those low nightclub tables, and he wanted her to come over and pick it up with her thighs like they do in some of those rough joints down on 12th Street. You didn't get the idea she had a lot of choice."

"And fifty dollars is a lot of money to an ambitious young chick," said Libba.

Teddy scowled at Libba before he continued. "So finally she walked over to the table where he and these three other hoodlums were sitting and raised her skirt up so you could see her underpants and she poked herself forward and squatted and squeezed that bill between her thighs and backed away with it. Then she grabbed it with her fingers and pulled her skirt down. O'Bannon watched her like a cobra, but he didn't try to touch her, and he even stopped his buddies from laughing.

"Then he asked for 'Melancholy Baby,' and we figured we were in the home stretch because that would be the last song. Terry sang it and when she was through he clapped slowly like this."

Teddy slapped his hand together four times very slowly. It was the beat of the funeral march, and the sound sent chills up my back.

"Then," said Teddy, "O'Bannon reached in his jacket and got his wallet again and pulled out another bill. This time it was a hundred. He bent the bill and set it on the edge of the table, like he had done before, and he told her he wanted her to take off her underpants and pick it up the way they do in those lowdown strip joints. He meant with her private parts.

"Terry had tears in her eyes. She told him she was a real singer who had studied voice at Fisk and this was a real music club and she was a nice girl and didn't do things like that."

Teddy paused and glanced at Libba, as if daring her to say something sarcastic.

"So O'Bannon started screaming at Terry and she began crying and I got into it and he started shouting at me and forgot Terry. She ran into the back of the club and went out the fire door. He called me some names and I called him some back, so O'Bannon told the piano player and the bartender to get on out, too, and then him and his buddies took me back into the manager's office and started hitting me and when I tried to fight back the three goons held me in the chair and O'Bannon had them take my right hand and stick it inside the desk drawer and he kicked it shut."

Teddy took in a slow, deep breath and exhaled heavily. Libba was looking at the floor, not saying a word, and I didn't know what to say either, so for what seemed like a long time, the room was silent.

Teddy finished off his drink and got up from the chair and walked over to the Victrola. In the bookcase next to it were several stacks of albums, the plain brown kind that hold ten or twelve records in thin pasteboard sleeves. He began flipping through the album the way you might flip through a book of photographs, and the second or third time the sleeves slapped together Libba said, "Teddy, stop that, you'll break my records."

Teddy nodded and raised his head to look at her. "My records too, Princess."

"Well, then, play one of *your* records," she said. I wondered if they had once lived together.

Teddy chose a record and put it on the turntable and turned the crank on the right side of the chest-high cabinet. When he got the record spinning at full speed, he lowered the arm until the steel needle was clicking on the outside of the disk. The groove grabbed it and pulled it in and Teddy began slapping his thigh as a piano chattered a brisk introduction and a big horn section skittered into an almost impossibly fast series of insistent riffs. Slowly, a grin took over Teddy's wide mouth, and he began tapping out the rhythms on his thighs with both hands.

"All right, brother Basie," he said. "All right, brother Page. Allll right, brother Webster." He pulled open the double doors in the belly of the cabinet and the music came out louder and richer, but Libba shook her head and pointed upstairs.

"Yes, dear," said Teddy closing the doors again, muffling the band. He slapped his leg as the bass drum kicked a hole in the ensemble to let the trumpet player slither through. "Oh brother Moten, you could have used me right there. Never should have let me go."

Teddy grinned and held his right hand up and flexed it, fingers writhing to the beat like the legs of a tarantula. He stared at his hand for a moment and then looked toward me. "Maybe they're not any different down here. Maybe they did cut Bennie's throat. That pissant tonight, that Morelli, he'd cut his *mother's* throat for ten cents."

Teddy sat back down and finished his drink and got himself another one as the Moten band romped through "Toby." It was, Libba said, recorded at RCA in New York in 1932 at what she now realized would be Bennie Moten's last session.

"In memoriam," she said, "I'll take another drink."

Teddy mixed a light one for Libba and then held the bottle up and looked inquiringly at me. I nodded and got up, holding out my glass, and he poured a couple of ounces into it. I mixed in an equal amount of water. By then, I was startled to see, we had drunk almost half a quart of whisky. And we still had plenty of water left in the pitcher.

The key-wound clock on the mantlepiece had just played its cumulative little four-part sonata all the way through and sounded the hour of four when I split the last inch or so in the bottle between my glass and Libba's. The water pitcher had been empty for at least an hour, but nobody had bothered to refill it.

By then, Teddy had finally succumbed to whisky and fatigue and sprawled over the easy chair, snoring lightly beneath his dark blue hat, legs and arms akimbo.

The Victrola was silent now. Teddy had played "Toby" twice and a version of "Somebody Stole My Gal" with a wordless "da-de-ya-da" vocal by Basie.

I was making my drinks progressively stronger, so I don't remember everything I heard that night, but I know for certain it was the first time I ever heard Billie Holiday. The songs were silly novelty tunes, but Benny Goodman and Jack Teagarden were backing her, and she already had that unforgettably scarred, dusky voice, the voice of an ancient child. She could turn farce into pathos and make love's sadness seem nearly unbearable.

It was barely three months later that John Hammond would summon Ben Webster to play behind Billie Holiday on those astonishing records that I carry with me and that are among those I play over and over on the phonograph in the ward room today: "I Wished on the Moon," "Miss Brown To You," "What a Little Moonlight Can Do."

By the time I poured the last drinks out of the bottle, I had been drinking for twelve hours or so without much to eat, and I must have been approaching that nutty psychological plane common to paranoiacs and religious and political fanatics where everything makes sense as part of a single obsessive vision, a private eschatology. The ceiling could have collapsed and Libba's mother come floating down in a brass bed singing duets with Nelson Eddy and my mind could have accommodated the event, and included the intruders from above in the greater scheme.

The greater scheme was that I was going to make love to Libba, either right there on the sofa or upstairs in her bedroom, whichever she preferred. I certainly did not want to seem pushy about locale, and I was dead certain she thirsted for my body as I thirsted for hers. Why else would she be sitting there next to me so enticingly, perfumed like my grandmother's Southern garden on the first of May, with just a hint of autumn's smoke? The loose belt of her dress had gotten looser and was showing more of her chocolate breasts, and she was smiling at me with her full red lips, her hair glistening as it fell in sleek black waves to brush the sweet curves where her high dark neck met her shoulders, her large brown eyes catching the light and tossing it right back to me.

When my recollection is stirred by a sufficient amount of whisky and jazz, I can revisualize the scene in embarrassing clarity, and it is obvious that she was just being friendly, warmed by the hour and the music and two or three drinks beyond her usual limit. She was safe in her own home, I was a school chum of Teddy's nephew, I didn't seem to manifest any of the more overt signs of bigotry, I was truly interested in her life's work and very eager to hear her talk about it. I was only a couple of years younger than she, but I must have seemed almost like a child, a child who had flattered her by his attention.

When I made my move, she had just finished telling me a long story about the day, three weeks after she had turned eighteen, that the piano player she had run away with had himself run away, and left her and a twelve-piece band in St. Louis at the beginning of a week's stay at the Plantation. The piano man's friend and roommate on the road had been a drummer named Teddy Wellington, and he had offered to let her continue to sleep in the twin bed she had shared with the departed piano player, no strings attached.

Then, Teddy had convinced the desperate bandleader that Libba, a talented amateur piano player, a music teacher's daughter, protege of a great if footloose band pianist, could read the charts and could play well (and quietly) enough to appear convincing (and gorgeous) at the piano while the band was tootling away, and could even fake it on a few eight-bar intros and breaks. And he was right.

Thirteen months later, when Teddy himself decided to stay in Chicago and let the band go on to Indianapolis, Columbus, and points east, she was doing a lot more than faking it and the bandleader gave her a ten-dollar-a-week raise to stay and keep turning out the bluesy but stomping arrangements that the young Lindy-hoppers loved, and that even seemed to please the middle-aged folks still trying to learn the Charleston.

"By then," she said, "I didn't need Teddy to protect me anymore, and I realized he was the kind of man who was always going to be on the move, so I didn't follow him. But I still missed him very much."

I realize now she assumed I knew what she was talking about, but then, besotted with alcohol and hormone-drunk, I had x-ray vision and saw right through mere information to destiny and truth. If Libba had her own hotel-room bed in the beginning, I figured, and did not follow Teddy at the end, the relationship must have essentially been that of brother and sister, with perhaps a brief blossoming of romance, let die by mutual agreement. She was telling me that she was available.

And what of Rachael, my one true love?

Well, Rachael was in New York. In ways, Libba and Rachael were very much alike: small but strong-boned (and strong-willed), with full breasts and high cheekbones. Both were darker and considerably more exotic than the German and Scots-Irish girls I'd known in Kansas. Both of them were forbidden. In fact, in the state of Missouri, Libba was illegal.

I would like to think that my life would not have been changed all that much (but how can I say?) if Libba had reacted more positively when I leaned toward her and put my right hand on her cheek and tried to pull her toward me for a kiss. Immediately her lips hardened and her neck stiffened. She did not jerk away, in fact she did not move at all, but her neck became like a steel pole, and the open, friendly look on her face vanished to be replaced in an instant by something close to contempt. It took a couple of seconds for the message to drill through the whisky and lust to the functioning parts my mind, and then I snatched my hand back as if it had been scorched by dry ice.

She stared at me, the glow in her eyes now frozen, and said very quietly and precisely, "Where I come from, nice colored girls don't mess around with white boys. Not anywhere, never, under no circumstances, you got that? Not in a mansion in Lake Forest, Illinois, not in a hotel suite at the Waldorf, and sure as hell not in my mother's house with my husband asleep in the same room."

Startled, I looked over at Teddy. The hat was still over his face, and he was still sprawled out as if in deep sleep. I looked back at Libba.

"Let me say this again," she said, wearily, her expression softening slightly, from detestation to simple dismissal. "I'm not interested."

She gestured toward the hall closet.

"You want to get your coat and let yourself out?" she said. "I hope you'll excuse me for not getting up. I've had a long night."

9

Kansas Grave Clings to Secret That
Might Stay Drastic Hand of Hitler

Someone at the *Journal-Post* had written an irresistible headline. Before looking inside for the crime items I had called in the night before, I lingered over the front page story.

An Iowa man was desperately searching for the grave of his German immigrant father. Our Marysville, Kansas, stringer had a flair for melodrama and a problem with compound sentences:

> If it can be shown that Podschadly was buried with Catholic rites or that his body reposes in a Catholic cemetery, this, the son believes, will convince Hitler that Podschadly was not a Jew. Otherwise, the dead man's daughter and her family will be forced to leave Germany and join the long procession that wends its way wearily toward Russia, banished from their homeland by the stern ruler who is embittered against the progeny of Isaac, Abraham and Jacob.

"Great little yarn, huh?" said O'Malley, suddenly appearing over my right shoulder. I must have twitched at the sound of his voice, because he patted me patronizingly on the cheek with cold fingers, making me twitch again. "You're jittery, lad," he said. "Too little sleep and too much jungle music."

He tapped me on the shoulder. "It's 11:45," he said. "Come on, let's go. You can bring the paper with you."

I gulped down my coffee, threw a nickel on the counter, tucked the paper under my arm and followed O'Malley out of the diner. It was chilly. I was glad to be wearing my sweater and raincoat and my tweed cap, even though the storm that had been forecast earlier apparently had petered out in Western Kansas, after forcing dense dust clouds south into Oklahoma.

O'Malley looked ready for golf (or burlesque) in plaid knickers, long argyle socks, a green polo shirt and a green tam o'shanter I had first seen the month before, on St. Patrick's Day. It occurred to me, as it had before, how difficult it must be to be a professional Irishman here on the edge of the dusty prairie, and I wondered if O'Malley and his friends got together from time to time to practice. If the New York Irish are more Irish than Dubliners, what feats of self-creation were required in Kansas City?

After we had settled into the ancient LaSalle that had belonged to his father and made a U-turn to point the long nose northward on Broadway, I told him the thing that was foremost on my mind.

"Rachael's coming home this weekend," I said.

"She's not sticking around New York for the big college peace strike?"

"She's leaving just as soon as it's over," I said.

O'Malley said, "You'd think a Jewish girl would *want* us to go to war with Hitler."

"It's complicated," I said. "Where are we going?"

"You'll see," said O'Malley. "It's a little surprise. I cooked it up for you after you told me about that raid by the boys from Alcohol, Tobacco and Firearms." He began whistling a lilting little tune, and left me alone for a minute or two with my warm (and slightly guilty) thoughts of Rachael.

We took the Hannibal bridge across the Missouri River and drove past the long cement runways of the new airport that city manager McElroy had built on a diked sandbar across from the confluence of the Kaw. Soon, we were the only car on a wide four-lane cement highway through greening cornfields.

"I get it," I said. "We're going to the horse races. Aren't we a couple of hours early?"

"Actually," said O'Malley, "we're going on a picnic."

O'Malley stayed on the virtually deserted highway for a few miles and then cut left onto an unpaved sandy road that wound through flat, budding fields and eventually ended up at the edge of a sandbar on the Missouri. O'Malley stopped while he was still on loam and hopped out. He unlocked the golf-bag door, which opened from the left side of the car into the lower part of the rumble seat, and pulled out a long, narrow wicker basket with double handles.

"You carry that," he said. The basket clinked as he handed it to me. "Careful," he said. "My mother put some food together for us, and I added a couple of quarts of beer from the icebox."

"Isn't it a little cold for a picnic?" I asked, the basket under my arm.

"You only get one day off a week, Michael," replied O'Malley, pulling a black imitation-leather suitcase about three feet long out of the golf-bag opening.

O'Malley hoisted the case by the handle. It looked heavy. "First, we eat lunch," he said. "Then I'll show you my surprise."

We sat on a decaying sycamore log thirty or forty feet from the water. By then, the sun had come out, breaking the chill, but it was still in the lower fifties, so I took off my coat and left my sweater on. Because of the surprising amount of rain in the northern Great Plains over the past few weeks, the river was flowing right along, the color of a chocolate malt. It curled in froth around a sandbar barely submerged in the middle, and swirled back upstream in front of us in a long eddy formed by a curve in the river bed just above where we stood. High above the river, two sea gulls darted at each other, shrieking like angry Siamese cats, one rising high and the other going even higher, then both tucking in their wings to drop like divers off high boards.

Otherwise, we were alone. Almost directly across the river was the high smokestack of a generating plant, and downstream in the distance you could see the city.

O'Malley set the long suitcase in the sand to his right and reached forward to open the picnic basket. He pulled back a checkered cloth to reveal fried chicken and cornbread.

I took a bite out of a thigh, and it was deliciously moist beneath the crusty coating and still warm near the bone.

O'Malley opened both quarts of beer and handed one to me. He grabbed a drumstick and took a bite, washing it down with beer.

"You know," he said, gesturing with the drumstick at the sliding gulls, "those damn birds ought to be down on the gulf gorging on fat mullet instead of up here, 1,000 miles from salt water, fighting over these skinny river shad. They follow the barges up here from New Orleans, Christ knows why." He took another bite out of the drumstick and pointed upstream with the bones.

"Little geography lesson, Michael," he said, and paused to swallow. "If you go that way on the river, you eventually end up in Montana near the Canadian border. That's why Kansas City is where it is. Did you know that?"

I said I hadn't known that and grabbed a half breast. O'Malley tossed the drumstick toward the river. He was short by five or ten feet.

" 'Tis a fact," he said, getting a piece of cornbread from the basket. "The river runs essentially east and west between St. Louis and Kansas City. But just above here the river turns north. Lewis and Clark found that out. So Kansas City was the logical place for a settlement— as far west as you could go by water without also going north. From here, people continued west by stagecoach.''

O'Malley took a long swig of beer and reached for the other half breast. His mother's chicken was delicious, spiced with pepper and salt and Crisco, as good as any I had eaten since the family had left North Carolina.

"You know, lad,'' said O'Malley, his chewing slowed to a philosophical pace, "Kansas City has always been a movie-set kind of place, a toy city. Look at the old buildings in the North End and out in Westport. Square-cut, two and three-story facades that look like there's nothing behind them, like a set for a cowboy movie. Perfect place for Bat Masterson and Wild Bill Hickock and all those rapscallions who were whoring around Kansas City sixty or seventy-five years ago.''

He paused for a long drink of beer. I took off my cap to let the sun warm my face and watched the sea gulls dance above the river. O'Malley said, "And those Missouri Confederate boys—Jesse and Frank James, William Clarke Quantrill—if that's not out of some nine-cent matinee shoot-'em-up, I don't know what is.''

O'Malley sucked on his teeth and drank some more beer. He belched.

"And when Tom Pendergast's older brother came down from St. Joe fifty or sixty years ago and started organizing it politically like an Eastern city, and opening it up to vice and frivolity, he made another kind of movie, rip-roaring as the last one. And now T. J. himself has put the finishing touches on it. It's like a toy city, Michael, New York in a bottle. It's almost a parody.

"Here's the setup,'' said O'Malley. "The politicians are Irish. The gangsters are Italian, plus a few micks and Jews left over from the previous movie. The cops are German and Irish—for the Lord's sake, you have a police chief named Otto Higgins.'' O'Malley grinned and treated himself to another swallow of beer.

"The Jews,'' he said, "mostly run clothing stores and drugstores and corner delicatessens, but some of them are becoming doctors and lawyers and they are starting their own country club. And who is the principal voice of reform in Kansas City? Rabbi Mayerberg. More chicken?''

I shook my head. There was nothing left but wings and a back anyway. I did grab another piece of cornbread before O'Malley shut the lid on the picnic basket and resumed his discourse.

"The colored folk take the streetcar out to the suburbs so they can cook and sweep, and in the evenings they dance and sing for the white people. And the Mexicans—everybody shits on the Mexicans, and they live, would you believe this, down by the railroad tracks. The Slavs, they just arrived last week and got jobs in the meat-packing plants.''

O'Malley belched again. We sat side by side on the log, full of chicken and cornbread and bubbly with beer, gazing out at the river and the two darting gulls. Despite the chill, I took my shoes and socks off and dug my feet into the sand. O'Malley, of course, still had on his argyle socks and the long, black, plain-toed priest's shoes that he almost always wore.

"A toy town," he said, almost dreamily. "And because it's a toy town, it can be run much tighter than New York or Chicago. T. J. has got 6,000 people on the city payroll. That's a lot in a city of 400,000, and that doesn't count the thousands of other jobs the machine creates. We're in a depression, lad, but Kansas City has stayed healthy on the wages of sin. Pile the recent largesse from Roosevelt on top of that, and we live in a boom town.''

"I see a lot of people lining up for the soup kitchens," I said.

"Pendergast soup kitchens," replied O'Malley. He gave a satisfied sigh. "Yep," he said, "it's a toy city. But what you fail to perceive is that all of us—potato eaters, spaghetti eaters, chitlin' eaters, chili eaters, gefilte fish eaters—we are all beholden to the Yorkshire pudding eaters.

"Your people own the banks and the packing plants and the newspapers." O'Malley hawked and spit. It seemed a rather melodramatic gesture, even for him. His pale face was beginning to flush.

"Hitler talks about the Jews and usury," said O'Malley, waving his beer bottle, "but the real usurers are the Saxons.''

He lifted the bottle to his lips, but what was left in the bottom had shaken into foam. "We'll have a use for this," he said, setting the bottle down in the sand behind the log.

"And that, Michael Holt, brings us to the real purpose of this little picnic. I have something educational to show you." He pushed the picnic basket out of the way and pulled the long black suitcase in front of him. He undid the metal clasps and opened the hinged lid.

Inside was what looked like a very long pistol, with a a wooden hand grip and a metal barrel that extended more than two feet in front of the trigger.

"What the hell is that?" I asked.

O'Malley held the device up in his left hand, and reached into the case with his right. He pulled out a hunk of polished wood about a foot and a half long. He shoved the narrow end of the piece of wood into a slot behind the handgrip of the weapon, and then it was quite clear what the thing was.

"You see, Michael," he said, holding the weapon up, "You press this little catch right here and slide in the butt and when it goes 'chunk' you have yourself a fully assembled model 1928A-1, forty-five-caliber Thompson submachine gun."

"Then," he said, reaching again into the case with his right hand, "you grab yourself one of these." He pulled out a long metal magazine. "And you press this thing-a-ma-jig right here—see where my thumb is?—and shove the clip straight up into the gun like this."

It made a heavy click.

O'Malley raised the gun to his right shoulder, right hand on the wooden pistol grip, left hand on a grooved wooden foregrip. He posed against the blue sky, grimacing at me. Except for his rather outlandish costume, he looked like a gangster or G-man in a movie.

I pointed to the magazine. "Isn't there usually a wheel-shaped thing there?"

"That is a fifty-round drum. Hard to come by. This"—he lightly slapped the long clip with his left hand—"is a twenty-round magazine."

"Now," he said, relaxing his pose, "this little beauty fires 600 rounds a minute when it is set on full automatic. That means within a couple of seconds you are out of bullets. So, unless you have the touch of a safecracker, or unless you have only one large thing to shoot at and you want to put a pretty sizable hole in it, you are wise to keep the gun set on semi-automatic. Stand up."

He turned the gun on its side. "See this little thumb lever here? Push it forward, fully automatic, *braaaaaack*. Push it back, semi-automatic, bang, bang, bang, bang. And the safety, which is right here, works in a similar way. If you really want to make a mess out of the fellow you are shooting at, everything goes forward—fire control lever, safety and bolt." He demonstrated. "Now you have a bullet in the chamber and are ready to mow the bastard down."

He grinned like a child showing off his brand-new Lionel.

"O'Malley," I said, "where the hell did you get that thing?"

"You'll just have to figure that out for yourself, Michael," he said. "Of course, if you tell anybody about this, I'll have to kill you." He smiled, but thinly.

O'Malley lifted the gun again to his right shoulder and, with his left thumb, moved the fire-control lever back to semi-automatic.

"Now," he said, "If you will throw a beer bottle in the river, I will demonstrate the use of this weapon." I grabbed O'Malley's empty and walked toward the river. The surface of the sandbar was warmed somewhat by the sun, but as soon as my bare feet broke through they touched colder, damp sand. A chill rose up my body, and then the odd, frightening notion struck me that O'Malley was behind me with a gun and was going to shoot me in the back. I fought the urge to turn around. I stopped about five feet from the water and tossed the quart bottle underhand and it sailed high and landed in the edge of the eddy about ten feet from shore. The bottle spun around, but stayed at about the same point in the river.

I turned around and walked back to the log, glancing at O'Malley, who still had the gun to his shoulder. "Thank you," he said, looking past me at the bottle. My legs were shaking, and I sat down on the log.

"Now watch," said O'Malley, as I brushed off my bare feet and began to put my socks and shoes back on.

He pressed the gun to his right shoulder and pointed it at the bottle and squeezed the trigger. *Chewww.* The bottle splintered and glass went flying as a small brownish-white gusher rose from the river. When it settled, the bottle had disappeared. The explosion had been loud, but not nearly as loud as I had expected it to be, nothing like my father's twelve-gauge shotgun, which was the only thing I had ever fired other than an air rifle.

O'Malley held the gun toward me. I finished tying my shoes and drank the last swallow or two of beer and stood up and looked at the malicious piece of machinery, hard and polished, put together from cured walnut and steel tubes and plates and levers and springs and knobs, smelling of oil and gunpowder. It looked lethal, and of course it was. Still, what the hell.

I took the gun from O'Malley. I was surprised at how light it was, and how small. Those things in the movies that roared and spit fire and chewed holes in people looked a lot larger and more fearsome. This gun seemed, somehow, comfortable. The pistol grip was skillfully rounded and grooved, so the lower three fingers of the right hand felt as if they belonged there, lightly squeezing the curved and polished wood. And the wooden foregrip was close enough so you did not have to extend your arm very far to reach it. You could cock the upper part of your left arm against the side of your chest and open your hand so the gun lay in it naturally. I pulled the gun in to my right shoulder and leaned my head down to sight it.

O'Malley tapped me on the shoulder. "Don't aim it like a rifle, not for now. I'll show you how to do that later. Just point it at the middle of the river and fire it like you would a shotgun."

I did as he said, looking out at the river. I squeezed the trigger and jumped at the soft explosion—*chewww*—but there was not as much recoil as I had anticipated. The barrel jumped a few inches, and that was all. I felt a shiver in my back, not of fright but of pleasure. It felt good to shoot a Thompson submachine gun.

I handed it, almost reluctantly, back to O'Malley, and followed him back to the log. He laid the gun carefully across the case, barrel slanted up, wooden butt resting on the sand.

"Before we leave, I'll fire it on automatic for you, just once. I've only got one other magazine, and I don't want to use it."

I sat down again on the sycamore log. "O'Malley," I said. "what's the gun for?"

"For killing Saxons and traitors," he said.

"I don't get it," I said.

"That's quite true, Michael, you don't," he said.

"The gun will be an Easter present for the boys in Ireland, a tradition begun years ago by my father and some friends. In about two weeks, it will be on its way, joining a couple of dozen more from other parts of America."

"How?"

"We have ways," said O'Malley. He grinned. "A few years ago, the football team from Derry toured America, and when they returned home they had fifteen or twenty of the damn things stuffed in among their equipment bags and steamer trunks."

"And who gets them?"

"The IRA, for Christ's sake, the Irish Republican Army."

"I didn't know there still was an IRA. I thought the war was over, and the IRA won."

"*Won?*" O'Malley shouted. "We didn't win a bloody damn thing. We were fighting for the thirty-two counties, and we didn't get the thirty-two counties, and we were fighting to get rid of the fucking English and we didn't get rid of the fucking English, not in the north we didn't."

O'Malley had begun pacing back and forth in front of me, going ten or fifteen feet in one direction, then turning on his heel and walking ten or fifteen feet in the other direction, like a man in a prison cell. Quickly, he had a well-marked path in the river sand.

I said, "Explain this to me, O'Malley. I thought the president of Ireland came from the IRA."

"His name is DeValera," said O'Malley as he paced. "And his name is a synonym for traitor. He betrayed us to the British with his deal to partition the country, and he continues to betray us."

He stopped pacing and faced me from four or five feet away, his back to the river. "His priests now deny the sacraments to anyone who joins the IRA."

O'Malley's face was pink now, and two rough circles of a deeper red had appeared on his temples. He put his hands on his hips and took a deep breath, letting it out slowly. He nodded his head.

"Well, Michael," he said, stepping past me and reaching for the gun, "I was going to show you automatic fire." He put the gun to his shoulder and turned toward the river.

With his left thumb, he flicked the fire control button forward. With his right thumb and index finger, he pulled up a folding sight made of two thin vertical strips of steel with a crosspiece between them. "This thing," he said, "is adjustable for windage and is supposed to make the damn gun accurate up to 600 yards, if you believe what they tell you. Actually, you can't hit anything more than seventy-five or 100 feet away with this bloody damn flamethrower. Here, I'll show you."

He put the gun to his shoulder and leaned his head in to look through the sight with his right eye. His hands were shaking slightly, and his face was still flushed. He pulled the gun into his shoulder and raised the barrel so it was pointing high above the river. When he pulled the trigger, the sound of rapid explosions was like an airplane engine kicking over. He held the trigger down and in an instant, it seemed, there was silence again.

O'Malley lowered the gun and looked out over the river. "Oh, Jesus," he said.

One of the white gulls was rising in a rapid, tight circle, shrieking as if in panic. And the other was falling, like a ball of feathers tied to a stone. It struck the water in the middle of the river, disappeared for an instant and then came back up, moving downstream with the rolling current. Soon, I could barely distinguish it from the froth and flotsam of the wide muddy river.

"I didn't mean to do that, Michael, I swear to heaven I didn't," said O'Malley, who looked suddenly pale and almost ill, as if someone had slugged him in the stomach.

"Oh Jesus," he said again. The other gull swooped down over the river, as if looking for its lost companion, shrieking like a child.

"We better go," said O'Malley.

He disassembled and packed the gun and I grabbed my raincoat and put the empty beer bottle in the wicker basket. We put the suitcase and the wicker basket back into the rumble seat through the golf-bag door and headed back to Kansas City. By then, there was traffic coming the other way, presumably horseplayers who wanted to make sure they were in plenty of time for the first race. O'Malley was silent for a mile or two, but then he spotted a roadhouse and bought us each a couple of beers, and by the time he had gotten to his second bottle he was a little more cheery. He still did not have much to say. He began singing that Irish song I had heard him hum and whistle and sing in snatches. I could tell he was performing for my benefit. He sang it more slowly than he usually did, almost at the tempo of a dirge:

"I am a jolly plowboy,
I plow the fields all day,
But now I'm off to Dublin town,
To join the IRA.
And we're off to Dublin in the green, in the green,
Our helmets gleaming in the sun,
Where the bayonets flash and the rifles clash
To the rattle of a Thompson gun."

10

"And what did that prove?" asked Rachael Loeb. She scooped the last of the vanilla ice cream from the bottom of one of Mrs. Stover's tall, fluted glasses and licked at it with the tip of her little pink tongue.

"Well. . ." I said, and tried to remember what I had planned to say next. Rachael smiled at the way I was staring speechless at her across the small glass-topped table.

"What did that prove?" she said again. "The straight pin in the dead man's coat? The one that made you suck the blood off your finger." She cleaned the spoon with her tongue like a cat.

I took a deep breath and let it out slowly.

"Well," I said. "I figured it proved the dead man was around the Sunset Club the night before Bennie Moten was killed. It's just a little more evidence that John Doe, unidentified Negro male, and Dr. Stone were one and the same person."

"One-and-the-same person," she mimicked. "Michael, that's serious Dashiell Hammett talk." She smiled and licked at her spoon again, even though all the ice cream was gone. I blushed.

Rachael had gotten into town Sunday morning, but this was the first time I had seen her. Her aunt and sister had picked her up at Union Station and they had gone immediately to the hospital, where her father seemed worse, slipping in and out of consciousness. Then they had gone to her house. Passover began Thursday, and out-of-town relatives were arriving to celebrate the seder with her family and visit her father for what would probably be the last time.

At first, she had seemed very depressed, and not just because of her father I soon surmised. She had attended the peace rally on Friday and told me with a flash of pride that 3,000 Columbia and Barnard students, the largest turnout in New York, had gathered in the gymnasium to hear Roger Baldwin of the Civil Liberties Union and a fiery little man from the British Labor Party.

The rally had ended with the burning of a swastika armband and then they had walked out on campus to discover that someone had replaced the school banner above the administration building with a Nazi flag.

"It had to have been those Irish Catholic boys from Fordham," she said. "Those bastards. Then. . . then I saw my father, and after that, at home—" She shook her head and reached up with a hand to brush a stray lock of her short hair back from her forehead.

"My aunt Ruth was telling terrible stories about friends and relatives in Germany who had been beaten by brown shirts and had their stores and home stoned."

Foolishly, perhaps trying to identify myself with her hurt, I told her about the Podschadly case, and my part in it—on Friday, on instructions from the city editor, I had made a futile search at the federal courthouse for naturalization papers that would indicate the dead man's religion. At that, her mood appeared to change from sadness to anguish.

"Don't you see, Michael," she said, "these people are in a horrible situation. They can only save themselves by denying their Judaism."

"But maybe they're not Jews," I said.

Rachael just stared at me for a moment, anger in her large brown eyes.

Then, thankfully, she changed the subject by asking me about Bennie Moten, and I told her about the man in the morgue and the suit and the pin and she seemed to cheer up as she ate her ice cream and entered into what she saw as the game of solving a mystery.

"So Michael," she said, "why would a doctor from Kansas City have a suit from San Francisco?"

"Maybe he bought it there," I said. "You don't see a lot of Negroes shopping at Klein Brothers."

"I bet they could if they wanted to," she said. "The Kleins are nice people."

I didn't say anything; I just gazed at her, aching to make love to her.

"Michael," she said, "I'm still hungry. Have you seen the waitress?"

I looked around and spotted the woman halfway across the large, tile-floored ice-cream parlor. I waved, but she did not seem to see me as she turned and walked through a set of pink swinging doors.

"What about the death certificate?" asked Rachael. "Did you go to the coroner's office?"

"O'Malley was right about that," I said. "The man who performed the autopsy told me to go to hell. He said he had already talked to the press and who was I to question his professional word, etc., etc. I think he's hiding something. I think they're all hiding something."

Rachael grinned at the detective-story cliché. I felt my face flush.

"That's not so farfetched," I said. "Listen to this. The feds have been looking into rumors that the syndicate and the Kansas City police department were all tied into the Union Station Massacre. Federal prosecutors tried to subpoena the police records of dozens of Kansas City gangsters, from the late Johnny Lazia on down. And you know something? All those records have disappeared."

I spotted the waitress again and tried to catch her eye. The woman didn't seem to notice my fingers treading the air. Rachael raised her right hand and made an abrupt motion, half way between a wave and an obscene gesture. The waitress was there like a bullet. A few months in New York does wonders for a girl.

"Yes, modom," said the waitress, her candy-striped pinafore slowly settling back down over its layers of crinoline. She stood with lips pursed and pencil poised.

"This time," said Rachael, "I think. . . I'll have a strawberry egg cream. A strawberry soda. With a scoop of vanil. . . no, strawberry ice cream. And a little more whipped cream this time, please."

"Yes, modom. And more coffee for the gentleman?"

I said yes and the waitress whisked away, her pinafore and crinolines rising like a parachute.

"Don't you want some ice cream?" asked Rachel.

"I'm afraid I'll spoil my supper," I joked.

"Yoah suppah?" Rachael mimicked. "Afraid to take the edge off your feast at White Castle?"

"I just find it hard to eat between meals."

"Drinking, however. . . ."

"Is a different matter." I looked at my watch. It was 3:17.

"Rachael," I said, "are people going to be at your house all week?"

"I'm afraid so," she said. She wrinkled her nose and forehead in a mock frown.

"And I'm sure you will then be heading back to New York in plenty of time for the big May Day parade."

Rachael smiled and shrugged. I didn't know what to do either. I certainly was not going to invite her to share my miserable hotel room. And Rachael Loeb was not exactly the type for a dampsheeted flagstone tourist cabin out on 40 Highway. And, I guess, neither was I.

"So," said Rachael. "Tell me more about your mystery."

"Let's see," I said. "I told you I called the hospital."

She nodded.

"Well, a couple of days later, I went by. It's an old ramshackle place in the colored Bowery, a couple of blocks west of Paseo. I thought I might be able to find something out if I just snooped around and asked questions."

The waitress arrived with the strawberry soda and poured more coffee into my cup. Very carefully, Rachael pushed the ball of ice cream to the bottom of the tall glass with her long-handled spoon, and poked at it until it spread up the fluted channels. The soda fizzed like a Bromo Seltzer as Rachael ate the whipped cream off the top. She nodded at me to continue.

"Well, I was pretty conspicuous in that hospital, being the only white person in the place. The administrator was on me like a dog and when he found out who I was he told me to get out of there and not come back."

"The power of the press," said Rachael, licking whipped cream off her lips.

"I left," I said, "but not before I saw something."

"Something interesting?" asked Rachael, raising her eyebrows.

"Something very interesting," I said. "The front hallway had half a dozen portraits hanging in it. One of them looked very much like someone I had seen before. Namely, John Doe, unidentified Negro male. There was a plaque on the frame. The name on the plaque was Dr. W. E. Stone."

"Michael!" said Rachael, swallowing a pink mouthful of ice cream and sparkling water. "That's your doctor. The plot thickens."

Rachael had carefully taken the maraschino cherry off the top of the whipped cream and placed it on a napkin. Now, with the soda half drunk, she put the cherry in her mouth and tugged the stem loose. A little of the red juice spilled out on her plump lower lip. She ran her tongue over the juice and then cleaned the rest of it off with her upper lip. She looked across the table at me. "Tell me more, Nick Charles," she said. "How about the man's family?"

"He's a bachelor," I said. "I found his address in the city directory and went by and knocked on the door of his house, but nobody answered."

Rachael's eyes glistened as she looked at me and sipped her soda. "Newspapers?" she asked.

"Aren't you swift?" I said. "He doesn't subscribe. According to the newsboy on the corner near the hospital, he picks them up on his way to and from the hospital, which is where he sees his patients. He tips the boy a dime every Friday."

"I'm impressed," said Rachael. I assumed she meant with me, not the tip. "Mail?" she asked.

"The postman received no instructions, so he keeps shoving mail through the slot in the door."

I looked at my watch again.

"I'll know more after tonight," I said. "I better run pretty soon. I have to be at work at four."

"And I have to be at the hospital," she said. She stirred the ice cream with her spoon and poured the rest of the lumpy soda into her mouth. "Woo," she said, when she had swallowed it all. "Too fast."

We split the check and I walked her to her little green Dodge. "Call me at work tomorrow?" I asked.

"Of course, Michael," she said. She was facing me, standing a foot away, and she reached over and touched the back of my hand. I reached up to pull her to me, but she backed away and left my hand hanging in the air.

"You sure you can't get out tonight?" I asked. "Earl Hines and his orchestra are in town for a couple of weeks. They're going to play between movies at the Main Street, but tonight's Blue Monday and they're going to have a jam session with the Moten Band at the Reno Club."

"I can't Michael, you know I can't. I'd like to be with you, although I am not totally enthralled by that kind of music."

"You prefer Franz Lehar."

"Only 'Yours is My Heart Alone,' " she said. "Otherwise, I'll take Rachmaninoff or Tchaikovsky."

"Don't be a snob," I said.

"I can't help preferring the music I grew up with. When I was a little girl and we lived in an apartment over my father's first drugstore, I used to sit in the living room for hours and listen to my grandmother from Odessa play the piano and dream of the land she missed terribly and was ever so grateful to have left."

I had hoped to leave work by eleven, but around 9:45 Sweeney called O'Malley and told him there had been another attempted kidnaping on the South Side, this time of a twelve-year-old girl walking home from ballet class, and it took a couple of hours to get the story.

It was almost one o'clock by the time I was clear. I picked up a couple of five-cent White Castle hamburgers on the way and headed for the Reno. It was on 12th Street, a couple of blocks east of the new Jackson County Courthouse. It was also two blocks north of 14th and Cherry, the palpitating center of the whorehouse district, and the trade spilled over into the rooms on the second floor above the Reno. There, for two dollars, you could get laid and listen to some of the best music in America drifting up through the floorboards.

The night before, Robert had called me at work. He said Seventeen would probably be at the jam session, and also that Teddy wanted to talk to me about something. That made me instantly nervous.

I asked Robert why he had not told me that Libba and Teddy were married and he said, "They might as well not be. They don't live together anymore, although Teddy sleeps at her place sometimes. They just never got divorced, because Libba didn't want to and Teddy didn't care. He's never going to get married again anyway. For Libba, being on the road with all those men eight, ten months out of the year, being married helps keep the jive artists and lounge lizards away."

"Thanks for telling me," I said.

The Reno was essentially a white club—even O'Malley had been there. It was run by Papa Sol Epstein, whose connections with Pendergast were so tight that the club had never been raided, I was told, even during the periodic—and strictly cosmetic—clean-up campaigns.

I squeezed into a parking place a block away. There must have been fifty people at the front door, shoving to get in. Robert had warned me that might happen and said to come—carefully—down the narrow alley just west of the club and ask for Teddy at the back door.

I tiptoed through the alley, lighting a match once when I heard a sound that turned out to be a cat.

I emerged into a vacant lot—and a scene that evangelist Billy Sunday might have conjured up to terrify the righteous. A man could commit every sin imaginable in that vacant lot, starting with gluttony. I could see Seventeen with this portable lunchwagon and his brain sandwiches, crawdads, and fried chicken. There was also a larger, more permanent looking lunchwagon, with ribs and hot dogs on a grill.

The lot was a courtyard, with buildings on every side and a floor of sandy dirt, packed down like a well-traveled country road. There were whores in low-cut, high-hiked satiny dresses standing in the glare of lights at the back entrance to the club, and, in a corner of the lot under a light, what looked like a crap game, the dice kicking up dust as they spun. A couple dozen men, some holding instrument cases, were standing around talking. This, Robert had told me, was the other, unofficial hiring hall of Local 627, the colored musicians union that Bennie Moten had founded.

The smell of sizzling short thighs—chicken thighs chopped in half and dropped into hot fat—and boiling Blue River crawdads and chili-flavored Kansas City barbecue was in the air, along with a thick, mildewy smoke that any boy who had grown up in a Kansas town hard by the Katy tracks recognized immediately as burning hemp, marijuana. There was, I found, a woman known only as The Old Lady who sold it, three sticks for a quarter, one dollar for a matchbox, three dollars for a lid—the amount that would fit level in the lid of a pound tobacco can. There were also stronger drugs for sale in that lot and in the rooms above, and never, at least since Papa Sol had owned the club, had there even been a narcotics arrest.

Above the back door was a loudspeaker that blasted out the music from inside. People, out-of-work musicians especially, hung out in the lot to hear the music for free. Somebody must have just put a nickel in the jukebox inside because over the loudspeaker came the click-click-click of a needle, then a solo trumpet flourish.

It was immediately recognizable, the most thrilling introduction in jazz. Robert Creech had played his record of it so many times for me that it wore out, and we went down to the record store in Lawrence and bought two more copies, one for each of us. It was the Louis Armstrong trumpet cadenza that led into "West End Blues," a series of fiery notes that soared high, dropped like ball bearings scuttling down a flight of stairs and rose once more to a stretched-out plateau where the Hot Five came in and the blues began.

My neck tingling, I looked around and saw Teddy Wellington, leaning against the back wall of the Reno not far from the door, talking to a man who, like eight or ten others in the lot, was wearing a dark blue suit and vest, a polka dot tie with matching handkerchief spilling out of his coat pocket and white shoes with black patent leather toe and heel trim.

The man had on a low, flat-crowned black hat, and his right hand rested on a tenor saxophone dangling from a lanyard around his neck. His skin was beige, a little darker than Teddy's, and splattered with freckles, like a brown chicken's egg. The man looked up as I approached. He did not move, but I sensed his hand tighten on the saxophone. He looked straight past me and said to Teddy out of the side of his mouth, "I feel a breeze." His voice was soft but had a cat's growl within it that came from deep in his throat.

Teddy looked up and saw me. He smiled, which was a relief.

"It's cool, Les, it's cool," Teddy said. "He's a friend of my nephew. Hey, Michael, glad you could fall by. This is Lester Young. Michael Holt. Michael works for the newspaper."

Lester Young nodded once, a greeting and a dismissal. His face was flat and expressionless as a tombstone. I started to ask Teddy if he would mind going with me to ask Seventeen a couple of questions when someone came up behind me and said, "Brother Lester! Want to get yourself straight?"

He was a tall, slightly stooped man with light, almost yellow skin, and crooked teeth that made little x's in the front of his mouth. He walked past me and handed Young a thin, hand-rolled cigarette. Smoke was curling from it. I took a couple of steps over to stand by Teddy, my hands in my pocket, trying to look blasé.

Lester took a couple of quick drags off the marijuana stick, sucking the smoke in deep. He passed the stick to Teddy.

"Niiiiice," said Lester Young as he exhaled smoke. "This isn't any of that salt-and-pepper shit."

The tall man said, "Les, I haven't seen you since you left Fletcher Henderson. You playing with Bennie's band again? Or is it Bus's band?"

"I'm playing around town," said Lester Young, softly. "Whoever needs a reed man. Bill Basie called me, so I'm with Bennie's band this week, maybe I'll be with some other band next week. Long as nobody tells me how to blow, like Fletcher did."

He spoke with a slow, dreamlike fluidity, as if his intent was less literal meaning than tone and nuance. The tall man said, "Is it true what I hear you told him when you left?"

Lester Young grinned. "I said, 'Would you give me a nice recommendation? I'm going back to Kansas City.' "

Teddy Wellington exhaled, sneezing a bit as smoke blew out of his nose, and passed the stick to me. I took it and stared at it. What the hell. I took a drag. It was stronger, more pungent, more medicinal tasting than the dried Kansas roadbed weed we used to roll up in wheatstraw paper. I held it in. Not harsh at all. Rough yet smooth, like Lester Young's voice. Just fine, I thought, absentmindedly holding the stick.

The tall man to my left reached for it, but he kept looking at Young.

"Take another toke," said Teddy. "Then pass it on." I did. My head was already starting to widen perceptibly and I felt a tiny tingle of paranoia, fear of the unknown, soon lost in the spreading flow of the drug.

From inside the club came the sound of a trumpet warming up, reaching for the high notes.

"Sounds like Lips is hot tonight," said Young. "I better go inside." He took a last drag off the stick and handed it to Teddy before he turned to go. The stick was almost gone now. Teddy took a drag. The butt was so tiny it looked as if it would burn him, but he held his hand out for me to take one final drag between his fingers. Then he rolled the butt into a tiny paper ball and popped it into his mouth like a pill.

The tall man and Teddy and I stood there under the lights and the loudspeaker, drifting, half-listening to the musicians warming up inside, taking in the scene. The lot behind the Reno, I mused, was like a medieval painting of a field filled with folk.

Teddy put his hand on my shoulder.

"Michael, I wanted you to meet Herman here. He used to play with Bennie Moten."

It took me a moment to think how I was supposed to respond to that.

"Herman," I finally said, "how did Bennie Moten die?"

Herman looked at me as if I was crazy. He glanced over at Teddy, who just shrugged. Then he looked back at me. He ran saliva around inside his mouth. He swallowed.

"Bennie Moten?" he said. "Bennie Moten bled to death on the operating table getting his tonsils out. I thought everybody knew that."

"The *Kansas City Star* said he died of heart failure," I said.

"Sheeit," said Herman, and he laughed and laughed and laughed.

He stopped to catch his breath. he said, "Anybody dies, it's heart failure, you hear what I'm saying?" He laughed again.

"Herman," said Teddy, "tell him about your girlfriend and the operation."

"One of my girlfriends," corrected Herman. "She's one of my girlfriends. She works down at that hospital, she's a scrub nurse, you dig? She was on duty in the operating room the morning they cut on Bennie. Broad says she's never seen so much blood in her life. It was pouring out of Bennie's mouth like that doctor hit an oil gusher. Yeah! I wouldn't lie."

He wouldn't lie. He's too high to lie. I giggled to myself. Stop that, I thought. Pull yourself together. Take a deep breath. Pursue this matter.

"Herman," I said, "I think Bennie Moten was murdered. I'd really like to meet your lady friend and ask her some questions."

Herman glared at me. He glared at Teddy. He glared at me again. Then he said, "I think I'm going to ease on inside and get myself a nice sweet rum and Coca-Cola."

He turned to walk away. I started to take a step after him but Teddy held my shoulder.

"Be cool, Michael. Don't be chasing that man." He leaned over and whispered in my ear. "Take a look around. But be cool about it." I don't know how cool I was, but I did take a look around, and what I saw sent a chill through me. There were at least half a dozen men and women close enough to hear my conversation with Herman, including a very big, very black man bursting out of a pin-stripe suit. He looked like a much darker version of the boxer Jack Johnson, and he was staring right at me.

"Now," said Teddy very softly, "look up." I did, squinting to see past the lights shining down, and saw several shadowy figures on the balcony right above us. My, my. Time to change the subject.

"Uh, is . . . Earl Hines here tonight?" I asked.

Teddy shook his head. "His boys are here, but Earl went home," he said. "Said he was tired. Besides, it's in his contract that he can't jam, he can only play for money, and the boys in Chicago have to get a piece of it. Those gangsters got Earl in a golden cage."

Teddy flexed the long, twisted fingers of his right hand and looked about ten feet past me at a woman in a red skirt that was slit halfway up her thigh. She was trying to get a white man, one of the few in the lot, to go upstairs with her. He said no, and she persisted, and finally he cursed her and she walked away, her ass swaying. "Looks like two pigs fighting under a blanket," said Teddy.

We stood there by the back wall of the Reno club, silent for a moment. The marijuana was settling in and leveling off and I was cruising right along, not molasses-brained the way you get with that railbed stuff but high and clarified, alert, aware of nuances. Even if there were no nuances.

I finally said something. "Why is it different here than Chicago?" I asked.

"One thing, I guess," said Teddy, "down here you got a lot of spades as middle men—Piney Brown, Felix Payne the lawyer. Billy Shaw, head of the union, Bennie Moten before they. . . before he died. Even the ofays that run clubs down here seem more respectful of the musicians. Hell, Milton Morris would do anything in the world for Bill Basie or Julia Lee."

He gave a little laugh through his nose, but he was not smiling. "And down here," he said, "these gangsters, they pretty much stick to killing each other."

"And voters," I said.

The sound of the musicians warming up inside was rising in a dissonant crescendo, and the people in the lot were slowly finding their way inside, although the crap game showed signs of enduring all distractions. The whore in the red dress had found a customer, a small, dark-skinned Negro in shirtsleeves carrying his suitcoat over his shoulder. The stairs creaked as they headed upstairs. As they passed over us, Teddy glanced up and grinned.

He winked at me. "Women shouldn't be allowed in public without underwear," he said.

A woman's voice came from above. "You shouldn't be standing under the stairs looking up, Teddy Wellington." Teddy laughed. He laced his fingers together in front of him and cracked his knuckles, and then stretched his joined hands high above his head. "It's about time to go in," he said. "Robert and Libba are holding us a table."

"Teddy," I said, flinching a bit at the sound of Libba's name, "I'd like to talk to that guy Herman again, about the nurse and the blood."

"Right," said Teddy. "I'll see what I can do. Let's go hear some music."

Inside, the Reno club was mobbed, with a couple hundred people sitting and standing in a room that had seats for about half that many. Robert and Libba were at a table for four on the edge of the small wooden parquet dance floor in front of the bandstand.

It took me a long time to say hello to Robert, whom I had seen less than a week before, but when I finally, nervously, turned to say hello to Libba, she reached her hand up to shake mine and smiled. She looked lovely in a black satin dress bunched at one shoulder under a jeweled pin, her glistening black hair falling in curls around her face, her lipstick deep red against her dark-chocolate skin.

Libba acted, then and always afterwards, as if nothing had happened between us. Our casual acquaintance picked up from where it had been a second before I reached for her than morning in her living room. It was as if she had locked a door, one that was going to stay locked. She was simply Libba again. At first, I was uneasy in her presence, but fairly soon, and quite unconsciously, I quit looking for little sparks of hostility and enjoyed being around her again.

The Moten band was ready to begin. They were shoved together, thirteen strong, on a small bandstand beneath a tin canopy painted in zebra stripes. The canopy sloped low in the back and there was a circular hole cut in it to leave room for the pegs and scroll of an upright bass.

A chubby Bus Moten stood at one side of the bandstand, and opposite him, at the baby grand piano, was Bill Basie, handsome like a black Clark Gable, with a wide mustache and white teeth sparkling against his buffed-ebony skin.

Bus Moten raised his baton and shook it, as if he was trying to dislodge some sticky foreign substance, and Lester Young rolled his eyes and let out a sarcastic little honk from his tenor sax. Bus frowned and started again and at the fifth beat the band was off, roaring and riff-driven as always, into the first tune. It soon became clear, as Bus drifted off to

117

one side, his baton useless now, who was really leading the band. You could see it the first time Lester Young and Herschel Evans locked into one of their fierce saxophone duels.

Lester, head cocked and sax held out to the side above his right hip, blew with a tone that was light and pure but had a hard bite to it, and he cut and skittered and lightfooted his way through the rhythms and riffs like a fancy scatback. And Herschel was the fullback, coming straight on and full of power, his tone resonant and muscular, his big tenor as mean and unstoppable as a Texas tornado. They went at each other furiously, and yet, if you listened and watched carefully, you could detect the complex messages Basie was giving them with chords from his flicking right hand—now this way, Herschel, now over here, now right there between the reeds and the brass, that's it, now Lester you come in, right through there, that's it, ride that rhythm from the bass, that's it, baby, that's it baby, that's *it*.

And at that, in would come Hot Lips Page, the mouthpiece of his trumpet engulfed in his wide mouth, riding to the attack with a burst of silver, climbing, leveling off, climbing again, scattering notes like a man throwing coins by the handful to a hungry crowd. By then, at the back of the bandstand, sweat would be rolling down Walter's Page's studious, round black face as he leaned over to yank the basic Kansas City steam-engine four/four out of the strings of his bass. Pretty soon, he would be yanking so hard the peg of the instrument would start to bounce on the wooden band platform and the big fat bass would walk forward until it began to come out of its hole in the canopy and Walter Page would finally catch himself, back up and start all over again. Basie would smile and hit a calming chord—take it easy, Big 'Un, we got all morning long.

Then Moten's singer, Jimmy Rushing, came on stage. He was the shape of a corner mailbox and had an Oklahoma City whine like the wind blowing across hundreds of flat, sand-dry miles from the mountains of New Mexico, and like that Sooner wind Rushing's voice was full of tricky twists and swirls.

You knew just listening to Rushing and Lester Young and Herschel Evans and Hot Lips Page and watching Basie that the band was something special, and what happened later now seems almost inevitable. Within six or eight months, it was Basie's band in name as well as in spirit. One January night in 1936, when John Hammond was in Chicago to produce records with Benny Goodman and Gene Krupa and Meade Lux Lewis, he turned on his car radio and heard Count Basie broadcasting from the Reno Club. Right away, Hammond drove to Kansas

City, signed Basie to a recording contact, and brought the band to New York. Two days before Christmas in 1938, Hammond put Basie and Lester Young and Jimmy Rushing in Carnegie Hall, along with Joe Turner and Pete Johnson and, it seemed, half the other great musicians in Kansas City.

On that night in April 1935, at the Reno Club in Kansas City, when it became clear who would be the heir to Bennie Moten, what did Jimmy Rushing sing? One song for sure:

> It takes a rocking chair to rock,
> It takes a rubber ball to roll,
> Takes a rocking chair to rock,
> And it takes a rubber ball to roll.
> It takes a Kansas City woman
> To satisfy my soul.
> I'm going to Kansas City
> Yes I'm going to Kansas City
> I'm going to Kansas City
> Where they sing the blues all night.

On and one and one, twelve or fifteen or twenty verses, some made up on the spot, others changed as he went along, so that Jimmy Rushing never sang the ancient "Kansas City Blues" the same way twice.

After the band played for well over an hour, there was a break. About half the crowd shoved out the front and back doors for a little relief from the smoky air, the other half pushed toward the bar. The musicians left the bandstand and Libba Monroe got up from our table and walked over to the piano. She spun the stool so it rose perhaps a foot from where it had been for Basie, sat and began playing pretty little runs with both hands, starting in the middle of the keyboard and working outwards.

Soon, Teddy joined her on stage and began tinkering with the drum set. Within a few minutes, the band's chairs had been shoved as far to the rear of the stand as they would go and there were five or six horn players standing there, ready to go.

Libba led it off with a long, strutting introduction at a medium-fast tempo. Her left hand was doing little else but beating time, hopping back and forth on the keyboard. As the introduction progressed, her right hand grew adventurous, making trills and surprising little leaps, falling back into silences for a beat or two and then catching up with a burst of notes or quick arpeggio. Somewhere in there one could detect hints of a melody—"Moten Swing." Her style was more intricate and subtle than Basie's, if less propulsively rhythmic. She sat straightbacked at the piano, her hands and arms doing all the work, and she seemed stiff and formal, almost uninvolved, until you looked at her dark face and saw little beds of sweat poised like tears below her eyes, which were half-closed, expectant, as if she was waiting for a kiss.

Then Teddy came in, riding the cymbal with a hard four/four, and they were off. Soon a bass player wandered over and the hornmen began to take their turns and there we were, at almost four in the morning in Kansas City and the joint was jumping.

The jam went on for a half-hour or more, same tune, and Robert and I sat at our table, drinking, half-listening, half-screaming at each other about some shared moments of college struggle and joy, when the background noise from the crowd lessened a few decibels. You could hear Teddy and Libba and the bass player laying down the foundation, but no horn was using it to take off from. I looked on stage. Standing there, looking quite small, a battered alto saxophone in his hand, was the kid from the Sunset, the kid from the funeral, the teenager who carried his instrument around in the bag his mother had made from pillow ticking.

Teddy looked over from the drums, frowning. He hit a hard, angry rim shot. As the kid watched, Libba leaned toward Teddy and said something. He shrugged and went back to a light, strong four/four on the cymbal, ching-ching-ching-ching. Libba nodded at the kid, restated the melody, romped through sixteen bars and left a hole.

The kid leaped in, surefooted and fleet, and for a few surprising moments it was magical. He played a little like Lester Young, but higher on the smaller horn, with more of a metallic shriek and more sense of the deep-down ancient blues. Libba's chords crept up on him from behind to push him higher, and he responded. For sixteen bars or so it flowed like quicksilver—and then something happened. The kid tried to double-time or shift chords or both, and his saxophone blurted out a quick series of squeaks and unintended harmonics. That clearly shook him and he lost his way and his horn squeaked again and again and finally, after a confused burst of unrelated notes, it fell silent.

Almost everyone in the crowded room stopped talking and looked at the stage. The kid stood there alone and silent and about all you could hear was the tinkling of bar glasses and ice and Teddy's tauntingly insistent four/four on the cymbal. Then Teddy stopped playing too and sat, as if waiting for the kid to leave the bandstand and let the grownups play. But the kid just stood there, his brown, vaguely Oriental face turned down toward the instrument that had betrayed him, his shoulders slumped, as if he were almost in shock. Finally, Teddy put both drumsticks in his left hand, reached up with his right, fiddled a moment with the cymbal, then lifted it off its supporting rod and, with a discus backhand, flung the bronze plate across the wooden bandstand.

It went "changggg" and slid to a halt inches from the kid's feet. His head snapped up and he looked around the crowded room at all the people staring at him in pity or disdain. There were tears in his eyes. Slowly, he walked off the stand, saxophone hanging low in his right hand, and turned toward the back door.

And that was the end of the jam session. Everyone, Teddy included, left the stand but Libba, who sat silently for a while, and then began picking out a slow, deep blues.

It was close to 4:30. Robert had to get a couple of hours of sleep and teach that day. And I wanted to go home to bed. We stayed about ten minutes more while I had a double bourbon to help me sleep. Robert put a couple of nickels in the jukebox and punched the same number twice—"West End Blues." Again, Robert and I marveled at Louis Armstrong's transcendent unaccompanied introduction.

Then we got up to leave, waving goodbye to Teddy, who was with other musicians at the bar, and Libba, who was still at the piano, playing the blues. We went out the back way.

The back lot was almost empty now, littered with dead half-pints and quart wine bottles and scraps of greasy, sauce-splashed newspaper. Even the crapshooters had disappeared. It was still dark, and the lights were still on, but the loudspeaker was silent. The hot-dog man was gone and his lunchwagon was shuttered, but Seventeen was still there. I had completely forgotten about him, with the whisky and the marijuana and the music.

Robert and I walked over to the little hunched man. He looked up at us with his good eye from under his worn gray wool cap. "You gennemen got Seventeen pins?" he said, in a tired rote voice.

We nodded.

"Seventeen," I asked, "how many of those pins do you give out a night?"

"Lemme see, lemme see now," he said. "I gets them by the box from Matlaw's Men's Furnishings over at 18th and Vine. I give the man a short thigh time to time. Let's see. How many's in a box?"

He reached in the pocket of the tattered old suitcoat he wore, way too large for him, and he pulled out a small orange box. He held it out so I could read the label.

"There's fifty in a box," I said.

"I goes through a box in about a week, I'm out four, five nights a week. I only gives them to strangers who buys something from me or who's with someone I know." Seventeen yawned. "Mister, I got a couple of short thighs left, maybe a few wings. You hungry?"

"So you give out ten or twelve a night," I said.

"That sound right, that sound right. More on weekends, less other times. You gennemen hungry?"

"Remember the night you gave pins to me and Robert?" I asked.

He raised his head to look me and Robert over, and I could see his clouded eye beneath the cap. "Now I can't rightly say I do," he said. "What night was that?"

"The night before Bennie Moten was killed," I said. Robert coughed, as if something had caught in his throat.

Seventeen didn't say anything, but the drooping eyelid squeezed shut as he squinted to see me more clearly with his good eye.

I said, "That night, Bennie Moten was around 12th and Vine with another man, a tall, light-skinned man in a suit and a black hat. Remember?"

"Mister, I see lots of men looks like that."

"Yeah," I said, "but this one ended up in an alley with this throat cut."

Seventeen sighed. He took one more look at me, then he turned his head so he could look past me. "You going to have to excuse me," he said. "Customer coming."

I looked over my right shoulder. A man was coming down the back stairs of the Reno club, very slowly. When he reached the ground, he came our way, walking like a figure in a dream. As he came into the glare of the streetlight over Seventeen's lunchwagon, I recognized him.

It was the kid with the alto saxophone. He was in his shirtsleeves in the chilly morning air and he was just buttoning his left cuff. His horn was hanging at his chest from a lanyard.

"Charles," said Robert. "Why don't you ever come to school anymore?"

He replied, dreamily, "I get kind of tired of Lincoln High School after a while, Mr. Creech." He spoke softly, but his voice had an edge of sarcasm. "I'm playing with a band now," he said. "The Deans of Swing."

"Yes," said Robert, "I heard you, over at the Kentucky Barbecue, and you're the sorriest man in that band. You've got talent, but you need to spend more time at school in the rehearsal room."

"Is that right?" he said. He grinned sleepily. "I get plenty of practice. Listen here, Mr. Creech. You play the saxophone. Can you play this?''

He raised the horn to his lips. He stood loosely, relaxed like a man after a steambath. His pupils were bull's-eyes.

His fingers began to move on the saxophone, and suddenly he did not look sleepy anymore. For a few seconds there was no sound, and then his cheeks puffed out and he began to blow. It was startling, like a burst from a machine gun. The notes came even faster than they had in the club, faster than Lester Young, and the notes were hard, harder than an alto should be played, and almost painful to listen to, as if they were torn from his throat. At first, the flood of notes made no sense, and then they started to come together and the realization hit me like a blow.

"Robert?" I whispered.

"Yeah," said Robert. "West End Blues."

It was Louis Armstrong's cadenza all right, but it had never been played that way before. Not only was the kid playing it at double or triple time, but he had tempered it and given it an edge that Armstrong had never imagined, and a bitter core of torment slid out like molten wire. What he had done, I realized, was take Armstrong's introduction to "West End Blues" and, for the first time, and at a speed that took your breath away, truly play it as the blues.

"Jesus, Lord Jesus," said Robert Creech. The moment was incandescent and over in a flash. The beat-up saxophone stuck on a note, the kid's stubby brown fingers began to stumble, he lost his embouchure for a second and then he lost everything in a triplet of squeaks.

He lowered the saxophone and let it dangle. His eyes opened wide and he smiled at us. He knew we could not ignore what he had just done.

He pulled a small silver coin out of his pocket and flipped it high in the air, so high it disappeared for an instant and then reappeared, spinning and glittering in the circle of light. He never looked up, but kept the black suns of his eyes on Robert Creech as the coin fell. He put out his right hand, still not looking, and the coin fell into it. He smiled and walked over to the lunchwagon and held the coin out to the little man with the one dead eye.

"Seventeen," he said, "give me some of that yardbird."

11

Drummond had left me a note about a $1,245 bar holdup, along with his best wishes and a queer smell in the air, and I was reading it when the phone rang.

I picked up the receiver. "Holt, *Journal-Post*."

"Mr. Holt, you're rather difficult to get in touch with," said a deep, cultivated voice. "I called your paper first, and had to wait several minutes while someone figured out who and where you were. Then, when I called this number an hour ago, I was subject to vulgar abuse from an ungrammatical gentleman who appeared to be intoxicated."

"I'm sorry," I said. "That would be my colleague Mr. Drummond. He is under a physician's care for an inner-ear disorder. The tonic makes him slur his syllables."

"I know inner-ear disorders quite thoroughly, Mr. Holt," the voice said, growing even more formal in tone. "That man was drunk."

The voice sounded authoritative. It also sounded slightly Negro.

"Who is this, please?" I asked.

"Dr. W. E. Stone," the man replied.

"Oh," I said.

"I have just returned from a a vacation in Mexico. Mr. Robinson at the hospital tells me you have been asking after me."

"O'Malley?" I said, hopefully.

"I beg your pardon?" This is not O'Malley, I thought. O'Malley could imitate Amos and Andy, but this sounded like the Negro equivalent of Franklin Delano Roosevelt. O'Malley chose to think such people did not exist.

"O . . . K . . ." I said, trying to think of what to say. "Did . . . are you the doctor who operated on Bennie Moten?

"I am," the voice said.

"I thought you were dead."

"If you thought I was dead, why were you looking for me?"

"I, uh . . . it's a long story. Could I see you?"

"Not if you wish to talk about the late Mr. Moten," the man said. "The doctor-patient relationship is a confidential one, and his family is entitled to the same privacy I would have shown him. But tell me, Mr. Holt, why did you think I was dead?"

"I . . . thought I saw your body in the morgue."

"Goodness," said the man. "That's rather chilling. But we have never met. What made you think you recognized my remains?"

"I saw you earlier that morning drinking and shooting pool with Bennie Moten."

There was a long silence. Finally, I broke it, stumbling ahead.

"Okay," I said. "What is a doctor doing out on the town with his patient a few hours before he's supposed to take his tonsils out?"

There was another silence. This time, the doctor broke it, his voice even deeper and more imperious than before. "Mr. Holt, I shall end this conversation in a moment. But first, tell me your imagined version of the events of April 2."

"Sure," I said. At that point, I was no longer certain what my version was, so I had a gulp of coffee and started thinking aloud.

"Okay. You were drunk in the operating room. Your hand slipped and cut the wrong thing, an artery or something, and Bennie Moten bled to death. You made a fatal mistake, one that could cost you your license. Maybe they could even try you for . . . for manslaughter. Or at least malpractice. So you left town until it blew over."

I paused. My throat was dry. I took the last swallow of coffee in the cup. The man on the phone said nothing.

"Okay," I said. "That's just one theory. An accident, a criminal accident. But there's another way it could have happened. Maybe somebody wanted Bennie Moten dead. And you. . . ."

"Mr. Holt," the man interrupted, his voice edged with a weary anger. "I have nothing further to say to you, and do not intend to listen further to your fantasies. But let me warn you. If I discover you have spread these speculative lies about me, or if you bother me in any way, I shall notify my attorney to prepare a suit for slander and whatever other charges he considers appropriate. Good day." He hung up.

Oh, swell, I thought. What does this mean? If the doctor is not dead, does it shoot my whole theory? Or does it matter? Maybe I was mistaken about the identity of the corpse in the morgue, but there still is something very fishy about Bennie Moten's death. All the musicians say so. Maybe the dope syndicate, whoever they may be, paid the doctor to kill Moten, and then the doctor went on the lam to Mexico until he was sure he had gotten away with it. But then, who was the hawk-nosed man in the morgue? And does that matter?

And what have I gotten myself into?

I still had not figured out much of anything when O'Malley came strolling in. He looked as if he had been at the races again. It was too warm and humid for the loud tweed coat, so he had switched to his rumpled seersucker suit—his Huey Long suit, he called it.

He was again wearing the green hat with the yellow feather and carrying his shooting stick over his shoulder like a rifle.

"You win?" I asked, distractedly.

"Michael, Michael," he said, with boozy expansiveness. "The Lord giveth and He taketh away. Today the Lord was in a taking mood. I was not the only loser, however, nor the biggest by far."

He took the shooting stick from his shoulder and flourished it at me like Captain Blood.

"I learned from a Sicilian gentleman of my acquaintance that the old man went zero for nine. You would think a man betting on his own horses at his own track could do better than that. But they say T. J. has been on a disastrous losing streak lately."

He lowered the shooting stick with his right hand until its point touched the floor, and he posed, wrist bent, hip sticking out to the left, like a swell at Saratoga with a gold-handled cane.

"He has even installed a horse wire in his office, and he bets long-distance. He lost so much to a big-time bookie from Newark that the man came out here personally to collect."

O'Malley leaned toward me and lowered his voice slightly, to something approaching normal conversational tones. "I am told that Pendergast lost another $125,000 to the man while he stood there waiting to be paid for the previous losses. I am also told that Charles V. Carollo had to make a tour of the gambling houses to come up with the loot."

"O'Malley," I said, "how do you know so much?"

He straightened up and took his weight off the shooting stick. "Let's just say I'm well connected," he said. He winked. When I failed to respond with a smile, he asked, "What's the matter with you? Off your feed?"

"Well," I said, "I just talked to Dr. Stone."

He looked puzzled for a moment. Then his brow went up and he said, "Oh, you mean the dead doctor? You just talked to the dead doctor?"

I nodded.

"Then perhaps he is not dead."

"Perhaps," I said.

'Where did he call from?" O'Malley asked. "Down there?" He tapped the floor with the point of the shooting stick. I couldn't tell if he meant the morgue or hell.

"Wheatley-Provident Hospital, I guess," I said.

"Hmmm," said O'Malley. He walked over to his side of the desk, laid the shooting stick across it and picked up his phone. He asked the police operator to get him Wheatley-Provident. While he waited, he tapped his foot and hummed an impromptu tune that seemed to mix horse racing and Celtic revolution.

When O'Malley was put through to the hospital, he asked if Dr. Stone had returned to duty. He paused for a reply. "Thank you," he said. "No need to speak with him just now. I'll see him on the golf course."

He hung up. "A miraculous recovery, Michael," he said. "Positively Lazarusian."

"That's not a word," I muttered.

"In any event, the dead man has risen. But part of your great vision remains in place. Somebody *is* bringing heroin into Kansas City, and it is not the usual folks."

O'Malley lowered himself into his wooden swivel chair. "A lot of heroin," he said.

"I hear the same thing from other people," I said. "Maybe you should talk to Robert Creech and Teddy Wellington."

"Who's Teddy Wellington?" said O'Malley, shoving the shooting stick aside so he could prop his feet up on the desk. "Some Brit?"

"A Negro musician," I replied.

"Is he funny or dangerous?"

"What?" I asked.

"In my experience, niggers are either funny or dangerous. Which is Teddy Wellington?"

"O'Malley, don't—" I stopped myself and changed the subject rather than start an argument.

"This may no longer be relevant," I said, "but I called Jeff City today about Bennie Moten's death certificate."

"Maybe it's relevant, maybe it isn't. What did they say?"

"It's in the mail."

"An ancient lie," said O'Malley, reaching forward to scratch his mangy ankle. "Well," he said, his eyelids fluttering in sensual reaction to the pleasurable pain his fingernails were initiating, "on to work. What's going on?"

Not much was going on. I told O'Malley I would probably follow up on the bar holdup out on Troost and he wished me luck. When he left to search for richer fodder, I called the bar and asked the question Drummond had suggested: how had a neighborhood tavern on Troost come by $1,245 in receipts?

Oh, the bartender replied, more than $1,100 had belonged to the bookie who worked in back. If I wanted to come out around 7:30, during the dinner-time lull, he would be happy to talk about it. The bar could use the publicity, and so could his brother-in-law, the bookie.

A wonderful town, Kansas City.

A little after six, Robert Creech called. First, he wanted to tell me Dr. Stone was alive. I told him I knew that. Robert said that he still thought there was something suspicious about Bennie Moten's death, and I agreed.

He had been heartbroken the other night, he said, to see Charles come down the back stairs of the Reno with his pupils dilated, clearly on the needle. He and Teddy had talked about all the heroin coming in, and agreed they wanted to do something to stop it. That included going to the police, if we could come up with some evidence that couldn't be laughed away.

Robert had a band concert that evening, but Teddy would like to get together with me before his gig at the Subway. He put Teddy on. I told him I would probably be out on Troost pretty soon and could take a dinner break around 8:30 and he said that was perfect and he would meet me at Milton's Tap Room.

Both Milton's and the bookie bar were on Troost around 35th Street, theoretically four blocks south of the line the gambling syndicate would not cross. But Troost was like a war zone extending into the peaceful petit-bourgeoise respectablity of that part of the city. On Troost, you could find horse-race machines and turf accountants and strip joints and jazz clubs and a tiny nest of cabarets where female impersonators performed.

I left the office around 7:15. After getting some usable quotes from the bartender about the holdup ("I ain't going to die for my brother-in-law's next Cadillac,") I drove down the block and parked in front of Milton's Tap Room.

Milton's was next to a small Piggly Wiggly grocery store. It had a chest-high tan brick facade topped by plate glass windows. A black-lettered sign in the window read: "Appearing nightly for cocktails: Julia Lee and Baby Lovett." From the sidewalk out front, I could hear a piano and the light sizzle of a cymbal stroked by brushes.

Inside, Milton's was dimly lit. There were two red-neon beer signs and an illuminated clock behind the bar, which was to the right as you entered, and to the left was a small spotlight that shone down from the ceiling on the piano player and the drummer beside her. I looked at the clock. It was almost 8:30.

The bartender, sticking a thick hand over the bar and speaking around a large red-banded cigar, introduced himself. Milton Morris had a face like the mask of comedy, topped off with big brown eyes, bushy eyebrows and curly dark-brown hair that was cut to the white on the sides and was thick on top, brilliantined back in a series of little waves.

He took the cigar out of his mouth. Remarkably, despite the seeming death grip his teeth had had on it, the end was round and unchewed. He gestured with the cigar.

"Can I get you something to drink?" he asked, the cigar wagging as he spoke.

"Budweiser," I said. He turned to the cooler.

I looked around. To my right were three men standing with their backs to the bar, listening to the music. There were a dozen or so low tables in the room, with people at about half of them. The woman barely visible behind the upright piano was playing and singing a fast jump tune. She had a pretty, plump beige-yellow face and long spitcurls that reached down her forehead.

Beside her, at a minimal drum set, was a little tobacco-skinned man with a thick topping of shellacked black hair, like something a taxidermist had plopped on his head.

The bartender set a bottle of beer, with foam puffing out the top, on the bar in front of me.

"That'll cost you ten cents," he said, wiping his right hand on the white apron that was tied around his waist. "Local beer's a nickel when the band ain't playing." He pulled the cigar out of his mouth and looked at me across the top of it, like a painter sighting in on a model with his thumb. "New in town?" he asked.

I nodded. "I'm here to see Teddy Wellington."

"Over there," said the man, gesturing with his cigar to the right of the piano player. I looked where he was pointing, but all I could make out was a table with a couple of people at it.

"Pretty dark in here," I said.

"I like it dark in my joints," he said, replacing the cigar in his mouth. "Makes it hard to tell what color people are."

He reached behind him and got a shot glass and a cocktail glass. He put ice in the cocktail glass and poured whisky in both of them.

"You a friend of Teddy's?" he asked, pouring water from a pitcher into the cocktail glass.

I nodded. "All right, then," he said. "You take those two glasses of whisky over there. You set the shot on top of the piano for Julia, and then you take the whisky and water over to that table where Teddy is sitting with that young girl. See where I mean?"

I looked again. My eyes were slowly getting adjusted to the dark, and if I squinted I could make out Teddy and someone else seated at one of two tables on a long, low platform to the right of the piano player. Teddy held up his hand when he saw me looking.

"Let me tell you about that platform," Milton said. "This is a white saloon in a white neighborhood, know what I mean? Colored people aren't supposed to drink in here. But Julia's got lots of colored fans. Bill Basie is in here almost every night if the Moten band ain't working. So I sit Bill Basie and the girls who come in to ogle Baby Lovett and the other colored people on that platform. Any peckerwood raises sand about it, I just tell them that's my bandstand and those people are part of my band. See what I'm saying? I guess that little chick is my new singer, huh?" He gave a wild, rambling laugh low in his throat.

At the piano, Julia Lee was romping to the end of the song and the little brown drummer was booting her along. She sang,

"Can't sleep for dreaming,
Just can't laugh for crying.
Can't sleep for dreaming,
Just can't laugh for crying.
The man I love,
Forever on my mind."

They ended the song with a quick burst of notes and a fast drum roll. There was a volley of applause and, over it, a man yelled, " 'Come Over to My House.' I wanna hear 'Come Over to My House.' "

I looked toward him. He was one of two men standing at the end of the bar near the door. They must have come in just after I did. They were leaning with their backs to the bar, both wearing double-breasted suits with overpadded shoulders and the wide brims of their gray hats were turned up all the way around.

"The boys do that so they can see 360 degrees," O'Malley once told me, half-joking. Sure enough, the suitcoat of the man closest to me bulged at the breast, as if there was a gun under there. It was too dark to tell much about their faces from where I was.

Julia Lee ignored the request. I carried the shot of whisky over and put it on top of the upright piano. Julia smiled up at me and reached up to take the glass.

She held it up in a toast. "Thanks, Milton," she said, her voice like a kitten's purr, and tossed the whisky down her throat with a flip of her hand. She swallowed easily, as if the bourbon was lemonade, and smacked her lips.

I went back to the bar and got Teddy's whisky and my beer. When I stepped up onto the platform, Teddy stood up. "Audrey," he said to the girl, who looked up from a straw poked into a tall glass of something with a cherry in it, "this is Michael."

I handed Teddy his drink and said hello to the girl, who nodded shyly.

She was young, seventeen or eighteen, and skinny, with protruding front teeth. She had on black satin cocktail gown that was too dressy for Milton's and a 1920s-style black cloche hat that fit her head like a bandage. Somehow, she looked as if she belonged in a flour-sack dress in a sharecropper's shack somewhere, or maybe in a country church choir robe, not in this white-man's jazz bar in Kansas City.

"Audrey," said Teddy, "could you go powder your nose for a minute or two while I talk to Michael alone? That's a sweetheart."

The girl reached up to touch her nose, puzzled. Gently, Teddy took her thin wrist. "Pussycat, don't you have to go to the ladies' room?"

She looked away, embarrassed, and then got up from the table and walked toward the rear of the bar, stumbling a bit in her high heels as she stepped down from the platform.

I sat down across the table from Teddy with my back to the bar. I heard a chair scrape and looked to my left. The two men from the bar were sitting down at the other table on the platform, a couple of feet away. They still had their hats on. In the dim light spilling from the piano directly in front of them, I could see that one man, the one with the lump in his coat, had a long scar on one cheek. Both men looked like extras in a gangster movie. In a way, given O'Malley's fanciful script, they were.

Teddy said to them, "That table's for the band."

"That's swell," said the man with the scar. He turned toward us and I could see that the scar sickled from just below his right eye down into the top of his mouth, and the whole lower right side of his face was puckered and pushed in as if some of the bone was missing from his cheek and jaw. When he spoke, only the left side of his mouth moved.

"We're musicians," he said. "Want to see our instruments?" He patted his bulging coat. Both men laughed. "Want to see my instrument?" he said again, this time to his buddy, and they both laughed again.

Julia Lee began playing boogie-woogie and Teddy reached across the table and tugged me toward him, so our heads were close.

"I caught up with Seventeen last night down at 18th and Vine," he said, just loudly enough for me to hear. "He didn't want to say anything at first, but we've known each other for a long time, and finally he opened up a little bit. The man in the green sharkskin suit was not Dr. Stone."

"I found that out, too," I said.

"But there *was* a man in a green sharkskin suit down there that night," Teddy said. "The first time, he was alone. Seventeen remembers him because of the fancy suit and because he spoke like a white man. He kidded Seventeen about selling trash like pork brains, but he bought a couple of short thighs and Seventeen gave him a pin."

I glanced over at the table next to us. The men were not paying attention to us or to Julia Lee's piano. They were leaning close to each other, talking in low tones, as if they, too, had secrets to share.

Teddy cleared his throat softly and continued.

"That was early, ten, eleven o'clock. Seventeen saw him again, several hours later. He came out of the Lone Star with a white man. Seventeen said he had seen the white man around a lot in the past month or two. Said he dresses like a Negro musician. He told me, 'That grey cat means only one thing—dope.' "

Teddy leaned forward dramatically and whispered the last word. It tickled my ear and sent a shiver through me.

"Teddy?" It was Audrey. Teddy gestured to the chair between us. She sat down, her back to the other table.

"Baby," said Teddy, pushing her drink across the table to her, "now you tell Michael what you told me about the doctor and all that blood in the operating room." The men at the other table still seemed to be deep in conversation, and Julia Lee was really pounding away now, so it seemed silly to keep trying to speak so softly.

"I told Herman I wouldn't tell nobody but you, Teddy," she said, in a whiny voice.

"Then you pretend Michael's not here, and you tell me again."

"Well. . ." the girl said, hesitating. "Well, all right." She glanced at me, and then fixed her eyes on Teddy as she spoke.

"Like I said, I haven't been working at the hospital long, but I never seen so much blood come out of one man in my life. It was pouring out of Mr. Moten's mouth like he'd drunk a quart of mulberry wine and was spitting it all back up."

"And tell me again about the doctor," said Teddy, his right hand lightly tapping along with the music, halving the bouncy eight beats in-to silky four/four.

"Well," she said, "I thought he was acting real strange. He was sweating a lot and he was kind of pale and once he looked like he was going to fall over and he had to hold himself up with his hand on the operating table."

She took a sip of her drink, her face puckered in memory.

"That was right after he shot Mr. Moten inside his throat with that long hypodermic needle. He stood there like he was having a fainting spell, and then he said, 'I'll be back in a minute.'

"He was gone for four or five minutes, not just one, and Mr. Moten seemed like he had gone to sleep. He was snoring when the doctor came back. And the doctor, he looked like a brand new man, like he was over whatever had been hurting him. He went right into Mr. Moten's mouth with these long pliers and clamped down on something and then he took out this pair of scissors and he stuck them down Mr. Moten's throat and Mr. Moten's eyes popped open and got real big and he jumped like he was trying to get away from the doctor and that blood started pouring out of Mr. Moten's mouth. The doctor yelled at me, 'Nurse, get me some help,' and I ran out of the operating room and found the head nurse. When we went back in, the doctor was working over Mr. Moten but there was blood all over the table and it seemed like he was dead."

The girl sucked on her drink until there was nothing in the straw but air bubbles. "Teddy," she said, "can I have something else to drink?"

"Baby," he said, "we got to go in a minute. Take a sip of my drink."

"Is that the whole story?" I asked her.

She took a drink of Teddy's whisky and water and made a sour face. She kept looking at Teddy as if she had not heard me. But she answered my question.

"I know they called for a pulmotor from the general hospital, but the head nurse told me later it was too late. I was out in the corridor when the doctor came out of the operating room. He was still in his gown with blood all over it and he was wearing his rubber gloves and his surgical cap and he walked out the front door of the hospital just like that. And I didn't see that man again until this morning, when he was back in his office at the hospital, seeing patients." She took a tiny sip of Teddy's drink. "And I guess that's it," she said.

Teddy reached for his drink and finished it while Julia Lee ended her song. Then, getting up, he said, "Michael, I got to get Audrey home and pick up Libba for work. I got her mother's car. Grudgingly loaned."

Teddy grinned and touched Audrey's hand. "Come on, baby," he said.

I stood up and watched as Teddy ushered Audrey to the bar, where he said goodbye to Milton, and then out the door. It was a little after nine. I had asked O'Malley to cover for me until 9:30, which meant I barely had time to grab a couple of burgers on the way in. I glanced at the other table as I passed. The men were silent, leaning back in their chairs, watching Julia Lee.

" 'Come Over to My House,' " the scar-faced man shouted again. I stopped at the bar to say goodbye to Milton. The man shouted the song title again. His companion was looking over his shoulder in my direction.

Julia Lee nodded so emphatically her spitcurls flounced on her forehead. "Tell you what, Mister," she chirped. "I'll play that one, and I'll play another one just for you."

I reached across the bar to shake Milton's hand. He held it for a moment. "Stick around and watch this. Have a beer on me."

I sipped a skunky bottle of local Country Club and watched as Julia Lee sang "Come Over to My House," the kind of risque Negro barrelhouse song that Sophie Tucker had stolen and gotten rich singing in her psuedo-black style. Julia Lee rolled through it, winking a couple of times at the men in the gangster hats, a kewpie-doll leer on her sweet round face.

She finished with an eight-to-the-bar flourish, and as she paused, she raised her hands high, wrists cocked like a showy concert pianist about to launch into something Slavic, and brought them down on the keyboard with a dramatic crash. She let the chords decay in the smoky air and then she swept, both hands pumping, into a brief, portentous introduction. Again, she let chords hang in the air as she gave the men another cute little grin.

Then, she slid into a sly medium-tempo blues. The drummer picked it up with his brushes and Julia Lee began to sing, her eyes never leaving the two men at the table where they did not belong.

"Laughter,
And what comes after,
When your games and your rackets
Are through?
At the end
Of the game
You'll get a number
For a name—

Wise guys,
There's few chumps like you.''

That was all there was to her version of the old song. She sang "Wise Guys" through twice, her taunting gaze never wavering, and she ended it with a doomful crash of minor notes.

The final funeral chord died slowly. Then, there was silence in the dark room except for a man and woman seated near the door who must have been too drunk to notice anything outside the focus of their immediate attention. They clapped and cheered and yelled for more. But the other fifteen or twenty people sat in silence as the scar-faced man reached with his right hand inside his coat and pulled out a squat black automatic pistol, his right index finger resting on the trigger guard. He raised the pistol until it was pointing at the ceiling and then, very slowly, he lowered the barrel until it was pointing straight at Julia Lee. All I could see above the back of the piano were her shoulders, bare in a strapless pink satin dress, her neck and her plump face, round like a target. The man's elbow was cocked, and as he slowly straightened it the gun slid forward smoothly, dead level, as if it moved on a track.

Out of the corner of my left eye I could see Milton take a couple of steps toward me and reach his hand under the bar. Julia Lee sat as if paralyzed, her face in the horrified remnants of a smile. Next to her, the little drummer was immobile, his head cocked to one side, poised as if he was ready to spring but had not yet determined in which direction. The couple near the door had stopped clapping.

The man with the gun slid his finger onto the trigger. He tilted his head slightly to sight down the barrel of the automatic. The phone behind the bar rang.

Julia Lee's head jerked for an instant at the sound and then she was still again, as if the spotlight and the barrel of the gun held her frozen. No one made a sound. The phone rang. Milton did not move. His right hand was still beneath the bar. The scar-faced man stretched his arm out even further, as if reaching for Julia Lee, and he squeezed the trigger.

Milton yelled, ''Duck, Julia!'' The phone rang. Julia Lee's head popped behind the back of the upright piano. There was a click from the trigger of the gun. The phone rang. Milton had a pistol in his right hand, pointed across the bar at the back of the head of the scar-faced man. The scar-faced man began laughing and lowered the gun to the table. The phone rang. ''I must have forgot to put bullets in it,'' the scar-faced man said to his companion. Julia Lee was still out of sight behind the piano. The phone rang, and Milton put his gun down on the bar and turned to answer it.

"Milton's Tap Room," he said. "Seats one thousand. Sixty-nine at a time."

The scar-faced man tucked his pistol back inside his coat, still laughing. His companion was laughing, too, as I could see when he turned to look toward the bar. The release of tension was audible, as if the whole place had exhaled. Julia Lee's face crept back up from behind the piano. She briefly looked to see that the man had put the gun away, and then her eyes turned down toward her hands and she began playing a series of nervous notes that quickly evolved into boogie-woogie.

The drummer picked up his brushes from where he had dropped them on his snare drum and began swishing them around. People started whispering to each other, and I said goodbye to Milton and left, with half the beer still in the bottle on the bar. I wanted alcohol, but I was too jittery to drink anything.

Outside at the curb in front of Milton's sat a long black Packard, the spare-tire cover behind the right front fender centered on a fire hydrant. It had not been there when I came in.

A light rain had begun to fall, and I pulled down the brim of my hat and turned up the collar of my serge sport coat. My Ford was twenty or thirty feet down the block. As I opened the door, I looked back and noticed the two wise guys were leaving Milton's. They climbed into the Packard.

When I started my car, the Packard's huge round headlights blazed into my mirror. I pulled away from the curb and headed north on Troost, toward work. The Packard followed.

Twenty-three blocks down Troost, at 12th, the Packard was still following me. It was never closer than a few car lengths, never farther than half a block, those huge headlights burning in my mirror.

I turned left on 12th. So did the Packard. As I approached Main, the green light went amber and I sped up and made a quick right turn just as it was turning red, skidding slightly on the wet pavement. The Packard cruised through the red light and around the corner onto Main like a yacht rounding a buoy. I heard a squeal of brakes behind me and saw in the rearview mirror a car skid to a halt in the middle of the intersection. The driver honked his horn as he sat there, watching the Packard roll past him.

The big car followed me all the way to city hall and stopped, headlights still on, about half a block up Main Street from the police parking lot, as if the driver knew where I was headed. When I pulled into the lot, the Packard's lights went out, but it stayed where it was, just beyond the circle of illumination from a streetlamp. I got out and stood behind my car, looking around for a policeman, but saw no one.

I kept glancing at the Packard as I hurried through the drizzle across Main and exhaled with relief as I went around the corner of the old stone building and headed down Fourth Street toward the police station.

12

My watch read 10:50. I was ten minutes early, but Rachael was already there, sitting alone in a semi-circular corner booth of padded red Leatherette, sipping a Coke out of a twelve-ounce beer mug. She had called from Menorah Hospital just after midnight to tell me through tears that her father was dead, and we had agreed to meet. A beer joint off a bowling alley seemed the last place her family's silk-stocking relatives and friends were likely to run into us on the Sabbath, even if the bar was on the edge of the Country Club Plaza.

On the drive from downtown, I might have seen the black Packard a half-block behind me at a stoplight, but I couldn't be sure because of the heavy rain and the mist on the windows and the fact that there were an unconscionable number of long dark sedans in Kansas City in those depression days. Only when I had parked at the curb and stuck my head out the car door, seeing no Packards to my rear, did it occur to me that, if I was in danger, I might be putting Rachael in danger as well. But I ached to see her.

In a small attempt at deception, I walked past the entrance to the bar and went into the bowling alley, which was filled with kids, and cut back through the swinging doors and there was Rachael, the only person in the place except for the bartender, who was setting up glasses up for Saturday afternoon.

I hung my raincoat and hat on a rack by the side door. Rachael saw me, and she smiled weakly in greeting as I came to the table. I stood for a moment and gazed at her. She looked tired and frail, her boyish face damp and pale, her combed-back hair softly illuminated from above by the indirect lighting. She was wearing a dark blue dress that looked as if it had been slept in, but her slack eyelids and pink-rimmed eyes and the wan appearance of her face suggested that she had not slept at all. As we looked at each other, a fleeting image of that night in her grandmother's canopied bed went through my mind. As if she had seen the image too, seen it flicker in my eyes, she reached up and rubbed my cheek, and then looked at her fingers.

"Today, no shmutz," she said, speaking so softly I could barely hear her.

I slid in beside her and kissed her warm forehead and a tear slid down her cheek. I kissed it and licked the salt from my lips. "Shvitz," I said.

She smiled. "Not exactly. Oh, Michael, I've missed you."

"I've missed you too," I said. "How about a drive in the park listening to the rain on the roof?" My concern about the men in the black Packard had been displaced by more compelling feelings.

She turned my wrist so she could see my watch. "Michael, I've got about half an hour. I have a lot to do. My mother has pretty much collapsed, and my father's funeral is tomorrow morning."

"A funeral on Easter Sunday?" I said.

Rachael tried not to laugh, but a couple of coughs into her hand would not suffice to release what had built up inside her, and when she started laughing it took her a while to stop, and more tears came to her eyes. Finally, she pulled a Kleenex out of the purse in her lap and wiped her eyes and the corners of her mouth. She was wearing neither lipstick nor makeup, and the laughter brought a glow to her face. She smiled at me, her eyes glistening. "Michael, what are we going to do with you?"

"We could make love to me," I replied.

"Can I get you lovebirds anything?" It was the bartender, standing over us.

"This time," said Rachael, "make mine a cherry Coke." I ordered a beer.

"Michael," Rachael said when the bartender had taken her empty mug and his smirk and left, "do you realize how complicated it is to have a Jewish funeral in the middle of Passover, which is a time of celebration? Even now my Aunt Goldie is awaiting an audience with Rabbi Mayerberg to settle disputes over ritual that have raged within my family for the last few days. At least my father had the grace to hold on until after we had the second-night seder."

"Nice of him," I said.

"Michael," warned Rachael, "before you say any more, I want to tell you this. I get to joke about my father's death and my family's religion. You don't."

"I'm sorry," I said.

She nodded. "And humor on my part is a necessity if I am going to get through the next week, more or less, depending on Rabbi Mayerberg's instructions, of being in a dark house full of female relatives wailing and tearing their clothes. If I know my family, the mourning will be carried to extraordinary lengths." Her ironic smile contained more than a little pride.

"And to give the scene some counterpoint, my Left Bank sister Judy will be hanging around making desperately inappropriate Myrna Loy cracks about outmoded forms of grief, meanwhile not lifting a finger to help me, which means I am going to be out in the kitchen up to my elbows in schmaltz while the wailing goes on around me."

She sighed. "Actually, I envy them the catharsis."

"It's rough being a modern woman," I said, God knows why.

"Don't give me that patronizing crap," she said, in an intense whisper, and for an instant she seemed furious enough to get up and walk out, but then her shoulders slumped and she blinked back tears.

"Michael," she said, "I'm too tired and confused for jokes. Please just shut up and put your arms around me before I start crying again."

I held her, her cheek against my chest. I could feel the dampness of tears through my shirt and she wrapped her arms around me. The bartender brought our drinks over and set them down on the table, saying nothing. We did not look up but stayed in our embrace, barely moving except that my fingers occasionally brushed through the feathery hair above her ear. I could feel her breathing and sense her heartbeat.

I wanted that sweet moment to last. It was sexual without the urgency of sex, and as warm and soothing as a summer's day by the sea. I drifted into a waking dream of us on the beach all alone, the only sound the roar and tumble and swoosh and whisper of the surf. The sound was hypnotic, exploding and subsiding, rising and falling like a waltz. I stayed in that worryless place as long as I could but finally my mind nagged me out of it and as I floated back up I realized that the sound I heard was real, and close. It was the muffled crash of pins and the sliding of balls from the bowling alley next door.

Feeling me stir, Rachael drew her head away from my chest, sniffed and wiped her eyes and nose again with a Kleenex. She took a sip of her Coke and let it linger on her tongue like vintage wine before she swallowed.

"So, Michael," she said, "it would be nice to talk about something else. What about your great mystery?"

I told her what had happened, about the doctor turning up alive, about the fact that a man who looked very much like him had been down around the Sunset the night before Bennie Moten had been killed, a man apparently involved with drugs, and I told her what the nurse had told me Wednesday night. And now these B-movie hoods in the Packard were following me. Sometimes. I told her I was confused and scared.

"Michael," she said, "back up a little bit." Rachael was tracing damp circles on the black surface of the table with a finger. "Back to the nurse. She said the doctor put a long hypodermic needle down Bennie Moten's throat, correct?"

"Right," I said.

"What was that?" she asked.

"A local anesthetic," I said.

"Why didn't he use ether? Why didn't he knock him out?"

"Good question," I said, a little embarrassed that I hadn't thought of it.

"They used ether when they took my tonsils out," said Rachael.

I shifted my leg so as much of its surface as possible was in contact with hers.

Watching the circles dry on the table, she said, slowly, "I'm not sure how the local anesthetic fits into the plot, but it. . . certainly seems peculiar. And another thing," she said, looking at me for a moment.

I went for a swim in her eyes.

"Michael, listen," she said, smiling and squeezing my hand. "When the doctor first came into the operating room he was pale and sweating and looked as if he was going to faint? Correct?"

I nodded.

"Right," she agreed, her eyes drifting away again. "And he left for a few minutes and when he came back he looked like 'a brand new man,' correct? Weren't those the nurse's words?"

"Yes," I said. Rachael took a long sip of her Coke. She was gazing across the room in thought. Her thigh felt good against mine, soft and firm at the same time, and very warm.

"And then," she said, "he proceeded to jam these sharp instruments down Bennie Moten's throat and Moten jerked upward as if he was hurt and the blood started pouring out of his mouth. Correct? And the nurse went to get some help and that's really all she saw until later the doctor left the hospital, still in his bloody clothes. Am I correct?"

"That's right," I said. "I love you."

"And I love you," she said, almost as an aside, staring intently ahead and chewing on a piece of ice. Still, her words were like someone stroking my naked back with a soft feather. I shivered. Rachael looked over at me and mouthed a kiss, and I lurched into a state approaching ecstasy.

She looked away again, gazing off in the middle distance, tugged along by her thoughts. I stayed where I was, warm and tingling, and listened.

"Suppose," she said, "the man who came back into the operating room was not the one who had left. Suppose it was, as the nurse said, 'a brand new man.' But a man who looked enough like the doctor to fool that inexperienced scrub nurse, as . . . the same man, lying dead in the morgue hours later, fooled you and . . . set you off on this quest for justice in the murder of an innocent Negro?"

I liked the way she threw in that little political speech at the end. "Rachael," I said, pulling about halfway out of my daze, "if the nurse had just seen the real doctor, she's not likely to be fooled that easily by a double." I did not want to think too hard. I was happy to play her straight man as long as I could hear her voice and feel her body beside me.

She held her glass up and tapped another small piece of ice into her mouth. She crunched it and swallowed and a slightly crazed grin came over her face.

"Michael," she said, still not looking at me, "did you ever see an operation?"

"No," I said.

"An operation," she said, "looks much like a holdup, correct? The surgeon is wearing a mask and holding a dangerous weapon. And they wear these white caps on their heads, correct? All you can see are their eyes and their foreheads, true? Think about it. The doctor and the dead man in the morgue looked enough alike for you to think they were the same man, and they were not even wearing masks." She turned to me with a proud grin. "*Voilá!*" she said. "QED."

"That sounds awfully complicated," I said.

"Ha!" she said. "Me complicated? You haven't exactly been using Occam's razor."

"True," I said. "God, I want to make love to you."

She pressed her hand over the place where our thighs met, but she continued to look across the narrow room, as if the Budweiser reproduction of "Custer's Last Stand" behind the bar held the key to recent events. I fervently hoped it didn't.

"Agatha Christie couldn't have plotted it better," she said. "There's this gentleman you want to get out of the way so you can peddle drugs untrammeled. You hear he's going in for an operation. Or. . . maybe you bribe a doctor to tell him he needs an operation. Then, in the middle of the operation, you bring in a double, a man who looks enough like the doctor to pass in a surgical mask. Maybe you hire a trained killer who is unknown in these parts, a man from, say, San Francisco.

Then, to keep the killer's mouth shut, you bump him off too." This time *she* shivered, presumably at the combination of ghastly images and the thrill of deduction. I hoped a little tingle of lust was in there too.

"OK, Miss Marple," I said. "How do you get the real doctor out of the way?"

"You slip him a mickey at some point, perhaps at the pool hall."

"A mickey timed to act three or four hours later?"

"How do we know such mickeys do not exist?" She slid another chip of ice into her mouth. Crunch.

She swallowed and exhaled to warm her tongue. "Listen. You put a sleeping pill in a dough ball. Or you have someone jab the doctor with a hypodermic right in the hospital. These are drug peddlers, they would know how to do those things."

"Maybe so," I said. "But wouldn't the doctor think something was odd when he woke up and discovered his patient was dead?"

"Perhaps that is exactly what happened," she said, "but the doctor had been up all night drinking with his patient and maybe he was terrified that he had actually performed the operation and then had blacked out. Doesn't Hammett have one like that? I don't know the details, Michael. You're the detective."

"Me?" I said. That was slick, I thought. Suddenly she has turned from Miss Marple into Harriett Vane and cast me as Peter Wimsey.

"You're a whiz," I said. "But I'm not a detective."

"Michael, you're right," Rachael said, turning and looking at me with her luminous brown eyes. "And because you have been acting as a detective, you are in danger. You must go to the police."

"I went to the police," I said. "Last night, after the Packard followed me back to the police station. I told Detective Sweeney the whole thing, and he and O'Malley and another policeman just laughed and said there was no murder, and who cared anyway, it was just some Negroes. Sweeney said, 'And there's lots of mugs driving around in black Packards.' "

I shook my head.

"Besides," I said, "the Kansas City police are as crooked as the gangsters. The federal grand jury last year reported that ten percent of the cops in Kansas City had criminal records. Those are the ones who got caught. The cops *are* the gangsters."

She nodded. "That's true. Rabbi Mayerberg says that. So listen. I've got another idea. Go to the Federal Bureau of Investigation."

"I'd thought of that, too," I said.

"Then do it," she said. "J. Edgar Hoover and his G-men. They're quite modern, and they don't owe anything to the Pendergast machine or the crime syndicate. They got John Dillinger and Pretty Boy Floyd and all those other big-time criminals. I'm sure they have an office right here in Kansas City. That's the answer.''

Maybe that *is* the answer, I thought.

Rachael took my wrist again, her fingers cool from the glass, and looked at my watch.

"Michael," she said, "I've got to go."

"Can I see you tomorrow?"

"Sweetheart, tomorrow's impossible, you should know that. I'll try to slip away Monday."

"Same time, same place?" I asked.

She smiled. "Same time, same place."

"Maybe it was the double all along," I said.

"What?"

"Maybe they slipped the doctor the mickey early in the morning and left him somewhere to sleep it off. Maybe when Bennie Moten was wheeled into the operating room, the killer was waiting for him in a surgical mask."

Rachael grinned. "I'm not sure that makes sense, but I think we're on the right track. Are you going to call the federal men today? I bet some of them are there on Saturdays."

"They damn well better be," I said. "I'll call the federal building from here, after you've gone. I don't want us to be seen leaving together anyway. Where are you parked?"

"Just across the street," she said.

"Okay. I'll watch you through the window. And you keep an eye out for black Packards. If you see anything suspicious, call the police. Tell them that men with guns are following you. And tell them you live on Ward Parkway. Ever since those crackers snatched the city manager's daughter, there's been a rash of silk-stocking kidnap attempts, and the cops have had their tails burned. They'll be there with riot guns in two minutes."

"Michael," she said, "this is getting serious, isn't it? Give me a quick kiss."

I kissed her. Her lips tasted of cherry and were a little chilled, but I held her when she tried to back away and kissed her lips again, until they were warm. Then she pushed me away and walked to the door.

I watched as she crossed to her little green Dodge, got in and drove away. It had almost stopped raining, and I was fairly certain that nobody was following her, at least nobody in a black Packard.

Special Agent Waldo P. Mitchell looked bored. He was tracing neat Palmer penmanship spirals on a long yellow legal pad and seemed barely listening to what I was telling him.

Special Agent Mitchell did not look much like a G-man. He was of average height and build and he had an almost pretty face beneath his close-cropped light brown hair. He had that vaguely feminine air of some men in certain occupations—navy petty officers, teachers at a boys' school, the priesthood—who have chosen to live in a male world not so much to master it as to hide in it. When he shook my hand, I noticed his fingers were as pink and manicured as a society dentist's. He was about twenty-five, probably fresh out of law school, and his teeth were smooth and pearly.

"I'd like to help you, Mr. . . ." He glanced at the legal pad, but he had apparently helixed right over my name, and he was momentarily speechless.

"Holt," I said.

"Mr. Holt," he said. "But murder is not a federal offense. Now if these fellows were to kidnap someone from Missouri—you, for example—and drive you into Kansas and kill you there, that would be a federal offense, although the killing would be incidental to our concerns." He smiled dazzlingly.

"There's more," I said. "I think this whole thing may be tied in with narcotics traffic."

"Well, then," Mitchell said, going back to his precision scribbling, "you would probably want to talk to one of Mr. Anslinger's people"— he said the name with mild contempt—"over at the Treasury Department. You certainly won't find anyone there after noon on Saturday of Easter weekend. In fact, I was planning on departing these premises myself very shortly."

He looked meaningfully across the desk at me.

"Okay," I said, "What if I told you I thought the Mafia was involved."

Mitchell sighed and reached into the top drawer of his walnut-veneered government issue desk and pulled out a manicure stick.

"The what?" he said politely, worrying the cuticle on his left thumb with the sharper end of the stick.

"The Mafia," I said. "The Black Hand. Al Capone. Johnny Lazia."

"Mr. Capone," said Special Agent Mitchell, moving the stick to his index finger, "is in prison for neglecting to pay his income taxes. And Mr. Lazia is dead, apparently as the result of some strictly local dispute over illegal gambling." He put the stick down and held his hands up, palms facing me, in a gesture he may have intended to suggest openness, but that conveyed the opposite impression.

"Actually, Mr. Holt," he said, "we at the bureau of investigation tend not to put too much credence in these reports of a secret nationwide crime syndicate headed by Italian immigrants. The director prefers to go after the big guns. Pretty Boy Floyd. John Dillinger. Baby—"

"I heard it was the East Chicago police who found John Dillinger," I said. O'Malley had told me that.

"Nonetheless, we gunned him down," said Mitchell, fondling the last three words. "Baby Face Nelson. The Karpis-Barker gang. We are doing very well without wasting our time on some hypothetical Black Hand or whatever you want to call it."

And that's the way it went. I tried to go through it all again—the two dead Negroes, at least one of them murdered for sure, the other's death quite suspicious; the disappearance for more than two weeks of the doctor; the two gangsters, at least one of them armed, following me last night in the Packard.

Mitchell said he certainly understood my reluctance to trust the local police, but he could not see how the bureau could involve itself at this point, and perhaps he could walk me to the elevator since he, too, had places to go and people to see.

I didn't spot the Packard on my drive to work, and I began to wonder if perhaps O'Malley was right to scoff at my fears. Perhaps the Wise Guys had followed me Friday night as some kind of rough joke. The incident with Julia Lee had certainly suggested they were capable of that. Regardless, I was in the middle of some kind of murder mystery, and I was determined to pursue it.

It was O'Malley's night off, so he didn't come in until around midnight. By then, I had called in a three-car collision on a slick Broadway intersection (one dead, one critical); a couple of stickups, and a nonfatal shooting. There also were several incidents—suspected arson in Kansas City's tiny garment district, an unprovoked beating of a Jewish peddler just two blocks from the police station, vandalism at a synagogue —that I futilely argued should be reported in a single roundup. This was Easter weekend, and today was Adolph's Hitler's much-publicized forty-sixth birthday.

"You'll just stir things up," said the night city editor. That didn't stop the papers from running stories on Hitler's venomous birthday speech on the Sunday front page.

When O'Malley arrived, thoroughly soused, he was carrying the entertainment section of the Sunday *Kansas City Star* under his raincoat. He

146

tore a long strip from one page and pasted it to the wall next to his side of the desk. I could read the headline from where I stood: "ABBEY PLAYERS COMING TO TOWN."

"Hmmm," I said, as he took a gulp of the beer he carried in his raincoat pocket.

"Hmmm yourself," he said. "They're coming Monday for a week at the Shubert."

"I suppose you will be visiting with them in the green room," I said.

"Indeed," said O'Malley, giving me a sloppy wink. "Michael, my lad, in the words of the bard of pessimism, Sean O'Casey, the world is chay-os. Total chay-os. But that doesn't mean we shouldn't keep trying to impose some moral order upon it."

"You get that last part from Hitler's birthday speech?" I said.

"Michael," he said, wagging his beer at me, "there's one very big thing to be said for Mr. Hitler. He hates the British." He quickly put the agitated bottle to his lips as foam rose over the top.

"O'Malley," I said, "let's go get drunk so I can tell you what a fascist cretin you are."

"Fine by me," he said, licking beer off his lips. "Actually, you may be half right."

13

I was awakened by the obscene tintinnabulation from the gold-domed cathedral a couple of blocks away. Eyes half open, head aching, I lay in the sagging middle of my bed, looking blearily at the flaking ceiling, hoping paranoiacally that no chips of paint would fall into my eye. The bells seemed twice as loud as usual, and I prayed for them to stop. God was not on my side.

Finally, I pushed myself to a sitting position, legs dangling over the right side of the bed. My indifferent gaze wandered down the faded flowered wallpaper in front of me, idly tracing the downward course of the watermarks that groped like weeds through the lifeless blossoms. When I reached the brown floor, I saw the envelope. It was about halfway between the bed and the door, and it had what appeared to be part of a footprint on it. The clerk must have slid it under the door after the Saturday mail delivery, and I must have unknowingly shoved it out of the way with my foot when I came in at, what, 3:30, four in the morning? I probably could have stumbled over the corpse of the Easter bunny and not noticed, after taking O'Malley's tour of 14th-street sporting houses. As I recall, all either of us did was drink.

We didn't even talk much about "my mystery," although after a few boilermakers I did tell O'Malley about my visit to Special Agent Waldo P. Mitchell, and he said I got exactly the shabby treatment I deserved.

"G-men," he had said, "aren't interested in real criminals. They like to grab headlines by chasing down semi-retarded hillbillies who serve the public by robbing banks. Just remember this, Michael. The Treasury Department got Al Capone. And J. Edgar Hoover got Ma Barker."

I got up from the bed and picked up the envelope and walked over to the window to make sure my Model A was still in the alley where I had parked it the night before. It was, parked at an angle that suggested emergency abandonment. I sat back down on the bed and tore the envelope open. It contained a photostat of Bennie Moten's death certificate.

I looked it over quickly. "Died, 4/2/35. 10:30 a.m. Autopsy performed. Principal causes of death and related causes . . . coronary sclerosis . . . chronic fibrous myocarditis . . . autopulmonary edema."

Silence hit like a tornado. I looked at my watch. 9:05. We had entered the eye of the hourly storm of bells. I needed an interpreter for the death certificate. At that point, I didn't really trust anybody but Rachael, and she was busy with her father's funeral and whatever came after. It still seemed strange, a funeral on the morning of those resurrection bells: Easter, Passover, a funeral, ceremonies of rebirth, deliverance and mourning all going on at once. Life mixes metaphors.

I got some clean underwear out of a torn paper bundle, went down the hall, and took a tepid bath in the cramped, rusting claw-footed tub. Back in the room, I made a pan of cowboy coffee on the hot plate I was not supposed to have. I brushed my teeth and had a cup of coffee and a Lucky while I shaved. Pulling a clean white shirt from another paper bundle, I got dressed, topping my Easter ensemble off with the green knit tie, brown slacks, and beige sport coat I had thrown on a chair the night before.

I tossed down the rest of the coffee, swallowing some loose grounds, and went down to the lobby to the pay phone. Since I couldn't call Rachael, I called Patrick O'Malley, whom I almost trusted.

O'Malley sounded way too cheery for the morning after. He said he was getting dressed to take his mother to ten o'clock Mass and afterward they were going to stop at Myron Green's Cafeteria. I said I really needed to talk to him. He said he would meet me at the office around noon.

That gave me more than two hours to kill. First, I called my parents and wished them a happy Easter, reversing the charges. Mother sounded as if she was already into the Easter sherry and told me how much she missed me. Dad asked me how the car was, and I said fine and Dad said it was real, real good to hear that.

The desk clerk had sold out of Sunday newspapers, so I went out into the drizzle and bought the final editions of both the *Star* and the *Journal-Post* and got two large pasteboard containers of coffee and a bag of jelly doughnuts and went back to my room and sat on the bed and had my Easter feast while I read.

Glenn Cunningham had finished second in the mile race at the Kansas Relays, blaming influenza for adding almost fifteen seconds to his world-record pace of 4:06. The Cards had beaten the Pirates four to one, but Frankie Frisch had been badly spiked in the hand and might miss a game or two at second base.

Eighteen thousand Missouri farms had been foreclosed between 1930 and 1934.

Four inches of rain had fallen in one afternoon in Garden City, Kansas, and more rain was expected throughout Kansas and Missouri. George Kern of Columbus City, Iowa, was the proud owner of a petrified ham: Believe It or Not.

The Bungalow hamburger chain was going after White Castle with a special three-day sale, two burgers for a nickel. A variant of "awry" is "ajee."

Finally, it was time to go to the police station. When I walked in, O'Malley was already there, scrubbed and pink and all dressed up in black and white, looking like a depraved altar boy. He was in his squeaky chair, leaning back, feet on the desk, drinking coffee from a brand new porcelain cup labeled Myron Green. He peered at me from under the brim of his fancy black hat, his Adam's apple bobbing like a pump handle as coffee went gulping down to puddle atop his lunch and communion wafer.

I slid the death certificate across the desk. It stopped against his right foot. He set the coffee cup on the floor, reached for the photostat and gave a little snicker when he saw what it was. But he looked it over and said, seemingly without irony, "What can I do to help?"

I said, "I need a doctor who can explain this to me. But I don't want to pay him and I don't want to answer a bunch of questions."

O'Malley sat up, sliding his feet to the floor. I caught of flash of garter above his black socks, which for once hid not only his ankles but his lower shins. "I've got just the man," he said, reaching for the phone.

"I thought you might," I said. After a brief telephone conversation, O'Malley hung up the earpiece and said, "Dr. Foster is in the middle of Sunday dinner. If we get there in about half an hour, he'll see us."

"Fine," I said. "And after we talk to him, I want to see that colored doctor." I reached down for the phone.

"Wait a minute," said O'Malley, holding up a hand. "I have something to tell you. Take a load off your feet."

My stomach was still jittery from my hangover and from nervousness about the unsettling things that had happened the last few days. But I felt myself begin to calm down as I took my familiar seat across the desk from Patrick O'Malley. I was glad he was finally going to help me, but, I realized, there was also something less frenetic about the room

—I had not heard the police radio once since I had arrived. Crime was taking a holiday.

"I have some info for you," said O'Malley. "On my way up the stairs, I ran into an ambulance chaser of my acquaintance. I asked him if a physician's confidentiality extended past the death of the patient.

"He wasn't sure. We ended up in the warrant office downstairs looking up the statute. I copied the relevant part down." He pulled a long black wallet from the breast pocket of his black Easter suit and took out a piece of paper. He read aloud:

" 'Persons Incompetent to Testify: a physician or surgeon, concerning any information which he may have acquired from any patient while attending him in a professional character, and which information was necessary to prescribe for such patient as a physician, or do any act for him as a surgeon.' That's it."

"Sounds like to me he just can't talk about things the patient told him," I said.

O'Malley nodded. "Or maybe stuff he found out about the man while poking around his body, a syphilitic boil, a vagina in his armpit. But there's certainly nothing to stop him from talking about how he screwed up an operation."

"Or slept through it," I said, reaching across the desk for the city directory. "Or used it as a subterfuge for murder."

"Subterfuge, huh?" said O'Malley.

There was no answer at Dr. Stone's home phone, so I called Provident-Wheatley Hospital. No, the doctor was not in, but he usually started his rounds on Sundays and holidays between 1:30 and 2 P.M. I said I would check back then.

I looked at the clock. It was 12:40. "We better go," I said.

Dr. Foster lived in the old Santa Fe Trail settlement of Independence, a few miles east of the city. It had been the Jackson County seat until Judge Truman decided, in the interests of urbanity and the Ready-Mixed Concrete Company, to build a vast new county courthouse in downtown Kansas City.

O'Malley drove, going out Independence Avenue, the dividing line between the old and unbound river city and the new one of puritanical right angles. We crossed the Blue River bridge and drove past the industrial plants of Blue Valley and into a pleasant town of old homes and majestic trees. For the moment, the rain had stopped, although more was promised by the dark and rolling clouds and the weight of the air.

Foster lived in a filigreed steamboat-gothic house surrounded by oaks and maples, with beds of flowers along the walks and flowering shrubs bordering the house. His azaleas were just starting to flame out and would be dazzling as soon was we had a few days of sun. Already, his forsythia could break your heart.

The doctor met us at the door. He was a tall man, six four, perhaps even six five, and his upper back had a slight hunch, as if from years of trying to avoid towering over his patients. He was perhaps sixty, with still-thick white hair, a high forehead, and a strong-planed face that reminded me of Stuart's George Washington.

Foster greeted O'Malley as an uncle would a favorite nephew, inquiring about the progress of his mother's journey toward sainthood.

"She just needs one more miracle," said O'Malley. "They're counting me as two."

O'Malley introduced us and Foster told me his first name was Stephen. "My parents came from Kentucky to this bleak frontier before I was born," he said, with a grin and a wave at his greening lawn, his budding trees, and the masses of jonquils and tulips that warmth and rain had popped out of the earth. "And they brought the oaks with them in a little cloth sack," he said as he shook my hand.

Foster ushered us through his formal living room, with a large portrait of a handsome blonde woman and a towheaded little boy above the mantel, and down a few steps into his den, clearly a later addition to the old house. The den had a brick fireplace with wood laid neatly beside it, and the walls were lined with bookshelves.

He was wearing a red smoking jacket, an open-necked white dress shirt, well-worn gray flannel pants and bedroom slippers over black silk socks. Gesturing for us to sit down, he took a pipe from a silver teething cup on the mantelpiece, filled it with tobacco and lit it with a kitchen match.

O'Malley and I sat on a small couch with the fireplace to our left and Foster sat facing us in a beige leather-covered easy chair. He seemed a man of implacable dignity—he must have had a very calming bedside manner—but I thought I detected sadness in him.

"Patrick tells me you would like to ask me some medical questions," he said, in a deep voice with a smoker's rasp to it.

"Yes, doctor, I would," I said. "I would like you to tell me how to perform a tonsillectomy."

He took a long, thoughtful draw on his pipe. The smoke was strong and pungent, without the slightest trace of perfume. At first, I liked the smell.

"That is something many doctors never learn," he said. "A tonsillectomy is, at the same time, one of the easiest and one of the trickiest operations a physician is called upon to perform, although the layman is coming to think of it as something done almost automatically to children. I should warn you that it has been years since I performed one. My area of speciality has been somewhat south of the mouth; I do see evidence of the mouth finding its way down there on occasion.''

He sent up another cloud of smoke with his pipe. O'Malley laughed politely, and then lapsed into an unusual silence that persisted almost throughout the interview. It was only later that I realized he was acting the well-behaved child in the presence of the closest thing he had to a living father.

Foster pointed at me with his pipe. ''Tell me, young Dr. Holt,'' he said, ''how old is your patient?''

''Thirty-eight,'' I said.

''Oh,'' he said. ''That presents a problem. As men and women grow older, a tonsillectomy becomes more perilous. In fact, unless the condition is chronic and causes serious problems, we often avoid adult tonsillectomy because of the danger if something goes wrong.''

Foster stood up. ''Let me show you something,'' he said, his tongue making tiny clucking noises as he spoke around the pipe clenched in his teeth. He stepped to a bookcase and reached without hesitation to a thick volume bound in blue. ''*Gray's Anatomy*,'' he said, hoisting the book.

He turned pages quickly and then lay the book open on the low coffee table in front of us. O'Malley and I leaned forward. Foster knelt on the rug and pointed with his index finger. ''See this diagram?''

We both nodded. It was a fine line drawing with the caption: *The mouth cavity. The cheeks have been slit transversely and the tongue pulled forward.*

It looked like the entrance to a cave, with the tongue sloping forward almost like a ramp and something labeled ''uvula'' sticking down from the roof like a short, fat stalactite. Beyond the uvula, darkness.

''See these two cavities to the right and left of the uvula?'' asked Foster, pointing with the tip of his pipe. ''And see this material that looks like sweetbreads in each of the cavities? Those are the Palatine tonsils. They are soft and creviced like the brain. If you poke your finger in there, it quivers. It feels like nothing so much as a ball of Missouri night crawlers.''

His knees creaked as he got to his feet. ''I guess one should kneel at least once on Easter Sunday,'' he said, grimacing and flexing his right leg.

He sat back down in his leather chair. ''We don't know exactly what the function of the tonsil is,'' he said. ''People live to be a hundred with them, and people live to be a hundred without them. But we feel that they have something to do with protecting the body from infection. Perhaps as a by-product of that, and because they are located in a part of the body that is touched by virtually everything that enters the system, they are very prone to infection themselves.

"That causes them to swell and ache and may result in a high fever. Usually, a few days in bed will take care of the problem. With occasional applications of ice cream to cool the inflamation and soothe the psyche."

He puffed on his pipe. It had gone out. He set it in an ashtray on the coffee table, which was fine with me. The strong smoke was starting to get to me.

"But the condition can become chronic and, in adults, can lead to other complications, from difficulty breathing and swallowing to, some physicians believe, arthritis and kidney infections. So, we take them out. How do we take them out?"

He leaned forward to put his right hand on the open anatomy book between us. "We go in here"—his right index finger crept across the page to point to one of the tonsils, nestled half in and half out of its cup of flesh. "And we get hold of it with a teneculum, a kind of forceps. We carefully pull the tonsil out of the cavity and, with a pair of long curved scissors, we go in behind it and snip off the tonsular attachments."

He snapped his fingers and sat back in his chair again. "The tonsil," he said, "is fed by several arteries, and there inevitably is hemorrhaging the moment it is cut loose. The snipping must be done very carefully to avoid unnecessary severing. And we must be ready immediately to clamp off whatever blood vessels are severed." He reached forward with his hand and swiftly brought his thumb and first two fingers together.

"Then we do the same thing on the other side. If it is done correctly, the patient can go home in a few days."

I asked, "Would you ever use a local anesthetic instead of ether?"

I didn't get the answer I had anticipated.

"With a thirty-eight-year-old man? Yes, that's the preferred way. You go in with a hypodermic at the base of the tonsil and give it a little shot. It deadens quickly."

"Why not put the man to sleep with ether?" I asked.

Foster stared at me and his head gave a tiny, irritated shake. He said, "How the hell are you going to get the tonsil out through the mask?"

"I don't understand," I said.

He gave the long sigh of a professional trapped with an inquisitive ignoramus.

"With a child," he said, picking up his pipe again and taking a reaming tool out of a side pocket, "you can knock the patient out with ether and have a good chance of him staying out until you cut off the tonsils and get out of there. But with an adult, particularly one with a lot of body mass, you have to keep feeding him ether to keep him under. Is this a big man?"

"Maybe 190, 200 pounds" I said.

"Well, then," he said, tapping an acrid residue of scorched tobacco into the ashtray, "you'd be amazed at how rapidly a 200-pound man can recover from a dose of ether. With an adult tonsillectomy, you have two choices. You can give him a local. Or you can pour so much ether down his throat that he is damn near dead, and try to work like hell before the ether wears off. And then you'll get the tonsil about half out and he'll start coming to, so you have to stop what you're doing and pour another half gallon of ether down his throat."

He filled his pipe from an oilcloth pouch and struck a kitchen match on the underside of the coffee table.

"It's very frustrating," he said, sucking on the pipe to light it, "and dangerous. It's much better to deaden the tonsil with a local and treat it almost like a tooth extraction."

Foster took a couple of long puffs on his pipe, adding so much smoke to the air around me that I couldn't imagine ever wanting a cigarette again. I was almost nauseous from the rich, pungent tobacco, or perhaps that came from the hangover and the cheap doughnuts and the general anxiety.

"Young man," he said, "would you tell me what this is all about?"

I reached in my breast pocket and pulled out the death certificate. I handed it to Foster. "I'm trying to figure out why this man died," I said.

He unfolded the photostat and began to read aloud. "Bennie Moten. Yes, that Negro bandleader. Wheatley-Provident. Well, that can be good or bad, depending on the physician. I've treated Negro patients there from time to time. Causes of death—coronary sclerosis, that's hardening of the arteries. Thirty-eight is a little young for that."

Foster looked up from the photostat. "You said he was overweight?"

"Yes," I said.

"Well," he said, "maybe."

"And he had been drinking that morning," I said.

"That's irregular," said Foster, frowning. He looked down again. "Second cause of death, chronic fibrous myocarditis. That means he had a diseased heart. Third cause of death, autopulmonary edema.''

Foster looked up again. "Fluid in the lungs," he said. "Am I to gather this happened during a tonsillectomy?"

"Yes," I said.

"Then the fluid would have been blood," he said. "The doctor's hand slipped or something jarred his arm and he cut more than he was prepared to clamp off. The blood would come spurting out, quickly filling the mouth. The physician could not see where to set the clamps, and if there was alcohol in the patient's blood, it would have a lessened tendency to clot. The man would begin breathing in the blood. The bad heart and the clogged arteries wouldn't have helped. Rapid loss of blood, not enough oxygen to the lungs, cardiovascular system weak already. Bing. He died. Drowned in his own blood. Or maybe his heart stopped before then. Regrettable. Do you happen to know who the doctor was?"

"A Dr. W. E. Stone," I said.

"Bill Stone?" said Foster. "Bill Stone is the best colored surgeon in town. Hell, I'd trust my wife to Bill Stone."

Foster took a furious, windy suck on his pipe, which seemed to be out again, and then pointed it at O'Malley. "Patrick, is this some kind of filthy exposé?"

"That's what I'm trying to prevent," said O'Malley. "Don't worry. You have my word nothing you say will be repeated."

"Hunh," said Foster. "I better not read any of that 'a prominent Independence physician' shit either. You people in the press have no idea how much harm you do." He moved the pipe like a pointer from O'Malley to me.

"Young man," he said, "have you talked to Bill Stone about this?"

"Briefly," I said. "I'm going to see him this afternoon."

"Well," said Foster. "You ask him about it and see if it didn't happen the way I said."

"There's another possibility," I said.

"What's that, son?" asked Foster.

"That somebody slipped the doctor a mickey and—"

"A *mickey*?" Foster roared. "Patrick, do you believe this child? He's been living on dime novels."

"Fifteen-cent matinees," said O'Malley.

I persisted. I was starting to perspire and my face was flushing and O'Malley tapped me twice on the forearm, but I persisted.

"It's possible that somebody fed him a drug that put him to sleep and then another man who looked superficially like him came into the operating room in a surgical mask and cap and cut those arteries in Bennie Moten's throat and sent the nurse out of the room while he watched him bleed to death.''

Foster glared at me. He was holding the bowl of his pipe in his right hand and began twisting the Bakelite mouthpiece with his left, back and forth, scouring my nerves with a sound like chalk on a blackboard. Finally, mercifully, he stopped and said, ''Could you do it?''

''Could I do what?''

''Could you go into that operating room and make just the precise wrong cut so it would look like an accident and you didn't end up severing the jugular vein or cutting the tongue in half and extracting a couple of wisdom teeth while you were in there flailing around?''

He took in a deep breath and let it out slowly. ''I told you how to do it,'' he said, poking the pipe at me again. ''Could you do it?''

I shrugged.

''Damn right you couldn't. So your hypothetical second man would be a doctor, too, or at least a pretty sharp medical student. And he or a confederate would have to administer a drug at just the right time to doctor number one so there could be a switch of identity that nobody noticed. Isn't that getting a little complicated? If somebody wanted to get rid of this bandleader, why didn't they just bop him over the head and shove him in a barrel of cement?''

''Maybe,'' I said, a little hoarsely, ''they wanted it to look like an accident.''

''Look like an accident! Oh, my Lord.'' He shook his head slowly as he laid the pipe back on the ashtray in a gesture that suggested finality. Then he looked at me and cackled.

''Son,'' he said, ''we are talking about Kansas City, Missouri. There must have been two or three dozen people gunned down in the streets in broad daylight in the past few years, including five one afternoon in front of a crowded railroad station and another four during a goddamned election. Did anybody try to make it look like Johnny Lazia slipped in the bathtub and hit his head? And he ran the goddamned syndicate. What's so special about this colored bandleader?''

Foster's long body sank wearily back into the easy chair. He took a long, deep breath, and then let it out slowly. He shook his head. Then he smiled slightly, and waved a hand at me in dismissal.

''Look,'' he said, ''you go talk to Bill Stone. And I'm trusting you to keep Patrick's promise that none of our conversation will be repeated, although God knows I haven't said anything I'm ashamed of. You all run along now. I'm going to have a brandy and soda and take my Sunday nap. This nonsense is bad for my heart.''

O'Malley drove us straight to Wheatley-Provident Hospital. He smoked a Bull Durham cigarette and said nothing, which was either kindness or smugness, or both. I was beginning to suspect that I was like a kid who had built a very elaborate treehouse out of grade-A lumber without noticing that the tree was rotten.

We got to the hospital about 2:20. We asked an attendant pushing a wheelchair where we might find Dr. Stone, and he suggested we try his office, pointing down the hall. I took another look at the doctor's portrait as we passed it. It still looked like the man in the drawer.

Stone was in his office, alone, seated in a high-backed wooden chair behind a desk, right thumb and forefinger pressed on his closed eyelids. He was wearing an unbuttoned white hospital smock, streaked and smudged with red, over a dark brown suit. Across the front of the vest was a small gold watch chain and, dangling from it, an academic key. He had skin about the color of unstained oak, with a dark red undertone; wavy, slightly sun-bleached reddish-brown hair and a long, slim hooked nose. I recognized him immediately from Blue Monday at the Sunset.

When we entered, he took his hand from his eyes and opened them slowly. He was an older and substantially less Elysian version of the portrait in the foyer, and a good fifteen years older and fifteen pounds heavier than the young man in the drawer at the morgue.

"Yes?" he asked. He seemed exhausted.

I told him who I was. O'Malley was silent.

Stone's neck stiffened. "I thought I told you to stop bothering me," he said, without much energy.

I replied that I had read the Missouri statutes, and I saw nothing to forbid him from discussing what happened during an operation. I mentioned the possibility of a subpoena, and started talking about getting a court order to have Bennie Moten's body dug up, and the doctor flinched. O'Malley broke in.

"Let me say something, doctor," he said, his tone very sympathetic. "We know you are sick of the rumors about this man's unfortunate death." Stone's eyes dropped. "We just want to get your side of it and clear up these questions once and for all. Then we will leave you alone."

The doctor looked up at O'Malley. "And you are?"

"O'Malley of the *Star*," he said, using the more impressive name of the parent paper. "I think you can trust the *Kansas City Star*."

"I doubt that," said Stone. "But have a seat. Both of you."

As we sat in straight-backed chairs facing him, Stone squeezed his eyes with his fingers again and then opened them and, not really looking at either of us, began to speak in a slow, precise, soft voice. "I'm going to tell you what happened on the morning of April 2, and then I trust you will leave me alone." He sighed.

"Bennie—Mr. Moten was an old and dear friend. On several occasions, when his tonsils were acting up, I urged him to let me remove them. He would agree, and then back out. Bennie Moten was afraid of nothing in the world except the surgeon's knife."

He paused for a moment, looking at his hands.

"This last time," he said, "his tonsils were worse than ever. He was supposed to check into the hospital the night before the operation. He did not. Around one in the morning, he called me from a club on Vine Street. He had been drinking, and had decided once again he could not face the knife."

Stone spoke slowly and steadily, as if this was a speech he had rehearsed many times in his mind and, now that the time had come to deliver it, it had acquired a sad and weary momentum of its own.

"So, I told Bennie to stay were he was and I went down to meet him. We visited several taverns and a pool hall while I tried to convince him to enter the hospital. I was drinking cola or coffee, and I tried to get Bennie to do the same, but I finally decided, rather than fight with him and take a chance on losing him, I would let him drink and pray the alcohol would make him more malleable."

Stone took a deep breath and exhaled with resignation. "As you may know, alcohol in the blood acts slightly as a decoagulant, but I thought it was worth some risk to get him finally into the hospital and get those infected tonsils out. I suppose I was in error."

The doctor looked at O'Malley, as if seeking some sign of judgment, but apparently got none. He looked down at his hands again.

"Finally," he said, his voice growing softer, "about dawn, after he had consumed a considerable amount of whisky, he began to get sleepy. I drove him myself to the hospital, and stayed with him through the preparation for the tonsillectomy. I tried to soothe him. I told him a million children a year had their tonsils out. I told him he would be home in a day or two, drinking iced beer. He seemed calm. By the time we wheeled him into the operating room, he was quite drowsy.

"I shot Novocain at the base of his tonsils and placed pillowed restraints at either side of his head. Then, while the anesthetic took effect, I left the operating room for a few moments and splashed cold water on my face and drank some coffee. I had not had much sleep the night before, either. When I returned, Ben—the patient's eyes were closed and he was breathing through his mouth, as if he were asleep."

The doctor had raised his head again, but his eyes were not focused on either of us. He was looking between us, toward the door of his office, as if the past was being reenacted there for his vision alone. His right hand, long and slim, with big knuckles and veins standing out blue against his tan skin, was curled around his left index finger and nervously twisting.

"I went into his mouth and pulled the right tonsil out of its cavity and was about ready to cut its base when his eyelids opened. I'll never forget how he looked at me with those large brown eyes. At first, they were glazed, like a man coming out of sleep. And then, terribly, they cleared and opened wider and suddenly he jerked his head violently to one side, as if to escape the knife. He jerked so hard he broke loose from the restraints and from the nurse who was supposed to make certain he did not move his head."

The nurse had left that part out when she told the story to Teddy and me, but it was obvious from the devastated look on the doctor's face that he was blaming no one but himself.

"The tonsil," he said, "ripped lose from its attachments and blood poured into his mouth. I could hear him breathing it into his lungs. I tried to clamp off the torn and severed vessels, but there were too many of them and I couldn't see what I was doing for all the blood."

"I—" Stone shook his head slowly. He looked down, and he must have realized that his hands were twisting together violently. He clasped them, as if to squeeze something between them, and raised his eyes, again looking between us.

"Finally, I was able to stop most of the flow. But by then Bennie had stopped breathing. I told the nurse, who was going into hysterics, to go out and get someone with a pulmotor. She was gone for what seemed like a very long time."

He closed his eyes, as if trying to avoid seeing something, and then opened them again, as if he realized he couldn't.

"Eventually, an intern dashed in with a pulmotor and we put the mask to Bennie's face and tried to pump oxygen into his lungs. For a moment or two it seemed to be working and his chest was rising and falling and he was breathing through the bubbling fluid in his lungs and then, with a horrible sound like a tire going flat, one of the rubber valves collapsed."

He smiled bitterly. "The pulmotor was old and rotten. Everything we have is old and rotten."

For a moment, he looked directly at O'Malley, and then his gaze drifted away as he resumed the story. "We called for a pulmotor from the white city hospital, figuring we had a better chance of getting a proper piece of equipment there. In the meantime, we tried artificial respiration, but by the time the pulmotor arrived, it was too late. He—my friend Bennie Moten was dead. And through it all, even after his heart had stopped beating and his lungs had collapsed, right up until the moment when I reached up and pulled his eyelids closed, he never stopped looking at me.''

The doctor wiped sweat off his forehead with a sleeve of his smock. His hands began moving again, his long fingers twisting at each other.

''When I was certain it was all over, I walked out of the operating room and out of the hospital and drove home and lay down on my bed in my bloody surgical clothes. I have been a surgeon for fifteen years, and I have seen many things that the layman would consider horrifying. I thought I was in control of my personal feelings, but I have never experienced such a shock and a tragedy so profound, having a close friend die on my operating table while he looked with terror and pleading into my face. I needed to get away. I had planned a vacation at the beginning of May, but I arranged to go immediately. I left the next morning.''

For the first time since he began the recitation, he looked directly at me.

''And now, Mr. Holt, if you have any questions, I wish you would ask them quickly. I need to attend to a patient, an East Texas child whose body is covered with the lesions of pellagra. His system will not hold the foods he needs to recover. Perhaps you would like to see him, and interview his mother. There's a story for your paper, Mr. Holt. There are thousands of children in southern America who are malnourished to the point of severe illness. Not just Negro children, Mr. Holt.''

He turned his eyes away from me and again looked past us. I had little doubt that the operation had gone as he had described it.

I began to speak, but O'Malley interrupted. ''Mike, let's get out of here,'' he said.

I said, ''Just let me ask a couple of questions. Dr. Stone, one of the things that puzzles me, one of the things that aroused my suspicions initially, is that you not only left town right after the operation, but you left the country as well. Why did you go to Mexico?''

''You're being stupid, Michael,'' said O'Malley.

''Perhaps ignorant would be the proper word,'' said Stone. ''I went to a seacoast resort in Mexico because they would have me. Where would you suggest? Biloxi, Mississippi?''

It was impossible to reply to that. So I asked my other question, although by this time it was as if I was also pleading for the man to understand why I had suspected him. ''Dr. Stone,'' I said, ''I just don't see how I could have been so mistaken. I was certain I saw you lying dead in a drawer in the police morgue, and I was even more certain of it when I saw your portrait in this hospital.''

An ironic smile came to his lips. He said, ''It is my understanding, Mr. Holt, that white men think *all* Negroes look alike.''

''Michael,'' said O'Malley, rising from his chair, ''it's time to go.''

14

We drove to the police station in silence, except for one brief exchange. I said, "I think Dr. Stone was telling the truth."

"Astute," said O'Malley.

I went up into the police station. O'Malley detoured by the 3.2 beer joint around the corner, since the Pleasant Dove was closed. There was no one in the press room that Easter afternoon. In a couple of minutes, O'Malley arrived with a sack holding six bottles of beer and set it in the middle of the vast desk. He opened two beers and we settled into our places.

"If we had a net and a ball," said O'Malley, loosening the laces on his black dress shoes, "we could play Ping Pong. If we had paddles."

He propped his feet on the desk, shoelaces dangling, and took a long swig of beer.

"So tell me," I said, feeling humiliated, "if there was nothing fishy about the death certificate, why did I have so much trouble getting it?"

"Bureaucratic incompetence," said O'Malley, fluttering his free hand in dismissal. "The girl over in vital statistics got her job because she is somebody's niece or hotsy-totsy, and you can bet she doesn't know how to file anything but her nails. She or somebody mislaid the damn thing. Or it's in some forgotten out box in the coroner's office. Damn, these garters itch."

He put his beer bottle down and pulled up his pant legs so he could unsnap and slide off his garters. He began scratching his upper calves with both hands. "Ahhhh," he said.

Alternately lightening his touch, and then briefly intensifying it as his fingernails found virgin territory, he scratched and continued his lecture. "Then, Michael," he said, "you started poking around and nobody knew who the hell you were or what the hell you were after.

You made them nervous. Anybody who works in this building does something illegal at least once a day. That's the way this city works. I tell you one thing, if some kind of fix was in to keep that death certificate from you, you sure as hell wouldn't have gotten it out of Jeff City. Tom Pendergast runs Jeff City, too.''

O'Malley quit strumming his calves and reached for his beer. He finished it off in one long swallow, and then ran the still-cold bottle along the side of his leg.

"So," he said, "nobody was going to give you anything you wanted, whether they had it or not. This whole thing has just been a dumb mistake, Michael. I tried to tell you that weeks ago."

My phone rang. It was the city desk. I saw by the wall clock that it was almost 3:45 P.M., and I began to apologize for not having called in and the editor told me not to worry, he didn't have any rewrite men anyway, and we were probably out of business until two guys came in at six.

"On Easter Sunday," he said, "this place is like a morgue."

No it's not, I thought.

I hung up the phone and leaned back in my chair, gazing past O'Malley's head at the large window of wire-meshed glass. The rain had been coming down pretty regularly for several weeks now and yet there was still grime caked on the outside of the window, as if it was baked into it. O'Malley opened his second beer, and I took a long drink out of my first, not wanting to fall too far behind. The radio crackled out a call for a car to investigate a citizen's report of a body on a vacant lot. I listened until I heard the locale—14th and Brooklyn.

"Okay," I said, "suppose this is all a stupid mix-up. Suppose Bennie Moten's death was a tragic accident and the doctor left town because he was heartbroken and he went to Mexico because there's no racial segregation there and I am as prejudiced as anybody else for not realizing that—"

"And for not being able to tell one spook from another," said O'Malley, belching and taking another long drink of beer.

"And the death certificate just slipped behind a filing cabinet—"

O'Malley nodded.

"And what about the guys in the Packard?"

"Have you seen them lately?"

"No," I said.

"Then it was just a couple of guys in a Packard, having some fun with you." He favored me with his wry grin.

"So," I said, "How could I have possibly have come up with a totally different explanation, a very complicated one that accounted for all these facts in such a logical way, and yet was all wrong?"

"Easy," said O'Malley. "You're a Protestant."

"The hell with you," I said.

"I'm quite serious," said O'Malley. "The Jesuits may not have taught me much, but they did beat one thing into my head. 'Life, Patrick,' a theology professor of mine used to say, 'is not a puzzle to be solved, it is a mystery to be revered.' "

"I don't see what the hell that has to do with my looking into a suspicious death," I said.

"Protestants think the world is a damned cosmic whodunit," he said. "There was, in fact, nothing suspicious about that bandleader's death."

"The hell there wasn't," I said, finishing my beer and banging the bottom of the empty on the desk. "Besides, you're not such a good Catholic."

O'Malley smiled and celebrated my *ad hominem* retreat by quickly drinking the rest of his beer. He opened a couple more and set the final one on his side of the desk.

"I sense the need for a resupply," he said, rising from his chair. He gathered the empties and put them in the sack, and shoved the beer he had just opened into his suitcoat pocket. "I'll be right back."

I was sipping my beer and sinking further toward despondency when my phone rang again. It was 4:17. I picked up the phone, prepared to explain that nothing was going on but a couple of fender benders, plus a geographically uninteresting corpse, but it was not the city desk. It was Robert Creech. I immediately told him I was almost certain Bennie Moten's death had been an accident, and he said, "That really doesn't matter anymore."

He and Teddy Wellington were at city hospital number two, where a young musician they both knew was in a coma from an overdose. Robert said he was "just a morphine popper who got mixed up with some heroin." I immediately thought of Charles, the young alto saxophonist who had so astonished us in back of the Reno, but this was a seventeen-year-old trumpet player, a former band student of Robert's. Teddy had known him pretty well too. Robert was distraught, and Teddy was angry, and they wanted to come over right away and talk to the police about the invasion of narcotics into Negro Kansas City. They were willing to put the finger on a couple of known dope peddlers, including, Robert said with anger, a substitute English teacher at Lincoln High School.

I told Robert policemen were hard to find at the police station on Easter

Sunday, and he said they were coming over anyway and they would damn well find one. I got the idea he wanted to get Teddy talking to a cop before he cooled down. I told Robert to come ahead and I would see what I could do. I was heading for the door to see if I could scare up a detective when O'Malley came in carrying a fresh sack of beer. He was followed by a detective, although not necessarily the one I would have chosen.

Sweeney had on a green-striped grey jacket with 1920s-style high, pointed lapels, and his jowls were popping up from a cruelly tight celluloid collar. He was wearing a green polka-dot bow tie, a bowler hat and a lapel carnation, and his too-short pants had the same dazzling pattern as his too-tight coat, so I assumed this was his Easter outfit.

He moaned wearily and tugged at his middle, and I saw beneath his white shirt the clear outline of a corset. He spotted the morris chair, just a few steps away, and collapsed toward it. Just before he sank into its maw, I saw terror flick across his florid face, as if he had realized in mid-fall that he might never rise again.

As Sweeney plunged into the rotten center of the chair, he folded up like an oriental fan, ending up with his lower legs sticking straight out. He wriggled his sausage arms and legs and heaved his body until he was able to rise to a more dignified, if precarious, perch, with his feet touching the floor, if barely. The bowler had not budged from his head.

I told O'Malley about Robert's phone call. He said, "Sweeney, this might be worth your time. Holt and his colored friends may actually be able to help us latch on to that new dope gang."

Sweeney nodded and listened attentively as I told him who Robert and Teddy were and what I had seen in their company, stressing that Robert was a respectable schoolteacher and Teddy a well-known musician. O'Malley opened the lukewarm beer on the desk for Sweeney and pulled colder beers for the two of us from his sack.

Robert and Teddy arrived by cab in less than ten minutes. Both were wearing dark suits, but Robert's blue one probably had cost twenty dollars and was wet, while Teddy's gray one would run three or four times that, and it had been protected from the rain by a black cashmere overcoat that he now wore flung over his shoulders like a cape.

After he had shaken hands with O'Malley, and Sweeney had extended his fat fingers like a grande dame, Teddy hung his overcoat and hat on wall hooks and pulled out a handkerchief. He bent down to wipe the water spots off the shiny surface of his black patent leather shoes.

He jerked upward as the radio came on with a barrage of static. A man dressed like the Easter bunny was pulling holdups near the Art

Institute.

"How can you stand that noise?" asked Teddy.

"What noise?" said O'Malley, leaning back in his squeaky chair. "Won't you gentlemen have a seat?"

The radio came back on to cancel the last call. Just some art students fooling around. Robert pulled a wooden chair out from the wall and sat down. Teddy stayed on his feet. Looking down at Sweeney, he said, "Detective, are you in charge of narcotics investigations?"

Sweeney's eyes rolled upward to contemplate Teddy. "I'm in charge of everything," he said. "Ain't I good enough for you?"

Quickly, I said, "Teddy, a detective can initiate any kind of investigation. But, correct me if I'm wrong Detective Sweeney, isn't narcotics officially under vice? And doesn't a corporal down there usually handle drug matters?"

"Becker," said Sweeney. He cleared his throat and I saw him eyeing the spittoon, but he must have decided it was too far, so he swallowed whatever disgusting mess he had pulled up to express his opinion of Becker.

"Eddie the Snake Becker," said O'Malley. "Very independent. We think he sees narcotics as a growing concern and plans on growing with it."

"Won't share the loot, huh?" I said, getting into my chair.

"Eddie the Snake?" said Sweeney, grinning. "I never heard that nickname."

"I just made it up," said O'Malley.

"Listen, gentlemen," said Teddy, elegantly rising on the toes of his shoes and then lowering his heels again without putting the slightest wrinkle in the mirrored surface, "I've just seen a friend in the hospital in a coma he may never come out of, and I have seen a great increase in the use of heroin by musicians over the past six months. I would like to do something to stop it before other friends end up in the hospital, or in their graves."

"You going to name some names?" asked O'Malley. "You know any?" I looked across the desk. His pasty face was turning pink, and he was staring at Teddy.

"Absolutely," said Teddy, not looking at O'Malley. "Detective," he said to Sweeney, "shouldn't you be ready to write this down?"

"Just tell me what you got," said Sweeney. "If it sounds interesting, you can come in tomorrow and we can fill out a report. Okay?"

"I shall be busy tomorrow," said Teddy, his face starting to darken, too.

"I'll come in tomorrow," said Robert. "I'm on Easter vacation. Teddy, why not just tell the detective what you know?"

"Right," said Teddy. He began by describing a tall white man with a southern accent who hung around musicians and sold heroin to them, probably including the young trumpet player who had overdosed.

The radio screeched again. More about the body at 14th and Brooklyn. I waited for Teddy to resume his tale, but he turned to me and said, "Michael, don't you have to do something about that? A body in a vacant lot? Call your paper and say, 'Sweetheart, give me rewrite!' Isn't that the way it goes?"

"What?" I said, and then I realized what he was talking about.

Teddy was smiling, guilelessly I thought, intrigued as so many people are by the fictionalized romance of the newspaper business.

"We'll probably pass on that one," said O'Malley, beginning to grin. "Wrong part of town."

Slowly, the smile left Teddy's face. He continued to look at me, the long, gnarled fingers of his right hand closing and opening and closing again. Finally, he said, "Michael, did you hear the one about Rastus and Mandy fucking in the swamp?"

"Ha," said O'Malley. Sweeney looked puzzled.

"Teddy, please," said Robert.

Teddy said to me, "Rastus is fucking Mandy in a mud puddle. He's working hard and not getting anywhere, you understand? So he says, 'Mandy, is I in you or is I in the mud?' And Mandy says, 'You is in me, Rastus.' "

Teddy paused, as if to add suspense. Sweeney was beginning to grin. He appreciated a good joke.

Robert was now staring at his shoes. I did not look at O'Malley, but I could almost feel enjoyment radiating across the desk from him.

Teddy's large brown eyes never left me. He let the silence build for another couple of beats and then, at exactly the right dramatic moment, he delivered the punch line:

" 'Well, Mandy,' said Rastus, 'Why don't you put me back in the mud?' "

Sweeney cackled.

"Boy, that's a new one on me," he said. "I thought I'd heard 'em all. 'Put me back in the mud.' " He laughed again, laughed until he starting coughing. When he had cleared his throat, he looked at Teddy, who was plucking his overcoat from the wall rack.

"Mister, you're okay," Sweeney said. "I'll be happy to help you find these dope peddlers."

Teddy didn't say a word. He put on his hat, swirled his coat so it hung over his shoulders, and walked out. Robert got up to follow him. At the door, he turned to me. Through his glasses, I could see tears in his eyes. He said, in a soft, hoarse voice, "I'll come by at three o'clock tomorrow and make that report, Michael. This is important."

After he was gone, Sweeney repeated the punch line once again, this time squealing like Stepin Fetchit. He shook his head in amusement.

"I tell you something, Holt. That Teddy's one funny Nigra."

O'Malley winked at me, and that was the last straw, although the Lord knows I should have been as furious with myself as I was with him.

I jumped up and started across the room. In retrospect, I am amazed that Sweeney, all corseted into his suit, was able to climb out of the morris chair and grab me from behind just as I was drawing back my fist to pop Patrick James O'Malley in the mouth.

"But I didn't say anything!" O'Malley protested, backing his chair up and holding his hands out in an attitude of Christ-like innocence.

"You said enough," I said, letting Sweeney pin my arms.

15

It's hard to trust a man called Snake. On the other hand, the moniker had just been created by O'Malley, and Corporal Eddie Becker was in charge of narcotics. I waited until 9 A.M. to call from the pay phone in the hotel lobby, even though I had popped awake sometime before eight to find myself lying diagonally across the bed with my shoes and socks and pants on and one of those adrenaline-stoked three-day hangovers rushing through me. I had two pans of cowboy coffee, which added torque to the express train in my head, but kept it from going completely off track on the curves.

Becker was expected any minute, I was told by the vice detective who answered. Was this about a story? I said it was about drugs and asked if Becker could call me as soon as he came in.

"You in the press room?" he asked.

I told him where I was and gave him the number of the pay phone. I hung up and lit a Lucky. I had smoked about half of it when the phone rang. It was Becker.

"Holt of the *Journal-Post*?" he asked with a Missouri Bootheel drawl. "How you been, old buddy?"

I took the friendliness as a good sign, despite the unsettling image of him his voice triggered in my memory—tall and extremely thin, with ingrown hips, indrawn shoulders and a narrow, elongated head. Definitely reptilian.

"How come you're staying in that dump?" he asked. "I thought you newspaper guys were rolling in dough."

"That's rich," I said, which was about as clever as I was going to get until some of the poisons had osmosed out of my cells.

"What's up?" said Becker.

I looked around. There was nobody else in the dark, dank lobby but the desk clerk, and he was busy sliding delinquent-rent notices into mail slots. I told Becker that a friend had some good information on dope peddling in the colored section, and could even identify a white man and a Negro school teacher as a drug distributors. I tried to make the case as strong as possible, saying that I had been with my friend at clubs where illegal drugs were clearly being sold. I told him my friend was coming to the police station around three, and Becker said, "As soon as he shows up, you boys come right on down the hall and see me. In the meantime, you be careful. Some of these dope peddlers are dangerous."

I went back upstairs and bathed and shaved and brushed my teeth again and got dressed. There was time for a doughnut and more coffee at the corner drugstore, and then I got my car, which had survived another perilous night in the alley, and headed south to meet Rachael.

There was a light, intermittent drizzle, but the clouds moving in from the west were dark and swollen, suggesting there was heavier rain to come. Shallow pools of water stood in depressions and dips in the road and along the curb, and I kept having to turn the windshield wipers on to clear the spray from other cars.

Rachael seemed forlorn in the solitary embrace of the blood-red booth. She was wearing no makeup, but one cheek was streaked with black, and she looked like a child who had rubbed her face after putting coal in a stove. Her eyes were red and moist. The collar of her dark blue dress was ripped at the neck seam and hung down above her breast. All she needed to complete the picture was a floppy Jackie Coogan hat like Seventeen wore.

She did not look up as I leaned over and kissed her cheek. "Shmutz," I said, licking my lips and tasting, faintly, charcoal.

She smiled slightly, but continued to look at her hands, resting on the table in front of her, and did not reply. I slid into the booth beside her. As my leg touched hers, she turned her head to me and said, "Michael, I only have a few minutes. Please don't make jokes."

I took one of her hands. "Did the funeral go well?" I asked. She made a tiny sound in her throat, like an exasperated chuckle.

"Let's talk about you, Michael. I could use a good mystery right now."

"It's not a mystery anymore," I said. "Not an Agatha Christie kind of mystery."

"I guess real-life mysteries usually aren't," she said, and for an instant I felt betrayed, as if she had pretended to help me search for a treasure that she secretly knew did not exist.

"Tell me what happened," she said.

I started with the G-man. She grimaced. Then I told her I hadn't seen the Packard for a couple of days, and repeated O'Malley's suggestion that it had just been a rough joke.

"Maybe those hoodlums just changed cars and got one that's not so showy," she said.

"I don't think so," I said, in a hurry to tell her what I had learned from Dr. Foster, and about our visit to Dr. Stone.

"Well," she said when I had finished. "And you think the colored doctor was telling the truth?"

I nodded. She nodded too. "It sounds like it. How very sad, to watch your friend die and not be able to do anything about it. And how tragic if you believe it was partly your fault."

For a minute or two, we just sat there beside each other, not saying anything, feeling warm. Once, the bartender looked over inquiringly, but I just shook my head, and he left us alone.

Then she said, "I have to go," and we walked together to the door. I waited while she put a large black scarf over her head and tied it at the throat. I held her yellow slicker for her while she put it on. She buttoned it up to the top and took my hand and squeezed it.

"When can I see you again?" I asked.

"We'll be together all summer, Michael. All this summer."

"But what about tomorrow?" I said.

"I'd better not," she said. "I'll call you in a few days."

She raised her head and kissed me quickly on the lips. Then she turned and went out the door.

I followed her outside and stood in the doorway and watched as she walked down the street in the light rain. She turned back once and looked toward me, her face small and wet beneath the large black scarf. And then she turned away again and went around a corner and she was gone.

My hands were shaking and my stomach was fluttering. I went back inside the bar and had two quick beers and made the third one a boilermaker. I took my time with it, sipping the whisky and letting the fizzy beer wash it off my tongue.

Feeling much calmer, I drove back to the hotel and was able to sleep, fitfully, until it was time to get up and drive to work.

As I turned the coupe onto Main Street and headed north, I thought I spotted the black Packard again, almost a block behind me. But when I had rubbed the mist off the rear-view mirror and slowed down to let the car gain on me, I saw through my rain-streaked rear window that it was just a Buick 90 sedan with side-mounted spares.

When I got to Market Square, I pulled into the police parking lot and found a spot two cars away from O'Malley's old LaSalle. On my way down the hall, I stuck my head into the small office occupied by the vice squad, but there was no one at any of the four desks.

O'Malley was in the press room, reading the *Journal-Post*. He looked up when I came in. I nodded brusquely in greeting.

"Hear you called Becker this morning," he said.

"You know everything, don't you?" I said.

"I know a lot," he said.

I hung up my hat and raincoat on the wall rack, next to a wire hanger with a long white-paper clothing sack on it.

"What's this?" I asked.

"My tuxedo," he said. "At least it's mine for the next twenty-four hours. The Honorable Judge J. Michael McGuire is throwing a black-tie reception at seven, before the play. Then there'll be drinks backstage at the Shubert, followed by a much more private gathering elsewhere."

"Don't you have to work tonight?" I asked, sliding into my chair.

"I'm working the day beat for McClellan and he's coming in at six to cover for me," said O'Malley, dropping the paper on the desk. I was relieved that I would not have to spend the whole evening with O'Malley. Things were still very touchy between us.

I loosened my tie and picked up the note Drummond had left me. "Christ," I said, "another unidentified body in the river?"

"It's a new epidemic," said O'Malley. "Replacing kidnaping. Why the hell did you call Becker?"

"Because the meeting between my friends and Sweeney did not go so well," I said. "Thanks in part to you."

"Michael, Michael," he said, shaking his head. He sighed. "Your friend Robert just called. Said he wouldn't be here until about four. He had to go by general hospital number two first, to visit a critically ill friend. Is the world losing another nigger?"

"O'Malley," I said, "if you ever say that word again, I really will hit you in the mouth."

"Hmmm," said O'Malley.

I looked at the clock on the wall. It was just a couple of minutes after three. O'Malley's chair squeaked as he rose to his feet. "I got to make the rounds," he said. "I'll see what I can find out about that floater. And I'll ignore that last remark."

"You better not," I said, as he walked past me and out the door.

It took me about forty-five minutes to read through both afternoon papers and tear out a couple of stories that seemed worth following up.

Twice, I asked the operator to ring vice, but nobody answered.

O'Malley had not returned when my phone rang. I was expecting the city editor's voice.

"Holt, *Journal-Post*," I said.

"Is this Michael Holt?" The man spoke with what sounded like an upper-class English accent, but there was a strange lilt to the words.

"O'Malley, go fuck yourself," I said.

"My name is not O'Malley," the man said, pronouncing "not" as if it was "naught."

"Well, who the hell is it then?" I said.

"Are you Michael Holt?"

"Yes," I said. "And who might you be?"

"Someone who needs to speak with you."

"Go ahead," I said.

"I would prefer to discuss this in person."

"What is this about?" I said. I felt a touch on my shoulder and looked up. It was Robert in a soaking wet cotton overcoat. I held up my left hand and gestured toward the phone at my right ear.

"I would like to see you immediately," said the man with the British accent. "You will have to come to me."

"I'm at work," I said.

"This is more important," he said. "My colleague will explain."

I looked up at Robert and rolled my eyes. Then, another voice came on the phone. This one, I was certain, belonged to a Negro.

"You better come on out and see us, and right away," he said. "We need to talk to you."

"What about?" I asked.

"About a dead man in an alley with a great big hole in his throat, and a few things like that. We got a lot to talk about."

The man had a drawl like Lester Young's, with a slight lisp. He said, "You been poking around in our business, and we better talk about that, too. You hear me?"

"Who the hell is this?" I said, looking up at Robert. He furrowed his brow inquisitively. I shrugged.

"You come on out and see us, and you'll find out," the man said.

"And what if I don't come on out and see you?" I said. I was not in the mood for games.

"Well, then," the man said, "you just might never see that little girlfriend of yours again."

At first, I was too startled to reply, and then, for a moment, I couldn't take what he was saying seriously. If life wasn't an Agatha Christie, it wasn't a Dashiell Hammett either.

"Stop fooling around," I said. "Who is this?"

"You'll find out," he said. "You got yourself a pretty little chick, and she looks cute as a bug in that black scarf and that yellow raincoat and driving around in that nifty little green Dodge. But you don't treat her right, meeting her in a bowling alley like that. So she decided to spend some time with us. You want to see her again, you get your ass right on out here."

Oh, Jesus, I thought.

"Okay," I said, "Now wait a minute. Where are you? Where's Rachael? What do you want?"

The man told me he wanted me to drive out to 63rd and Brookside, about fifteen blocks south of the Plaza. He described a route that involved cutting back and forth a couple of times between the parallel southbound streets of Broadway and Main.

He said, "We want to be sure that black Buick isn't following, you understand what I'm saying? Wasn't for that Buick, we could have talked to you before and we wouldn't have to involve your little chick at all. Although she is some nice company."

"Okay," I said, baffled by the reference to the black Buick. "Listen, just don't hurt her. I'll do whatever you want. Will Rachael be at 63rd and Brookside?" I felt Robert grip my left shoulder and squeeze it.

"Let's not get too far ahead of ourselves here," the man said. "When you get there, you'll see a phone booth on the northwest corner. In thirty minutes from right now, that phone is going to ring, and you better make sure you are there to answer it. And if there is somebody using that phone, you better throw their ass out in the street. I don't want to hear any busy signals when I call to tell you where to go next. You hear me?"

"Okay, wait a minute, don't hang up." My mind was scrambling around, trying to figure out what to say. Robert squeezed my shoulder again.

The man said, "I tell you what. My watch says it's five minutes after four. I'll give you a little extra time to do all that driving back and forth. You be at that phone at 4:45. And you better not bring any cops with you, or that little girl is dead."

"Look," I said, "how do I know you're telling the truth? How do I know you've really got Rachael? How do I know you didn't just see her with me and that's how you know what she's wearing and even what her car looks like? Let me call her house and see if she's there."

The voice came back, harsher than before. "You don't have to do that, shithead. Just tell me one thing. That little girlfriend of yours, she got a cute little mole on her left thigh right up near her pussy? If so, you got thirty-nine minutes to get to 63rd and Brookside.'' The phone clicked dead.

16

"What are you going to do with this thing?" asked Robert, as I sped across Independence Avenue on the yellow light. "Hit somebody over the head with it?"

"I fired it once," I said, cutting around a Plymouth that had stalled in a shallow pond near the curb. The wind was gusting and the rain was falling heavier than ever. The storm sewers were backing up and water was a half-foot deep or more in low spots in the street.

The single overhead wiper on my side was not keeping up with the rain, and I had to keep rubbing the steam off the inside of the window with the back of my hand.

"Robert, could you do something about the windshield?"

"Anything you want, Ugly Boy Floyd," said Robert, putting the Thompson submachine gun on the floor. He rested the soles of his high-topped black shoes on either side of the twenty-shot magazine.

Pulling out his handkerchief, he wiped the inside of the windshield and left me a patch of relative transparency. Now, I could see almost a half-block ahead.

"Thanks," I said. "Hit it again in a minute or so. Please. And you can leave me your handkerchief when I drop you at the 18th Street trolley-car stop. There's even a little shelter there."

"I think I'll stick with you," said Robert. "You better step on it, or you're going to miss that light up ahead."

I sped up, but the light turned red a second or two before I hit the intersection. I kept going. Fortunately, there wasn't much traffic downtown.

"Look," I said, "how am I going to explain you? The guy on the phone said not to bring any cops."

177

"You think I look like a policeman?" I glanced over at Robert, who was squinting blindly downward as he tried to wipe the fog off his glasses with the front of his damp shirt. He looked like a schoolteacher. A colored schoolteacher. I had heard there were a few Negro policemen on the Kansas City force, but I had never actually seen one.

"And they sure as hell aren't going to think I'm a federal agent," he said.

"You're right about that," I said, still figuring I'd better get rid of Robert at some point along the way. "Okay. You want to help out? I've got to turn over to Broadway up here at 16th Street. When I do, check out the rear window and see if you spot a black Buick following us. Or a black Packard."

Robert ran his damp handkerchief over the rear window, leaving little chains of water streaking the cleared surface. I checked quickly and couldn't see much of anything behind us, and then I had to concentrate on making the turn and staying in the middle of the street to avoid drowning the ignition system in a lake-sized puddle.

"I don't see a car behind us at all," said Robert. "Not a lot of other fools out in this mess. Are the bad guys in a Buick or in a Packard?"

"I don't know who's in what," I said. I checked the tiny clock clamped to the right side of the rear view mirror. It read 4:17. I had about forty-five blocks and another dogleg to go before 4:45. It had taken us a few extra minutes to get the tire iron from the toolbox under my front seat and jimmy the golfbag door on O'Malley's LaSalle. We had gotten drenched doing it, and our clothes were undoubtedly adding to the dewiness of the car's interior.

"I don't know what these guys are going to say when they see you," I said.

"Answer me this," said Robert. "Would you rather try to explain me, or go out there alone?"

I turned left onto Broadway and didn't reply. My mind was scrambling in several directions, trying to figure out just what was going on. It didn't seem real, speeding through the rain to ransom my girl from an aristocratic Englishman and a cool-talking Negro. And what was I going to ransom her with? What did I have that they wanted?

Actually, I was afraid I knew the answer to that one. They obviously thought I knew a hell of a lot more than I really did about them, and the man they had killed and left in an alley, and their drug dealings, and whatever else they were up to.

"Robert," I said, "I'm supposed to cut back over to Main at the next cross street. Check the rear again, will you?"

Robert balled up his wet handkerchief and ran it over the rear window again. I made the left turn too tight and too fast and the car began to skid, but I jerked my foot off the accelerator and straightened the car out. I hit the accelerator again and sped along the cross street. I glanced up at the clock. 4:24.

"No Buick, no Packard, no cars at all behind us," said Robert. "An ice truck and some fool on a motorcyle with another fool drowning in the sidecar."

"What the hell do you think this is all about?" I asked Robert.

"It's not too hard to figure out," he said, leaning over in front of me to clear the windshield.

"You've stumbled into the middle of some kind of war over drugs. These fellows want to find out what you know, and how you found out, and who else knows anything. Then they're going to kill you."

Robert wrung his handkerchief out, dripping water on my right shoe.

"Do you think a cop might have tipped them off?" he said. "Told them you had set up a meeting to identify a couple of dope peddlers?"

"Maybe," I said. "Half the Kansas City police force is for sale. Becker could have called them, Becker or the other vice cop I talked to. I wish I knew. God, I hope it wasn't Sweeney. Or—"

"Or maybe," said Robert, "one of these fellows saw you snooping around at the Reno, asking questions. Heck, maybe Seventeen told them you were nosing around. Maybe they wanted to grab you right away, but something scared them off."

"The car following me," I said.

"Yeah, maybe the other side in the drug war has been following you in a Buick, or a Packard. Maybe they've got two cars." Robert turned his head and swiped with his handkerchief at the rear window.

"Nobody's following you now," he said. "And that's what those guys wanted, to make you shake the car that was on your tail. Make sense?"

I shrugged. "In the movies."

"Well, maybe they've been watching a lot of movies."

"I hope we've been watching the same ones," I said.

The stoplight at Main was red. The clock hand moved from 4:26 to 4:27 before the light changed. I had about thirty-five blocks to go. I kept my eyes out for police cars. I certainly did not want to be pulled over.

When I had hung up the phone, I had considered telling a policeman about the call. What stopped me was not so much the kidnapper's warning as my feeling that the police would either screw things up so badly they would get Rachael killed or they would actually be in cahoots with the kidnappers. In Kansas City, I thought, the cops are either funny or dangerous.

I honked my horn and the old Franklin in front of me edged over into the water swirling out from the curb. I went around him straddling the middle line.

If I had seen O'Malley, I probably would have told him about the call. I even peeked into the Pleasant Dove before I broke into his car, but he wasn't there.

I knew what I was doing was stupid, that these guys probably just wanted to get me alone so they could kill me, but I couldn't figure any other way to respond to the threat to Rachael's life.

"Listen. I know you're nervous," said Robert, "but stop talking to yourself."

I nodded as we began the long downhill run toward the Plaza. I left the car in high gear and pushed down the accelerator. It was 4:29.

We sped down the rain-slick hill. The car was briefly airborne as we went over the streetcar tracks near the bottom, and then it slammed to the pavement. Robert's feet flew up and the barrel of the submachine gun banged into the underside of the dashboard. Robert shoved it back down and put his rainy-day clodhoppers on top of it again.

I got stopped again by the stoplight at 43rd. "Last chance to get out," I said to Robert, as the sparse crosstown traffic rolled by.

"I'll stay," he said, clearing the windshield. "Maybe I owe you something for getting those frat boys off my back," he said.

"I thought you got them off my back," I said, nervously tapping the steering wheel.

"Anyway," said Robert, "I was partly responsible for getting you into this. I asked you to set up the meeting with the police. But I warn you. If I get killed, you damn well better put it in the paper. None of this niggers-don't-count shit."

It was 4:31 when I crossed the low bridge over Brush Creek. The rain and wind had slackened a little bit, enough so we could crack our windows open to clear some of the vapor from the car, but it was still coming down steadily. The laughable trickle that Pendergast had paved was turning into a major tributary. The creek had swollen almost to the edges of its seventy-foot-wide cradle of pavement and was roaring east, sweeping along small tree limbs and branches and other flotsam.

Shifting into second as Main rose steeply out of the Country Club Plaza, I tacked around a bakery truck double parked in front of a delicatessan. Just past the crest of the hill, I got stuck behind an ancient Model T. I honked, but it didn't speed up or move over. It was 4:34. Fifteen blocks to go. I slid around the Ford and back into the right lane a few feet ahead of a collison with an oncoming, honking delivery van.

With the luck of who-knows-what, no one hit us, and it was not quite 4:45 when I slid to a stop across from the phone booth at 63rd and Brookside. I handed Robert the key to the rumble seat. He grabbed the machine gun and pushed open the door, and I hopped out the other side and ran across 63rd, pulling my raincoat over my head. Southwest High School was a block or so away, and with the accordion door closed, the phone booth smelled of stale sweat and cheap perfume and old sack lunches. I dug a half-dry Lucky out of the pack in my shirt and went through half a dozen wet matches before I got one to strike.

The cigarette smoke dispelled some of the odor and made me feel a little less like battering my fist through the glass pane in the door. The rain had settled into a steady downpour, the kind of spring rain that might keep up all day. I kept looking at my watch, which was so far living up to its billing as water resistant. And I thought about Rachael, and about the last time I had seen her, walking away from me and then turning back, looking like a little girl who was holding onto childhood for a moment longer before she had to go off and act like a grown-up. I better act like one, too, I thought, or we might both be dead before the day was over.

The phone rang at 4:49. It was the smooth Negro voice again, and I was instructed to proceed south to a roadhouse out on Prospect just past 79th, a few blocks beyond Fairyland amusement park. This time, I had no doglegs to make. I had been given another deadline: the roadhouse at 5:15.

I didn't make it. The winds had knocked down a power line on 75th street, and the roadway was blocked. Cars in front of me were trying to make U-turns or back up on the wet pavement. Before I could turn around, a car behind me skidded trying to stop and ended up sideways across the road, and a panel truck smashed into him. It took me more than ten minutes to retreat past the resulting tangle, backing up on 75th for almost a block with my head stuck out the window in the pouring rain, my horn honking, until I found an alley I could escape through.

If anybody was following me by then, they must have been some kind of wizard at the wheel. An invisible wizard.

It was 5:20 when I passed Fairyland Park. Despite the rain, the empty Ferris wheel was turning, lit and sparkling like a giant jeweled ring in the middle of the air.

"Libba's band starts there next week," said Robert. "Be nice to be around to hear them."

Three minutes later, I pulled into the graveled lot of the roadhouse, a small one-story white shingled building with neon beer signs glowing in the two front windows. There were three empty cars parked out in front. I stopped, parallel with the road and facing south, lights on, motor running, as I had been instructed.

My eyes flicked up to the clock. 5:24. I was nine minutes late. I rolled down the window and stuck my head out in the rain again, looking both ways, but nobody was in sight. There was still was no break in the thick, rolling layer of clouds, and the light was fading.

"What are you going to do when somebody comes?" said Robert, blowing on his cupped hands. It was getting chilly, and we were soaking wet. Robert had taken his sopping summer topcoat off and put it on the floor. I was still wearing my raincoat, but my hair was wet, the lower legs of my flannel pants were soaked, and my socks held water like sponges. My useless hat was a wet ball on the shelf behind the seat.

"First," I said, "I thought I would try to explain that this was all a mistake."

"And say you're sorry?" said Robert, grinning.

"Shit, Robert," I said, checking the clock. 5:26. "I'll just say I thought there was this murder, and there wasn't, and I'm perfectly willing to forget about the rest of it if they will just let Rachael go. Anyway, I don't really know anything that would hurt these guys."

"I doubt if they will believe you," said Robert. "Besides, *I* know something."

"Yeah, but how much? Is that damn clock moving?" It still read 5:26. I reached up and yanked on the winding string.

"Don't break it," said Robert. "You said one of the men had an English accent?"

"Yeah," I said, peering desperately out at the road, praying for a headlight.

"I think I know who that is," said Robert.

I looked over at him. He had his arms folded across his chest, trying to keep warm, which was probably futile in a wet cotton shirt and suit. In the dim light, his lips looked bloodless gray against his dark brown skin.

"You going to tell me?" I asked.

"I'm probably wrong," he said. "Look over there."

I looked to my left and saw a man come out of the roadhouse, dark slicker pulled over his head. He got into one of the parked cars and drove away.

It was 5:28. Maybe the men had left when I hadn't showed up at 5:15. Maybe they had killed Rachael. Maybe her body was already lying in a ditch, covered with muddy water.

"Kidnapping," I said, shaking my head. "Why the hell would they do that? These fellows have been reading too many dime novels."

"Or tabloid newspapers," said Robert.

"You think they've already killed her?" I said. "Like they killed the Lindbergh baby? Don't most kidnappers kill their hostages?"

"Mary McElroy is still alive," said Robert.

"Think that's the guy?" I asked.

Dimly through the rain and gathering dark, I could see a man wearing a cap and jacket step out from behind the side of the roadhouse. He stood there looking straight ahead, apparently at us. Quickly I blinked my lights. I had not been told to do that, but I was desperate.

For a moment, the man continued to look in our direction through the rain. Then, he walked toward us. He signaled for me to crank down the window. As he leaned close, I could smell stale beer on his breath. He had a wet black felt cap pulled down low over his face, and it was too dark to make out his features, except to see that he was a Negro.

"Who that with you?" he asked, in a thick Deep South accent.

"A friend," I said. "Unarmed. He's not a policeman. I was told not to bring any police. But I was afraid to come out here alone." I hoped that last line would be a little disarming.

"They not goin' like it," the man said. "But that ain't my worry. You follow me."

He walked back to the roadhouse and disappeared around the side. In a moment, headlights came on and a car pulled out, cut in front of us and began moving very slowly south on Prospect. I put my car in gear and followed. How close was I supposed to be? As I drove out Prospect, I settled on three to four car lengths.

The car was not a Buick, nor a Packard. It was a Model A Ford sedan, black like mine and million more on the road, with a standard black metal trunk affixed to the rear. That car could have followed me for a month and I probably would not have noticed it.

He braked for a curve, and the single taillamp went amber to reveal the only thing remotely distinctive about the car. It had a Louisiana license plate. I slowed down to avoid crawling up its back.

"That's not either of the men on the phone," I said.

"That farm boy barely knows how to drive a car," said Robert. "He's just some field nigger."

"Would you please not use that word!" I said.

"When did you get so particular?" asked Robert.

"Quite recently," I said. I lit the last Lucky from the damp pack and threw the match on the wet floor, where it sizzled for an instant. The car in front of me continued its slow pace out Prospect for a few blocks, turned left—east—for eight or ten blocks, and then went south again, on a concrete-paved two-lane country road.

We went along it for two or three minutes, passing only one car going in the other direction and only a few houses. I was surprised a road this far out was even paved—although I shouldn't have been.

Robert unbuttoned the front of his shirt and wiped his glasses on his undershirt. He put them back on and tried to peer through the windshield, which was awash on his side. Neither of us spoke.

The Ford's brake light came on again and it lurched to a halt. I saw something dark waving from the window on the driver's side. When I got almost close enough to touch bumpers, I saw it was the farm boy's hand. He was signaling for a right turn. I blinked my lights.

We turned up a narrow gravel road through a ravine that rose curved to the right. We both were in second gear now. Water was streaming from the muddy hillsides that flanked us, and gushing down the ditches at either side of the high-crowned roadbed.

We reached the top of a hill and came to an open field. The Ford sedan drove on a gravel strip straight across the field for perhaps fifty yards and then passed through a gate in a chain-link fence. I followed. I was able, in the glare of the Ford's headlights, to see we were heading for a wall of rock on the side of a high hill. The Ford drove straight for the wall, going about fifteen miles an hour, and disappeared.

In a couple of seconds, the Ford's headlights circled back into view. By then, I had slowed to a crawl and I was close enough to see that there was a mouth-like opening in the rock wall, perhaps fifteen feet high and twenty or twenty-five feet wide, illuminated from inside by the lights of the Ford. Just to the right of the entrance a truck was parked. As we passed it, I could recognize the lettering on the side: "Ready-Mixed Concrete Co."

Then I was inside the cave. I stopped. The Ford was parked to my left and a little ahead of me, and now I saw the driver standing in front of it, signaling me to pull up towards him. The wiper began squeaking against dry glass. I turned it off and eased the car ahead until the headlights of the Ford were shining directly on my door. The man shouted, "Now both of you get out." He was standing about ten feet in front of my car, and he had a revolver in his hand.

Robert and I got out of the car. I could feel the soles of my shoes crunch on loose gravel above a stone floor. In the illumination cast by the car lights, I could see that the ceiling was twelve or fourteen feet high, and here and there was supported by stout pillars that appeared to have been chiseled out of the gray rock. And then I realized what kind of place this was.

This was not a cave, but a quarry, a rock mine carved out of the Bethany shelf: a thick mattress of limestone that runs under the western part of the state all the way to the Missouri River, 100 or more blocks from where we stood. Out of this quarry had come thousands of tons of lime and stone for the cement and concrete to build Tom Pendergast's Kansas City.

The driver of the Ford stood where the headlights intersected. He was wearing a long black rain slicker buttoned to the chin and rubber boots. His black cap was soaking wet and pulled down over his face.

"Y'all go stand over there in the light, over there by that post," he said, waving in the direction the headlights of his car were pointing, at a pillar in the middle of this vast entry room. I crossed in front of my car. Robert was walking ahead of me.

"Now both of you put your hands in front of you, put them on that post."

Robert and I were facing the pillar at right angles to each other. I put my hands on the cold, damp, gritty limestone. Robert put his hands forward, too, and briefly pressed the back of my right hand with his left before he slid it over and placed it flat against the pillar.

Robert said, very softly but not whispering, "Push hard enough and we can bring this whole place tumbling down." A nervous snicker escaped through my nose. I could see the side of Robert's face, dark wet skin shining, and the headlights picked out drops of water in his kinky hair and made them glisten. I looked past him, but I could not see a wall—the light just disappeared into the black distance. I could hear the rain falling outside, and water dripping somewhere inside the cavern.

There was a metallic squeak, and I figured the man must have jerked my car door open to let his headlights shine on the interior. My heart fluttered as I heard him raise the front seat to check the tool compartment underneath. Then I heard him slam it closed. He began rustling around in the interior of the car.

My fingers were growing numb, and my upper body, with just a thin raincoat over a shirt, was getting stiff from the cold. I regretted leaving my jacket in the press room, but I had not been thinking about a cave expedition when I had dashed out the door.

After a minute or so, I heard the other car door open. There was more rustling, and the sound of something wet plopping down. Then I heard gravel crunch as the man began walking towards us. Involuntarily, as if to jerk away from a bullet, I arched my back until my stomach touched the cold pillar. I could hear Robert's breath quicken.

Then the man was right behind me and I could hear his breath, fast and phlegmy, as if he had TB. Something cold and metallic brushed the back of my neck, and I gasped.

The man tittered. "Don't worry," he said, "ain't going kill you, not yet anyhow."

Robert was right, he sounded like a Southern fieldhand. And he sounded very young. Up close, he had a strong smell of patent medicine about him, a smell I remembered from someplace long ago and associated with poverty.

"Where's Rachael?" I asked.

"Don't worry, you'll see her directly." He held the gun to the base of my skull and, with his free hand, slapped the pockets of my raincoat.

'Lift up your coat," he said. I gathered the bottom of my raincoat in both hands and he reached around and patted my chest and then rubbed his hand down over my pants pockets. He giggled as he touched my groin, sending shivers through my pelvis.

He moved the gun to Robert's neck and he checked his coat and pants for weapons. "You all wet, cousin," he said. He pronounced it "cuddin."

Then, I could hear him backing away from us. "Turn around and walk to your car," he said from nearby. "Get in and follow me."

I turned and saw him standing about ten feet behind me, the gun pointed at my face.

"Don't get out of the car," he said. "Or I come back and shoot you. And then I might go shoot that lady."

He waved with the revolver for me and Robert to walk in front of him. As we passed, he said, "You better follow me close, or you get lost." I heard his feet crunch as he began walking behind us. "I know my way around. I built this place."

There was a child's pride in that strange verb. When I climbed back in the car, I noticed that both door pockets had been ransacked. Scattered on the floor on my side were the crumpled Lucky pack, a half-used stenographer's notebook, a pencil with the eraser chewed off, a roll of friction tape, a spark plug taped inside a spark plug wrench and a small tin of aspirin. On Robert's side, a Kansas City map and a beer opener were lying on top of his crumpled topcoat.

The farm boy got into the sedan and tried to put it into reverse. The engine was racing because he had the choke or the hand throttle open too far, and he gave up after gears had crashed a couple of times. He managed to get it in second and lurched forward past us. He made a U-turn around the pillar we had stood by and drove past us. I followed. We went deeper into the quarry, driving between two rows of pillars. Robert turned around and knelt on the seat. He began twisting the small T-handle that rolled down the rear window.

He said, "You were right about the tool chest."

I had hoped that whoever came to meet us would check under the front seat, but wouldn't think about us being able to get into the rumble seat from the cab. More than half of the Model A coupes on the road, the older models, had fixed rear windows, as did all the sedans.

"We were lucky they sent the farm boy, Robert," I said.

He grunted as he tried to stretch his right arm through the open window and reach the handle of the rumble seat. Ahead, I could see the sedan slow down as it approached a wall. It made a lurching right turn, and now I could see its headlights were clearly pointed downward at an angle of ten or fifteen degrees.

Robert grunted again. He had both arms and his head past the rear window, and he was wriggling to get his shoulders into it. I made the right turn and slowed down to let the sedan get three or four car lengths ahead of me. We were now in a sloping tunnel that was about twice as wide as the cars, with a ceiling that couldn't have been more than eight or nine feet high.

"I got it!" Robert's voice was muffled because his body was stuffed in the window past the armpits. The amber light in front of me went on as the sedan slowed, apparently because I was getting too far behind.

"Shhhh," I said, as I pulled to within a car length of the sedan. With my lights shining on him, I was certain he couldn't see what Robert was doing.

We continued to descend while Robert wriggled to get his shoulders back into the car. A tunnel opened to the right, but the sedan continued to follow the left wall.

Robert set the submachine gun on the floor and took a deep breath before diving into the window again. We were still descending, driving at under ten miles an hour. I was in second, letting the engine keep the car from rolling too fast, adjusting the spark retard to try to keep it from backfiring in that stone vault. The farm boy must have been in third because he kept having to hit his brake.

Robert twisted back through the window with a couple of heavy tools in his hands. After what seemed like several hundred yards of slow descent, we reached a leveling off spot. The wall on the right disappeared and we were driving between the left wall and a row of pillars spaced about thirty or forty feet apart. The sedan continued for another hundred yards or so, and then for an instant its headlights went out and I glimpsed a glow, off to the right and perhaps hundred yards ahead.

By then, Robert was seated next to me and the submachine gun was on the floor under his wet coat. I hoped it was as water resistant as my watch. I had a tire tool in my lap, and Robert was holding a monkey wrench.

"Robert, who do you figure does the work in these quarries?" I asked.

"The same men who fix the roads," he said. "Prisoners from the Jackson County Farm."

"I bet you're right," I said. "Working for Boss Pendergast."

I turned the steering wheel to the right as the sedan began angling off that way, cutting through a field of chiseled stone pillars. The glow grew brighter, and then the sedan's lights went out. The farm boy circled left past a couple of battered, dusty dump trucks and an old red Chevy pickup.

He pulled to a stop facing a huge semi-circular alcove. We seemed to be at the intersection of the man-made cave and a real one of water-shaped flowstone that had taken millions of years to develop.

I turned my lights off and stopped about twenty feet behind the sedan. The driver signaled with his hand for me to pull to his left. I drove up and parked facing the alcove. It was thirty or forty feet across and about twenty feet deep at its midpoint, and the ceiling was as high as the dome of a cathedral.

In an area about ten feet deep and fifteen feet across at the front of the alcove, a relatively flat floor had been created with sledgehammer and concrete, but the rest was a gnarled forest of multicolored dolomitic limestone. Many of the small stalgmites, particularly those within an easy hammer's swipe of the paved floor, had had their tops broken off, leaving sharp edges. Most of the others were only a few feet high, but several were as tall as spruces, and there was one in a nave at the rear of the alcove that had fused with a stalactite, and it soared until in vanished into the darkened ceiling, like a redwood disappearing into storm clouds.

Tall steel spikes were driven into the stone at the four corners of the man-made portion of the floor, and high-intensity lanterns were hanging from the tops of them. This niche in the cave was as bright as an operating theater in a hospital, and the fiery lights picked out the crystals scattered throughout the stone. Elsewhere, the walls had seemed a dull, powdery gray-brown, but here they rippled and glistened and glowed in yellows and oranges and pinks and reds.

I did not see Rachael.

Two men were seated in metal chairs, facing us across a folding table with metal legs and a wooden top. Two other chairs sat empty near the table. On the table were what appeared to be some metal tools, a half-empty quart of whisky and a pile of cardboard wrappings from White Castle. What looked like two long stone drills were lying on the floor off to the left of the table.

After I had turned off the engine, the farm boy got out of the sedan and walked between the two cars into the alcove. He put the revolver on the table and picked up a short, thick knife. The other men stood up.

"Shit," said Robert. I glanced over at him, but he kept his eyes on the alcove.

The man to the left was white, except for his swollen nose, which was mostly purple. One of his eyelids was drooping, almost like Seventeen's. He was wearing a lavender shirt open at the throat and high-waisted, purple-and-gray checked pants held up by strangely mottled gray suspenders. His sleeves were rolled above his elbows, and there seemed to be dirt or clay smeared on his hands and lower arms, and on the knees of his pants. He was wearing a gray, low-brimmed hat. The high, loose ride of his pants made him seem slim, but his forearms and wrists were as thick as an oarsman's, and he had the neck of a bulldog. I thought I had seen him before, somewhere in the East Side nightclub district, and I felt the same way about the other man.

He was even taller, perhaps six-four or six-five, and he had the build of a heavyweight boxer. In fact, with his large oval head, wide mouth and gapped teeth, he looked like Jack Johnson, except that his skin was much darker, a deep ebony. He was as black as any man I had ever seen, with an inky shine to his skin. He was wearing a dark blue, conservatively cut pinstripe suit. A red silk foulard was loosened at his open collar, and the barrel of his torso seemed too bulky ever to have been constrained inside his jacket and vest, now both unbuttoned. Neither man appeared to have dressed that morning for a cave.

In the middle, with his black cap still pulled forward over his eyes, was the skinny farm boy. He was wearing well-washed overalls and he had opened his slicker to reveal the soiled top half of a suit of longjohns. His skin was dark brown, about the color of Robert's, and he looked very young, eighteen or nineteen at the most. And I saw where that odor had come from, and remembered where I had smelled it before. Past the low bill of his cap, I could see that he was wearing a cutoff stocking over his head, the way poor Carolina kids did when their hair had been shaved off and their skulls smeared with ringworm ointment.

Jack Johnson stuck his big right hand in the air and waved for us to come toward him. As we got out of the car and stepped around the doors, leaving them both half open, he reached to the table and picked up a double-barreled shotgun. He put the butt under his right armpit and let the barrel rest across his forearm, like a gentleman out for grouse.

By then, Robert and I were standing in front of my car, near the edge of the cement section of the alcove. The white man nervously snatched up the revolver from the table. I expected him to tell us in an English accent what we had to do to save Rachael.

I heard the English accent, all right, but it came from the black man. And it only took a few words to realize that he was in charge, not, as I had assumed, the white man.

"Now it all becomes clear," said the black man, looking at Robert. "You're the fly in the oinment."

"Where's Rachael?" I said.

"She had to cut out," said the white man, trying to sound cool, but unable to disguise the nervousness catching at his throat. He held the revolver tensely at his side, his index finger tight on the trigger guard.

The white man was the one who spoke like a Negro jazz musician.

His flat hat was pushed back on his head and the front of his curly hair was heavily pomaded and combed straight back, almost as if he had had it processed, and now I could see a tiny bluesman's goatee just below his lower lip. I could almost hear Teddy Wellington pronounce judgment: another nigger lover.

The black man squeezed his elbow to his side, gripping the shotgun tighter, and spoke to Robert. "Another six weeks, and I would have moved on. American children will talk, won't they?"

Robert said, "It's not just that, you bastard. I saw you last week in the band room, saw you hand a bag of that shit to a sixteen-year-old boy. You come from Nassau with all that Marcus Garvey African pride jive, and while you're bullshitting, you're murdering our race with those poison needles. You filthy motherfucker." The word sounded very strange coming from Robert.

The Bahamian smiled. "If I don't get rich selling it, the white people will," he said. There was a sweet lyricism in his accent that was startling in contrast to his words.

The young Negro in overalls ran his callused thumb over the blade of what I now saw was a linoleum knife, with a short round wooden handle and a thick curved blade about four inches long, hooked like a hawk's beat. It was the kind of knife that could cut and rip at the same time, the kind of knife that could tear a roughly circular hole in a man's throat. It had been sharpened to a razor's edge, and I thought I saw a dark blotch, like a strawberry birthmark, staining the thick shiny blade.

"Rachael!" I yelled. The white man's eyes nervously shifted to his right. I followed his gaze and saw the wide, high mouth of a real cave.

"*Rachael!*" I screamed into the darkness, refusing for a moment to believe that she could be dead out there somewhere. And then, I was certain she must be. And in my mind's eye, I saw her lying on the cold stone floor with her arms flung out, covered with blood, her dress ripped apart and her head at an impossible angle, her throat slashed by the hooked knife. But first, they would have raped her.

"You bastards!" I shouted. "Where's Rachael?"

"It doesn't matter," said the Bahamian, grasping the foregrip of the shotgun with his left hand and sliding his right hand back toward the trigger. I reached behind me under my raincoat.

The Bahamian was pressing the gun to his shoulder when I jerked the tire tool out of my waistband and hurled it at him. He twisted the shotgun up in front of his face, as if we were stick fighting. The tire tool clanged into the side of the gun and I saw him wince as the vibrations hit his hands. The tool dropped to the floor.

Robert had more luck with the monkey wrench. It hit the white man on the temple with a sound like a rimshot, and he fell to his right into the table. The revolver was knocked from his hand. The farm boy took a step toward Robert and the Bahamian raised the gun to his shoulder again, now looking at me.

I turned and ran for the car. I reached the door within four steps and was just going around it when I slipped for a second on a loose chunk of rock and the shotgun went off with a roar that battered my eardrums in the stone vault. The door exploded behind me. Glass showered the side of my face and neck, and the edge of the door slammed into my spine and then rebounded. I flung myself forward across the front seat of the coupe as the second barrel of the gun went off, showering me with glass from the windshield.

As I lay there, reaching beneath Robert's topcoat for the submachine gun, trying to bend my knees to get my lower legs and feet fully into the car, the backs of my legs felt as if they had been fiercely scalded Then the pain sharpened and it was as if someone was jamming red-hot wires into my legs. I wriggled out of the ripped raincoat and saw both pant legs were shredded and blood was beginning to rise from the flesh all along the back of my right leg.

I blinked my eyes and wiped them with my shoulder and my vision cleared enough for me to decide the stinging in my eyes came from sweat and blood from my forehead, not from cuts in the eyeball.

For a moment, as the echo of the second explosion died slowly in the cave, I heard nothing. Then it was so quiet I could hear the hissing of the lanterns, and I fought against the insane urge to slide off the seat and onto the floor and just lie there, pressed against the fire wall. Then, I heard a sound I recognized from the autumns of my childhood, the sound of a shotgun being opened at the breech. As if a film soundtrack had returned after a momentary breakdown, there was a flurry of noise to the rear of my car, shouts and a curse and feet scrambling in the loose rock and the sound of a fist hitting flesh. A man grunted with exertion and then something heavy slammed into the hollow metal of the rumble seat, shaking the little coupe.

Hoping all that was a distraction, I grabbed the submachine gun and scrambled backward out of the car. As my feet hit the stone floor, my right leg collapsed. I pushed myself up on my knees and shoved with my left leg, scrambling forward, beyond the shattered door. The rough stone surface must have slashed my knees as I turned on them to face the alcove again, but I did not feel a thing except adrenaline surging through my body. I rose stiffly on my left knee and saw that the Bahamian was pushing a shell into the opened breech of the shotgun.

On the other side of the table, the white man had the revolver in his right hand again. It was hanging limply at his side, and he was looking past me into the black distance of the cave as if in shock. I heard a sound halfway between a scream and a squeal from somewhere behind me, and something heavy slammed into the rear of my car again.

The Bahamian shoved the second shell into the jackknifed gun and snapped the breech shut. He was raising it again to his shoulder when I swung the Thompson toward him and thumbed everything forward, as I had rehearsed in my mind a hundred times in the past hour.

I held the trigger down and swept the barrel across the man's body, as if I was spraying a friend with a hose on a July day. The first few slugs missed to the left and ripped chunks out of the forest of limestone behind him, sending powder flying in the air, and then the gunfire reached the edge of its softer target and shattered the Bahamian's lower right arm, knocking the shotgun from his grasp.

The submachine gun, now seemingly on its own, continued to rise and sweep slowly across his chest, ripping a bloody diagonal streak that slanted up from his hip like a Sam Browne belt. When his shoulder exploded in a shower of red and pink and gray, I forced my finger from the trigger. I felt as if I was fighting the will of the gun, as if I was trying to stop in the middle of an orgasm.

The Bahamian toppled backward, blood pumping from his chest. The sounds of the explosions rattled through the cave like a departing freight train. His huge left hand reached back for the table to stop his fall. Its rear legs collapsed under the pressure and it fell backwards out of his grasp. He flailed his arms, trying with whatever was left of his will to keep his balance, but he could not swim in the air and toppled onto his back. His head smacked into the concrete and then he lay still, blood pumping from the red sash across his chest.

How easy it was to kill.

I looked down at the submachine gun in my hands. The chamber was still closed, so there was at least one bullet left. But my hands began shaking so badly I could no longer hold the gun, and it dropped to the stone floor in front of me. I looked down at myself and saw rough circles of blood on the gray stone around my knees. Blood-soaked rags covered the lower part of my right leg.

My left knee was supporting most of my weight, and I felt it weaken. But as I tried to lower myself partly onto my right knee, it collapsed, and I slumped onto my right hip and arm. I had no idea how much damage had been done to my legs, but the pain was coming back, fiercer than before, and I could not bear to look again at all the blood. I used the sleeve of my shirt to wipe my eyes, and then it too was smeared with blood.

I reached to my neck and pulled out a long thorn of glass. When I saw how much blood started flowing out of the cut, I crazily considered sticking the piece back in to plug the flow. Instead, I pressed the torn collar of my shirt onto it and held it there with my hand.

I was getting dizzy. I looked toward the alcove and saw that the white man was standing over the Bahamian, looking down at his shattered chest. He still had the revolver in his hand, hanging at his side, but the limpness of his grasp and the dazed look on his face suggested he had forgotten what it was for. He looked down at the Bahamian as if hypnotized by the blood, still rising in spurts from the man's chest. I crouched there, near the fender of my car, the adrenaline of fear and rage slowly draining away, feeling as if I was slipping toward unconsciousness.

I heard the sound of flesh slapping metal, looked to my right, and saw Robert standing between the two cars, his right arm and hand covered with blood and holding some dripping thing that looked to me, in my dazed state, as if it had been ripped from inside a man. I blinked and looked again and saw that the bloody object in his hand was the linoleum knife.

He looked at me and smiled. "How you doing?" he wheezed. I shook my head.

"How do your legs feel?" he asked, squinting.

"They hurt," I said.

"That's good," he said.

"What about your arm?" I asked, and the exertion of speaking left me lightheaded and gasping for breath.

Robert took a a deep breath and let it out slowly. "That's his blood, not mine," he said. "He's just a farm boy. I'm from Beale Street." He took another deep breath and, for a moment, a fierce grin spread over his face. Then, it disappeared into a wince of pain.

"I did bang the hell out of my leg back there," he said. "And he kicked me a couple of time in the chest."

Robert transferred the knife to his left hand and slid his right hand along the fender of the sedan until he could grab onto the headlight bar. He pulled himself forward so he was half-leaning, half-sitting on the fender. He looked very strange, like a lunatic whose eyes had retreated into deep hollows to hide from the light, and then I realized he must have lost or broken his glasses in the fight with the farm boy.

"How much can you see?" I asked. I looked toward the alcove. The white man was kneeling next to the body of the Bahamian, looking in our direction, blinking to focus his eyes like a man coming out of a dream.

"A blob," said Robert. "A white blob."

I tried to rise, to get back up on my knees, but my lower body had no strength left in it, and little feeling. I slumped back down. My mind was slipping away. I closed my eyes to hang on to it.

Robert coughed. I opened my eyes and saw his face was twisted with pain. Gingerly, he cleared his throat. "I may have broken a couple of ribs," he said. "Damn, that hurts."

A shoe scraped on the grainy concrete. Robert said, "Michael, the white blob is moving."

The white man had risen to his feet beside the bloody corpse. He appeared to have me in focus now, and I could see his right hand tighten on the gun and his finger move onto the trigger. He began to raise the gun, moving like a zombie in some horror movie. I looked down at the submachine gun at my knees and tried to grab it but my hand was too weak.

I heard a gasp and I looked up and saw the white man try to clap his hands over his mouth, but he was too late and vomit came spewing out, spraying over his hands and the gun and his pants and shoes. He jerked his head to the right, as if reflexively trying to avoid getting any more on himself, and a mouthful of vomit splashed onto the corpse. The man looked down, and another wave of nausea hit him. This time he threw up until he had nothing left but dry heaves.

He still held the gun, but it hung loosely at his side. He looked pathetic, gazing down in apparent despair at the vomit down the front of his lavender shirt. My mind, freed again from urgency, began to drift, and I found myself feeling vaguely sorry for the man.

"It sounds like that guy's out of action for a bit," said Robert. "Must have been those greasy damn White Castles."

"Concussion," I said, weakly. "Concussion makes you throw up."

"Maybe," said Robert.

The white man still had the revolver, and I realized dimly that I probably should pick up the gun and shoot him before he recovered again, but he looked so pathetic it almost made me cry. I had been forced to kill a stranger, or had forced myself to, but I couldn't kill this man. This man and I should have been friends, hanging out in back of the Reno together, passing a reefer, digging Lester Young.

"Poor bastard," I murmured, on the edge of passing out.

'What?" Robert said. "What the hell are you talking about? Listen. Where you figure Rachael is?"

"Don't know," I said. "Cave somewhere." I fought to stay awake.

I watched through a haze as the white man sank slowly to the concrete floor, his hand now lying palm up on top of the pistol. I tried to force myself out of an enveloping lethargy by telling myself that he was the man who had told me over the phone about the mole on Rachael's thigh. But the small jolt of anger that sent through me soon dissipated to be replaced by a weary sorrow that included Rachael and the man weeping on the floor and even the dead Bahamian, a sorrow at the awful things people did to each other.

By then, I am sure, I had lost enough blood and was weary and weak enough that I would have agreed to almost any notion, now matter how strange and inappropriate and dangerous, as long as I was left alone to sleep.

Dimly, I heard Robert say something about not being able to search for Rachael without his glasses, about needing me to help him. I gave a slow little nod in agreement, but I could feel myself slipping further away.

When I heard my car start, I jerked momentarily awake. I couldn't believe my ears, and even when I saw the car begin to move past me, I was so dazed that what I was watching seemed like a hallucination.

The white man must have heard the car too, heard it coming, because he looked up from his seated position and then tried to grab the bumper as it came toward him. Model A's don't move very fast in first gear, and if the man had been thinking clearly, if he hadn't been slammed in the head with a monkey wrench and jolted by the sight of violent death and humiliated by his reaction to it, he might have been able to scramble out of the way, or even lie flat and let the car roll over him. But instead he raised his hands as if to fend off the heavy steel bumper. It smashed through his hands and slammed into his chest. He screamed and held on desperately, wrapping his elbows over the bumper, his lower spine scraping along the rough concrete floor, his legs dragging under the front axle, until the accelerating car rammed him into the low forest of stalagmites, crushed his body and impaled him like a thrush on a barbed-wire fence.

I suppose the shock of that gave my system its final blood-pumping surge, one more than it could stand. When the coupe had come to a halt, past its fenders in the tangle of crushed stone, my red-webbed vision faded out and I slid into a soft gray sea. It was a restful sea, and I drifted in it for what seemed like a long time, until I felt rough hands on my legs.

As if I was watching a silent movie on a screen far away in the fog, I could tell that Robert was wrapping a belt around my upper thigh, and then I drifted, and awakened again when someone wiped my face and neck with a cloth that stung and smelled of whisky. I sensed the cloth being pressed to my neck, being held there.

Looking up as if through fish scales, I saw a face above me that was not Robert's. For a moment, it seemed to be the nurse who had awakened me and fed me ice cream after the doctor had taken out my tonsils. And then I realized it was my mother, and I was so grateful to see her this one last time that I did not mind dying at all. As my vision began to fade again, I murmured, "I'm so tired."

"Then I shall take you home," said Rachael Loeb.

17

I would like to end the story there, end it with her name. And I don't have much time left before we go to sea again. But I need to say some more things, as quickly as possible, and trust that later I—or someone— can smooth them into the narrative.

Rachael drove straight to Menorah Hospital. I remember nothing of the ride in the back seat of the sedan, and very little of the next two days, except that, when I awakened from the morphine on Wednesday evening, I knew Rachael and Robert had been there time and again, and O'Malley had visited wearing a tux.

I had lost a great deal of blood. Rachael, I am told, offered hers. The doctors said she was in no condition for that, even before they checked our blood types. Rachael's is AB. I have type A blood, like forty-one percent of the people in the world. So does Robert Creech.

I vaguely remember—or is it that I want so much to remember?— Robert lying on a cot beside my bed, his arm stretched out and angled toward me with his hand open, his fingers curled as if to catch something he was afraid might fall. We have since discussed the transfusion, and we are not certain such a thing would have been done in any other hospital in Kansas City, then or now. As Robert points out, not only had he achieved his goal of integrating a hospital, he had even integrated me.

Menorah even patched up the farm boy, who was near death from cuts inflicted by his own hawk-beaked knife, and perhaps from bouncing around for half an hour in the trunk of a Model A sedan.

Weeks later, Robert and I sat baking in the west Tennessee sun in a tiny, high-fenced backyard that was, indeed, barely a block off Beale Street, and he recalled for me some of the words that James Scott, the patriarchal ragtime pianist, had delivered at the funeral of his one-time student, Bennie Moten: "I came to see that Mr. Moten had not deserted ragtime, he had permitted it to live, embodied in a new orchestral music that in times to come will be the basis for the concertos and symphonies and operas of our race."

Beyond friendship and the feeling that he was partly responsible for Rachael's kidnapping, Robert had gone with me that rain-slashed Monday evening to stop the spread of the drug that threatened to destroy young musicians, the ones who would grow up to compose and perform the great music of his race.

Sadly, looking back more than seven years later, I don't think we accomplished that, anymore than you stop the flow of penny sweets by burning down the corner candy store. The tragic irony is that we made it easier for the robber barons to move into the narcotics trade. Indeed, that may have been our purpose, quite unknown to us.

For that, I blame O'Malley. Sometimes I blame him a great deal, and hate him. At other times, I think of him only with a bitter melancholy. Occasionally, I miss him.

O'Malley came to see me almost every day of the first of the two weeks I lay in Menorah Hospital, my legs wrapped in thick layers of gauze, stitches and bandages criss-crossing my face and neck, slowly regaining my strength, healed by salves, soup, and the blood of a friend.

Right off, O'Malley wanted me to know that he and detective Sweeney had tried to follow me Monday afternoon. They had driven directly to 63rd and Brookside and had arrived in time to see me dash back to my car and set out for my next destination. They tried to stay with me, but I vanished into a terrible tangle of vehicles on 75th Street. They had radioed a description of my car and last known location to the dispatcher, and gone back to the police station to wait for news.

"I missed opening night at the Shubert," he said, with a pout that seemed less of a joke than he tried to make it.

I asked how he and Sweeney had found out I was going to 63rd and Brookside. Because, he said, the police operator listened in on my calls. "We wanted to protect you."

I was still very weak during his first two or three visits, and the hospital staff cut them short after five or ten minutes. So O'Malley would leave me with a morsel like that and I would ruminate on it between long stretches of sleep.

He told me that he had been to the cave late on the night I had been brought to the hospital, and he thought I had done a hell of a job with his Thompson submachine gun. He reminded me of his theory that men with hangovers act heedlessly, with more grace and courage than they normally possess, and thus took half-joking credit not only for providing me with the weapon, but with the emotional force I needed to win the battle.

A couple of days later, he kidded me about being so obsessed with the Packard that it had not occurred to me that the two hoodlums might switch cars. "The boss only lets them use the Packard on special occasions," he said, with a grin and a wink.

By then, I had recuperated enough to ask him why the hoodlums didn't just come up and introduce themselves, since they were supposed to protect me.

"Be reasonable, Michael," O'Malley said. "We wanted you to flush those other birds out. We knew somebody from out of town was selling drugs. We just weren't sure who it was, until you started poking around mindlessly on that Bennie Moten thing. We wanted you to keep poking around. Mindlessly."

He told me who I had "flushed out": a schoolteacher from the Bahamas who had moved to New Orleans because he wanted to be rich like all Americans and soon decided tenth-grade English composition was not his swiftest route; the greedy white owner of a small Rampart Street jazz club who probably was also a heroin addict; and an uneducated Louisiana tenant-farmer's son who had bragged all over New Orleans about how easy it was to take money from rich Kansas City Negroes, not mentioning that he had spent most of his time there on a prison work gang.

The heroin they were selling had come from California through a Negro gangster and his crony, a Japanese-American seaman, but then the Bahamian had decided they could eliminate those middle men.

I asked O'Malley how he had first found out I was in Menorah Hospital.

"The call came over the police radio about 7:30," he said. "A half-hour before curtain time."

"So you came right over here and saw me," I said.

He nodded. "You weren't talking, but your friends were."

"And then you went to the cave?"

"Yep," he said.

"Why?"

"I'm a reporter," he said.

"Among other things," I said. "Was the gun damaged?"

He winked, but he did not smile. "Those Thompsons are pretty tough," he said.

"And Sweeney made sure nobody objected when you picked it up?"

"I let the cops keep it for a couple of days. For the inquest. Then, who knows? Things disappear."

"Yeah," I said. "I almost disappeared, along with my two best friends."

After a couple of more visits like that, he quit coming. I couldn't blame him, at least not for that. What I could blame him for, of course, was almost getting Rachael and me and Robert killed so he could do a service for someone whose precise identity I did not know, but whose connections were easily imagined.

They became obvious four years later, at federal drug trials in Kansas City. Narcotics agents testified that Kansas City had become the second-largest heroin distribution center in the country, with customers as far away as New Orleans and Seattle. The Kansas City crime syndicate had taken control of the heroin trade in 1934, after Mafia boss Johnny Lazia had been gunned down and his lieutenant, Charles Carollo, took over. The opium base for the heroin came from the Japanese section of Tsientsien, China.

That information, crawling with its own ironies, is among the hundreds of newspaper clippings in the three thick scrapbooks I lugged onto this vast ocean-going landing strip, where I have much free time to contemplate and recreate the past. Two of the scrapbooks are from Kansas City papers. The third is made up of stories about Kansas City from the *St. Louis Post-Dispatch*. That is where I worked from 1936 until early in 1941, when I enlisted, figuring we would be at war with Hitler within a year. I chose the navy, because although I had grown up in Kansas, I had childhood memories of the sea.

Nine months later, as I was finishing air-combat intelligence training at Quonset Point, R. I., the Japanese bombed Pearl Harbor. And here I am, working at a Royal upright in the ward room and reading again about such things as the narcotics trials of 1939.

Several Kansas City policemen were tried, but not Corporal Edward Becker. His body had been found early in 1936, lying in an alley off 14th street. He had two bullets in his head and a child's rubber snake tied around his neck.

I never asked O'Malley about Becker's killing. In late June of 1935, when I returned to the *Journal-Post*, a cub even fresher than I had taken over the police beat, and I seldom saw my former mentor. In any event, we had barely spoken since the day, just before I came back to work, that I joined him for a beer at the Pleasant Dove.

By then, he was reacting to my resentment of him by resenting me back. He began needling me about my friendship with Robert and my love of jazz. He started talking about the white man who had died in the cave, and suggested that the man must have been a lot like me.

"For instance?" I asked, with an inkling of what he would say.

"Well," O'Malley said, "he liked to hang out with—" he paused and winked, "with colored people."

I nodded and took a drink of beer, hoping he was through.

"And," said O'Malley, "it appears that you and he had the same taste in women."

I don't know whether I am proud or ashamed that I stopped myself from smashing him in the face with the beer bottle and merely set it down on the table and walked away.

Rachael's story came out slowly, over many weeks. I heard parts of it five or six times, and some of it she never told me.

The three men grabbed her a little before noon from a parking lot of the Plaza. After they arrived at the mouth of the cave, the white man dragged her farther in. She fought, but he was stronger, and when he pulled the linoleum knife from his pocket and jammed the point against her throat, she let him pull her along.

They went down a well-worn path into a narrowing passageway and stopped in a small, low-ceilinged room covered with chunks of limestone. Obscenities had been smoked onto the walls, and broken glass littered the floor. The room smelled of urine.

He propped his flashlight in a cluster of rocks and smashed the back of his fist across her face. He grabbed her by the upper arm before she could recover from the blow, squeezing nerves to the bone with one hand, and holding the knife at her throat with the other. He forced her down onto a large flat stone covered with a thin layer of dirt and mud.

Afterward, the man lay back on the rock next to her and asked her name. When she told him, he smiled and yawned and she jammed two stiff fingers in his right eye. She could feel a fingernail slice through a slippery surface. The man squealed and rose toward her. She smashed the heel of her hand into his nose. His head flew back and hit the rock, and the eye that was still open slid shut. He lay stunned, blood leaking from a nostril.

She jumped up and grabbed the flashlight and ran into a narrow passageway that led further into the cave.

Rachael must have run almost without stopping for five or ten minutes, the weakening beam of the flashlight just bright enough to show her what was a few feet ahead as she slid between towering formations, ducked low ceilings, and climbed around boulders, going deeper and deeper and lower and lower into the cave.

Once, she heard the man scream her name, and she quickened her pace, but when she had gone for a long time without hearing pursuit, she began to feel safe enough to stop and catch her breath. She turned off the flashlight. Then there was darkness and silence in all directions.

Rachael crouched against a wall of stone and tried to see with her mind. She had never been inside a limestone cave, but she had read *Tom Sawyer*. Her thoughts, undistracted by sight, began drifting toward images of the boy and girl lost in the vast Missouri cave, hiding from Injun Joe.

For a moment she visualized the little girl reaching down a hand to help her. The thought of Becky Thatcher as her guardian angel cheered her up, and she had to stifle a nervous burst of laughter.

After crouching there for several minutes, hearing nothing, she turned on the light and headed in the direction she had been going, terrified to go back, hoping she could find another way out, as Tom Sawyer had.

The light had grown so dim it was almost useless by the time she had crawled on her hands and knees down a steep hill to a stream that seemed to gush out of a rock wall to her left.

On her knees she drank from the stream, and then, somewhat refreshed, decided to wade across. It did not seem to be very wide. She went forward and in a few seconds the cold water was up to her waist. A powerful current swept the rubber soles of her oxfords off the slick rock bottom. She had to paddle desperately to keep afloat, and the flashlight slipped from her grasp.

She fought the current until she felt her feet touch rock again. Then she stumbled into shallow water and onto a flat shelf of rock. She was panting and tried to rub warmth into her cold, numb hands and legs, but she was overtaken by uncontrollable shivering.

She wrapped her arms around herself and her mood plunged. She again thought of Becky Thatcher, but that image was far too lighthearted to pull her out of the deep gloom. So she forced herself to remember the man who slapped her, and she made herself live, moment by moment, through what had happened next, building her anger.

In the blackness, cold and wet and hungry, hearing only the constant and hypnotic roar of falling water, Rachael began dreaming of revenge.

Using her teeth she tore strips from her shredded wool skirt and tied them around her cut knees and hands, leaving her fingers free. Bunching up the remaining tatters of the skirt, she tied them at her waist.

She began crawling away from the underground river. When she reached what felt like a canyon wall, she crawled along it upstream until she found a stone trough. As she ascended the trough, the sides flattened out and the incline lessened. After a few minutes on her hands and knees, she pushed herself to her feet to stretch her aching muscles.

She was, she decided, going along the dried bed of an ancient tributary of the river flowing below. If so, could she follow it upward to its original aboveground source?

Perhaps. She had been taught to trust rivers.

Alone among his friends, Rachael's father was a canoeist and fisherman, and once or twice every year he would take her canoeing on an Ozark river. Now she remembered something her father had taught her.

You couldn't always see the best route through rocks and rough water, but if you kept the boat in the center of the fastest current, moving straight ahead, it would find the main channel almost by itself. You could practically do it with your eyes shut, he said.

She remembered something else. She was standing with her father on a hill outside of Kansas City, and he was showing her where traces of the old Santa Fe Trail cut right through a farm town. The best way to see it, her father told her, was to relax and let it reveal itself.

It was only much later, when she told me about her vision of Becky Thatcher, that Rachael realized who her real guardian angel had been on that long and perilous Passover journey.

Rachael walked slowly, with her hands in front her, feeling forward with each foot before she put weight on it, moving steadily up what she now envisioned as a dry stream bed, five or ten feet wide. She climbed for an hour or two, skirting boulders or huge sharp cylinders of fallen rock, angling back toward the center when she seemed to be drifting into rougher terrain. Having a plan that seemed rational kept her going, seeking higher ground.

Sometimes anger and hatred so stirred her imagination that she would stop paying attention to where she was walking and would twist her ankle stepping into a hole or bang her knee against a protruding rock. If it hadn't hurt so much, she said later, she might have laughed at the slapstick.

After being in the dark for hours, she didn't trust her eyes when she saw a dim glow emerge from the blackness ahead. As she stood and watched, it slowly grew until it was like a light in a window miles away on an unexpected shore.

The light lasted for only twenty or thirty seconds, then flickered and faded until she couldn't see it anymore. Then, when she held her hand in front of her face, she could see a small patch of gray. Illumination was leaking in from somewhere in front of her.

She walked for a long time—half an hour, perhaps an hour—before she saw the light again. It was off to her left, brighter and closer than before, like a single planet low in the evening sky. It faded again, but it left a residual glow, as if buried in a fog bank. She could see it if she relaxed and let it find her eyes.

She followed the light, leaving the creek bed. Now there were many loose stones to stumble over and larger boulders to work around. The closer she got to the light, the more impediments she encountered. She could see them now, ghostly hulks all around her.

A hundred yards ahead of her, up a steep incline, Rachael saw a crescent-shaped hole in the rock wall. She worked her way up the incline toward it. The footing was treacherous, not just with loose rock, but with chunks of concrete, hunks of electrical cable, broken boards, and jagged pieces of tin. Rachael dropped down again on all fours to make her way through the debris, grateful for the wool pads on her hands and knees.

When she was about halfway up, light flared through the hole, piercing her eyes. As she dropped to her stomach, she heard the crunch of car tires and laboring engines. After a few seconds, the light dimmed and the car sounds faded away.

Rachael began working her way toward the top again, crawling and pulling herself up what seemd to be some kind of construction dump on a rock slide.

She was startled by an explosion from the other side of the hole. For an instant, she was terrified that workmen were blasting above her and she would be buried in an avalanche. The explosion was dying in its own echoes when there was a second one. When nothing came through the hole except motes of dust dancing in slanting light, she quickly scrambled the rest of the way to the top.

The hole was half-blocked with rubble and as she was tugging at rocks to clear a crawlway, she heard another frightening sound—a rapid series of smaller explosions, as if someone had kicked over the engine of a motorcycle. It caught and roared for a few seconds and then stopped, leaving a string of dying echoes.

She wriggled through the hole to find herself emerging from the base of a wall, with a rough roadbed just in front of her. With only her head and shoulders out, she could see, perhaps fifty yards ahead, two automobiles. Beyond them was the alcove from which she had been dragged hours before.

One of the cars, she realized, was the sedan that had brought her to the cave. The other was a Ford coupe. She decided it must be mine.

She crawled the rest of the way out, pushed herself to her feet, and began trotting across the cave toward the cars. Half-naked, covered with gray muck and streaked with blood like a tent-show Amazon, she rose on the toes of her rubber soles and broke into a run, gritting her teeth against the pain that jolted through her legs with every footfall.

As she approached, she could see one of her kidnappers lying on his back near the rear of the sedan. His eyes were closed and his head and shirt were covered with blood.

Rachael slowed down and crept up behind my car. She climbed on the rear bumper and looked over the top. The first thing she saw was the white man, seated on the floor of the alcove. Next to him was the torn, blood-splashed body of the Bahamian. And between them, near the white man's right hand, lay a pistol.

She was startled to hear my voice say "poor bastard," and she looked to her left to see me lying on the ground a few feet from the shattered door of the car, with blood spread like fingers down the side of my face and neck.

Then she heard another voice, a man telling me he'd lost his glasses. She looked to her right and saw a young Negro with a bloody arm leaning weakly against the front of the sedan, squinting blindly into the light.

She decided she had to stop the white man before he picked up the gun and shot us. She looked through the rear window. My keys were in the ignition.

As I recall the scene in the cave at approximately that moment, the man was sitting on the floor sobbing, covered with his own vomit, one eye closed and the other lifeless. His hand was lying like a dead carp on the floor near the gun, and the only person he seemed in a condition to shoot was himself.

But I was almost unconscious from the loss of blood and saw everything as if through a dense fog. And Rachael had only a few seconds to make a judgment and act. I have never felt I had the need, the desire, or even the right to argue with Rachael Loeb about what she did next.

Epilogue

My darling Rachael:

Here's the book.

Before putting it in the hands of the friend who is bringing it to you, I had time to read it over very quickly. How strange, I thought afterwards, but also how appropriate if it ended up serving two main purposes: to confess to my notoriously unforgiving wife, while safely thousands of miles away at sea, that I had made a pass at another woman, and to reassure my son someday, if he hears cruel speculation, that his parents had slept together before they were married.

Now, we are in drydock for a few days, and then we will go back to sea. As usual, don't worry about me unless you hear bad news from the navy department.

I got a note from Robert, with glowing reports on the intelligence and good humor of his godchild. I'm so glad he was able to come to St. Louis for Bobby's birthday, and am both sorry and angry about the incident at the restaurant.

Robert tells me that he recently was in New York to visit his uncle. Libba and Teddy are still married and still live separately most of the time. Libba is playing in a small supper club in Greenwich Village and writing arrangements for Basie and Goodman. Teddy is working a variety of jobs and jamming every night in Harlem with some very advanced young musicians.

I have spent a great deal of time contemplating the events of that sad and joyous spring. I see that I was wrong—we were wrong—to blame the death of Bennie Moten on some complex conspiracy by evil white people. But the result is the same: the man, a musical genius, is dead, and white prejudice is partly to blame. The collapsed tubing on an out-dated pulmotor is hardly as dramatic as a burning cross, but it can symbolize the same thing.

I cherish the snapshots of little Rose. She is so small and so beautiful in her pictures, and I am certain your mother would have been proud to have passed on her name to so precious a baby.

Rachael, I need a new picture of you. My eyes have practically worn out the one in the locket, although in my memory I will have always have another image of you, so bittersweet it brings me to tears. I see you on that April day in 1935, standing wet and waiflike inside that large black scarf before returning to your house to mourn for your father. You looked back at me for a moment, and then you turned and walked away in the rain.

As Robert and I drove to find you through that terrible storm, I was afraid I would never see you again, and I locked that image away like a treasure. Now, when it comes to mind, as it often does, somehow your face becomes blurred with that early portrait we have of your grandmother, and I am left with the imaginary image of a young girl who looks like you arriving by ship at Ellis Island, a forlorn but brave immigrant dispatched to cousins in the promised land of America, sad to leave her family and missing her home, but safe from the recurring pogroms of Odessa and eager to step into the New World.

Sometimes I will stand on the flight deck and gaze at the ocean and my mind will drift to other sea voyages and other arrivals, of my own great-grandfather escaping conscription into the ever-assembling armies of the Germans, of O'Malley's parents and grandparents fleeing famine and oppression in Ireland. And, inevitably, I think of the much crueler passage to Charleston Bay of the ancestors of Teddy and Libba and Robert.

But then I think of other things, the music and good times in Kansas City and raucous evenings in the Pleasant Dove. And that night with you in your grandmother's four-poster bed, when we knew for the first time that we were really in love.

Most of all, my beloved Rachael, I think of you, and I find myself praying that we can be together again very soon. Yours is my heart alone.

Love,
Michael

Afterword

This story is fiction, but it is based on actual events in Kansas City in 1935. All material quoted from the *Kansas City Star*, the *Kansas City Times*, the *Kansas City Journal-Post*, and the *Kansas City Call* actually appeared there. In a few cases, there have been minor editing changes for brevity or clarity, and there has been some tightening of the time frame for novelistic purposes.

All of the prominent jazz musicians who appear in the novel played in Kansas City in 1935, although some chronological liberties have been taken to get them all together at specific times during the three weeks of the main narrative. For example, the Earl Hines band and the Bennie Moten band, led by Bus Moten, actually did appear at the Labor Temple on a Monday night in April 1935, and it is logical that there would have been a jam session afterward, but the actual concert was on April 22 rather than April 15.

Libba Monroe and Teddy Wellington are fictional characters, partly based on Mary Lou Williams and Jo Jones. The young saxophonist named Charles is a fictional character partly based on Charlie Parker. The real Charlie Parker was four months shy of his fifteenth birthday in April 1935. Although he was probably already hanging out in the black nightclub district listening to music, most of the things that happen to the fictional Charles, including his use of heroin and the famous incident of the tossed cymbal, happened a year or two later to the real Charlie Parker.

Bandleader Bennie Moten actually died during a tonsil operation on April 2, 1935, at Wheatley-Provident Hospital. Dr. W. E. Stone is a fictitious character. However, it is historically accurate that questions were raised at the time about the performance of the operating surgeon, and musicians did report seeing the surgeon and Moten together in the nightclub district on the night before the operation. Interviews with musicians and others from the Moten era confirm what Moten/Basie trumpeter Ed Lewis told jazz historian Frank Driggs (the interview appeared in 1959 in *Jazz Review*):

"[Bennie] had a wonderful surgeon. . . one of the finest in the Midwest. A lot of people blamed [the doctor] for Bennie's death, but it wasn't his fault. Bennie was a nervous type person, and they had to use Novocain because he wouldn't let them put him to sleep. He got frightened when he felt the knife, and jumped, severed an artery and bled to death. It wasn't really [the doctor's] fault, but people in Kansas City were so hurt over it that the poor fellow had to leave town."

The doctor who operated on Bennie Moten moved to Washington, D. C. in 1938 and became one of the leading surgeons at that city's black general hospital. He died in Washington in 1962.

In May 1936 a New York record producer named John Hammond came to Kansas City in person to listen to some of the music he had been hearing on late-night radio broadcasts. It was, Hammond told me, "the most exciting musical experience of my life." By then what was essentially the Bennie Moten band had re-formed under Count Basie at the Reno Club and Hammond started the evening there.

"I stayed until four, when they closed," he recalled. "Then Basie and I went over to the Sunset Club to hear Joe Turner and Pete Johnson. We ended up at a joint on 18th Street where Lester Young sat in."

Two years later, Hammond produced the first of his "Spirituals to Swing" concerts at Carnegie Hall. A number of Kansas City musicians, including Basie and his band (featuring Lester Young), Pete Johnson, Joe Turner, and Hot Lips Page were featured and were well on their way to national fame.

In April 1939 a federal grand jury handed down thirty-three narcotics indictments as part of a sweeping campaign against Kansas City's political machine and crime syndicate. A month later, the Pendergast era officially ended—Thomas J. Pendergast was sentenced to fifteen months in federal prison for income tax evasion. Many of his associates, including crime boss Charles Carollo and police chief Otto Higgins, also went to prison on corruption-related charges.

On the night of February 18, 1950, in a performance at St. Nick's ballroom in New York City, Charles "Yardbird" Parker paused for an instant in the middle of a solo on a bebop tune called "Visa" and then interpolated, almost note for note but at two or three times the original speed, the Louis Armstrong trumpet introduction to "West End Blues." Five years and one month later, Parker was dead, his heart diseased, his stomach perforated, his liver ravaged by alcoholism, his arms covered with scars from the heroin injections he had begun as a teenager in Kansas City.

In the mid-1980s Bennie Moten's death certificate was still missing from the records at city hall in Kansas City, although it could be found on file with the state of Missouri in Jefferson City.

The historical background of *Blue Monday* is partly based on the author's discussions about Kansas City jazz and the Pendergast era with dozens of people, including Count Basie, Dave Dexter, Charles "Crook" Goodwin, John Hammond, Carroll Jenkins, Milton Morris, Martin Quigley, Belle Ritenour, Dr. Kip Robinson, Herb Smith, Herman Walder and Mary Lou Williams.

Many books were consulted, including *Hear Me Talkin' to Ya* by Nat Hentoff and Nat Shapiro, *The World of Count Basie* by Stanley Dance, *Bird: the Legend of Charlie Parker* by Robert Reisner, *Jazz Style in Kansas City and the Southwest* and *Bird Lives!* by Ross Russell, *Going to Kansas City* by Mary Lee Hester, *Goin' to Kansas City* by Nathan Pearson, *Playback* by Dave Dexter, *Celebrating Bird: The Triumph of Charlie Parker* by Gary Giddins, *John Hammond on Record* by John Hammond with Irving Townsend, *Stomping the Blues* and *Good Morning Blues: the Autobiography of Count Basie* by Albert Murray, *Mr. Blood's Last Night* by Martin Quigley, *Tom's Town* by William Reddig, and *K.C. : A History of Kansas City, Missouri* by A. Theodore Brown and Lyle W. Dorsett.

Everyone who has written about Kansas City jazz owes a debt to Frank Driggs and his pioneering articles in jazz publications. And the story has never been told better than in Bruce Ricker's movie, *The Last of the Blue Devils*, which was an invaluable resource for *Blue Monday*.

The staffs of the Missouri Historical Society in St. Louis and the Missouri Valley and periodical sections of the Kansas City Public Library were very helpful.

Particular thanks are due Judith Newmark, John Cournoyer, Michael Eastman, and especially Jan Stauffacher for her help, inspiration, and sacrifice.

Photo by Michael Eastman

Harper Barnes is critic-at-large for the *St. Louis Post-Dispatch*. He was the editor of the *Phoenix* in Boston, and has written for the *Atlantic Monthly, Rolling Stone, Village Voice,* and other publications. A former police reporter, he is currently at work on a novel about depression-era outlaw Charles ("Pretty Boy") Floyd.